LASHKAR

An alumnus of La Martiniere College, Lucknow, the National Defence Academy, Pune and the Indian Military Academy, Dehra Doon, Mukul Deva was commissioned in December 1981 into the Sikh Light Infantry of the Indian Army. After fifteen years of service – including active combat duty/operations in India and overseas – as a Major in the Indian Army, he opted for premature retirement. His previously published works include, *Time after Time*, S.T.R.I.P.T.E.A.S.E. – *The Art of Corporate Warfare*, and M.O.D.E.L. – *The Return of the Employee*.

Praise for *Lashkar*

'An edge-of-the-seat-thriller'

– *The Hindustan Times*

'Exciting... with some action, some introspection, some retrospection... A racy read'

– *The Times of India*

'For the first time, an Indian thriller set in contemporary times... a gripping tale'

– *The Pioneer*

'*Lashkar* tries to make sense of the terror that surrounds our lives'

– *The Hindu*

'Ludlumesque'

– *The Tribune*

'A glance is enough to discover... this is a Tom Clancy on the LOC'

– *Time Out*

'A real page-turner… a riveting read'

– *Business Standard*

'Written with style and panache'

– *Sahara Time*

'A real-life take on how the so-called jehadis are picked up from anonymous Indian streets... *Lashkar* tells many tales with great ease'

– *MetroPlus*

'Lashkar is gripping... racy and visually captivating'

– *Indo Asian News Service*

'Magnificently paced, rich and real in imagery… Deva is a visionary'

– Sarthak Dasgupta, filmmaker

LASHKAR

Into the Heart of Terror

Mukul Deva

HarperCollins *Publishers* India

First published in India in 2008 by
HarperCollins *Publishers* India
A-75, Sector 57, Noida, Uttar Pradesh 201301, India
www.harpercollins.co.in

1 2 3 4 5 6 7 8 9 10

P-ISBN: 978-81-7223-665-6
E-ISBN: 978-93-5029-592-2

Typeset in 11.5/14 Meridien
Nikita Overseas Pvt. Ltd.

For Mehtab, my favourite elder daughter –
Despite the fact that you do strange things like studying to be a lawyer, you make us proud, kid.

And to the thousands of men, women and children who have been sacrificed on the wanton altar of terrorism.

AUTHOR'S NOTE

This book is a work of fiction although some of the events mentioned here have actually taken place.

All characters, places and organizations described or mentioned in this book are fictitious or have been used fictitiously and any resemblance to any person, living or dead, is absolutely unintentional.

I have taken the liberty of using my alma mater, La Martiniere College, Lucknow, as a backdrop for a part of the story since I am inordinately proud of my association with this great institution; the school and its memories occupy a huge place in my mind.

The technical details, specifications and methodologies relating to bomb-making, weaponry and tactics employed by any police, military or militant organization, and all criminal, forensic and investigative procedures mentioned herein have been deliberately kept vague, inaccurate and/or incomplete to prevent there being any misuse of the information – accidental or otherwise.

There is no malice intended against any religion, race, caste, creed, nation, organization or people.

Part One

THE TERROR BEGINS

GROUND ZERO

1802 hours, 29 October 2005, Sarojini Nagar Market, New Delhi.

The plump, middle-aged lady had just bent to pick up the bright red table cover with small mirrors embroidered on it when the bomb placed five feet away detonated. There was nothing between her and the bomb to cushion the effect of the explosion. Her head and a large part of her neck were ripped right off, spraying the pretty teenaged girl standing directly behind her with gore and flesh. The lady's stout body shielded the girl from the blast but the explosion totally deafened her; the sharp, ringing sound echoing in her ears. The blood splattered all around her had yet to register when the second bomb placed twelve feet away exploded and the LPG *cylinder near which the bomb had been placed ignited in sympathetic detonation. A flaming, almost perfectly triangular, piece of metal splintered from somewhere in the centre of the exploding* LPG *cylinder. It sliced through the turbulent air and embedded itself in the teenager's chest with tremendous force. The young girl looked down and stared at the shard of blood red metal jutting out of her chest in disbelief. Life left her body as she crumpled slowly to the ground and came to rest in an untidy heap, inches from her mother's headless corpse.*

The firestorm that had been unleashed by the two bombs and the exploding LPG *cylinder scythed through the dense crowd of shoppers and shopkeepers gathered around. Forty-seven of them died on the spot. Another twenty-nine succumbed to their injuries at various hospitals in the days that followed. Each lost and crippled life would wreak a terrible toll on those it left behind. But it was Hamida, the middle-aged lady who had been beheaded, and her teenage daughter, Navaz, whose deaths were to matter the most.*

1840 hours, 29 October 2005, Muzaffarabad Terrorist Training Camp, Pakistan Occupied Kashmir (POK).

It was the first flurry of the season. The light snowfall outside matched the snowy picture on the black and white TV monitor that glowed bleakly inside the room. Though the images on the screen were blurred, the shock and horror in the voice of the dazed news reporter came through with chilling clarity.

Maulana Fazlur Rehman's attention was riveted to the television when his satellite phone began to ring. He snatched it up and nodded at Brigadier Murad Salim when he saw the number displayed on the phone. 'It's him. Furkan.'

'I thought he had been instructed not to make any calls.' The Brigadier's face tightened in anger.

'Maybe there is a problem,' the Maulana replied defensively as he muted the television and picked up the phone – he quite understood how triumphant Furkan was feeling – and listened to him with a slowly widening smile.

Just then the camp's instructors ushered in the twelve new graduates. The freshly-trained terror recruits were headed for the Pakistan Army post at Chakoti, on the Line of Control (LOC), to be slipped back across the border that very night. Back to India. Their arduous, six-month-long training was over. It was time for them to play their part in the jihad to free their land. What better way for their training to come to an end than on this glorious footnote?

The Maulana put down the phone and turned to face the young men as they trooped in and arranged themselves awkwardly by the wall. 'Look!' He pointed at the muted television. 'See what heroic deeds we are capable of.'

The boys looked at the images of havoc and destruction.

'What you are seeing today is the result of months of careful planning and training. It should inspire and motivate you. After all, it is fearless young men like you, trained at this very camp, who carried out the operation.'

Maulana Fazlur Rehman's words struck deep into the hearts of the youths. The punishing training routine, the horrors of the earthquake, the danger to their lives – all seemed suddenly worthwhile.

Brigadier Salim stood in the shadows studying the new recruits. Though Fazlur Rehman didn't introduce him to the new trainees there were few in the jihadi circuit in Pakistan who had not heard his dreaded name. Sizing up each adolescent face, the Brigadier's gaze came to rest on Iqbal's. Perhaps because his was the only face that registered a slight revulsion at the images of carnage on TV.

THE STRIKE

Border Town of Khajewala, Rajasthan, India. There are a dozen ways in which one can get hold of explosives in India, or in any country for that matter. All it requires is a little ingenuity and a lot of money. However there is always a strong possibility that such efforts would be detected by intelligence agencies and alert them to the possibility of an imminent operation. That is why this time it was decided that even a pin required for the mission would be brought in from outside.

Afzal carried the RDX, the detonators, the timers, the pistols and the ammunition across the Indo–Pakistan border in the Rajasthan sector. He used one of the many convoluted, nondescript desert trails that straddle the international border between India and Pakistan. Since this time the mission was to kill a really large number, so too was the quantity of RDX involved; it took six trips over as many weeks before Afzal was able to ferry it all across the border.

Tall and reedy with a pockmarked face, his morals as dirty and loose as the clothes he wore, Afzal was a man with a single need. Money. He didn't like spending it. Just getting his hands on it.

'We will pay you double the usual rate for this operation,' the man who had briefed Afzal at Fort

Abbas in Pakistan told him. 'You must be twice as careful and handle the items we give you with great care. Don't do anything dumb or you will blow yourself to pieces. And you will not talk to anyone about it.'

What an idiot! As though I am going to talk about this to anybody, thought Afzal but he kept his face expressionless and his mouth shut; there was something cold and dangerous about the tall, hard-looking man standing opposite him.

The RDX, detonators and timers had stayed hidden in the loft of his two-room house in Khajewala till the last week of October 2005. Up until the day he got a call on his mobile phone late one afternoon. 'A letter will arrive by courier tomorrow morning. In it you will find the photograph of a man and his address. Memorize it and destroy the letter immediately. Then take the items down to Delhi and deliver them to him. Have you got that?'

'Yes,' Afzal replied.

'Good. And remember, you must pack the stuff the way we had showed you and ensure it is delivered to him latest by the evening of 27th October. Call the number you have been given as soon as you have handed over the materials.' The caller hung up.

A couple of days later, Afzal was ferrying the deadly cargo to Delhi in his small truck, neatly packed inside a consignment of Rajasthani quilts that not only concealed but also cushioned the detonators and the RDX during the long, bumpy drive. Afzal was not too bucked about carrying explosives in his truck. But

Afzal also knew his handlers would not take kindly to his failing to deliver. Incurring the displeasure of such people had sinister terminal implications, which Afzal feared more than being inadvertently blown up in his truck. So he and his assistant, who also happened to be his nephew, left for Delhi as instructed.

His nephew-assistant was a gangly young man not blessed with much by way of brains. But then that was the primary reason Afzal used him. The idiot boy not only put up with all the abuse that Afzal routinely heaped on him, he never asked too many questions and was willing to work for a salary so meagre it would have shamed a starving Ethiopian.

26 October 2005, National Capital Region of Delhi. At about the time that Afzal's truck cleared the city of Bikaner en route to Delhi, a Tata Indica car was stolen from Ghaziabad, a Maruti Esteem from Gurgaon and a Bajaj Caliber motorcycle from Faridabad. All the vehicles stolen were battered looking machines well past their prime. Clearly not the kind a thief would normally target and certainly not the kind that would attract a second glance. *Only pick up vehicles from the small satellite towns around Delhi. They are not likely to feature in police lists very soon. Also, police jurisdictional issues will slow down the search for them. This is also why you must steal the vehicles as close to the day of the strike as possible.* This is what they had been told to do and this is what they ensured.

Do not take the stolen vehicles back to where you are staying. Change the licence plates and hand them over for servicing and repairs to different garages. Pick small garages that are not doing too well. They are always hungry for business and don't ask questions even if they happen to notice something amiss. Make sure every vehicle is properly checked and serviced. We don't want any vehicle breaking down.

They chose three different garages from amongst the plethora of small garages in the Savita Nagar area in South Delhi, close enough to be administratively convenient and yet at a safe distance from where the strike teams were actually staying. All three handed over an adequate advance to the workshop owners. The advance paid was not large enough to attract special attention but substantial enough to ensure they had the undivided attention of the garage owners.

1905 hours, 27 October 2005, Interstate Border between Haryana and Delhi.

About an hour after sunset, Afzal crossed Gurgaon and drove up to Delhi. He was duly stopped at the octroi post on the city border and spent a stress-filled hour waiting in the kilometre-long queue. The extremely alert officials manning the checkpost were not impressed either by Afzal or his truck. However, Afzal was a veteran of no mean standing and he had done this route often enough to know how things worked. 'I have a letter from Rangarajan Sahib,' he told the toll tax inspector who was waiting at the barrier when his turn came.

'*Kyoon bhai*? Only one letter?' the toll tax inspector asked brazenly.

Afzal gave a sly, ingratiating smile. 'Would I have the audacity to come to you with just one letter? There are ten of them.' He handed a small roll of notes to the inspector. The barrier was opened and Afzal was through. He heaved a sigh of relief as he saw the border checkpost vanish in the darkness in his rear-view mirror.

'Who is Rangarajan Sahib?' His nephew-helper asked a bit later, deeply impressed with the way the whole thing had been handled by his uncle.

'He was the Governor of the Reserve Bank of India.'

'Wow!' The dim lad whistled in awe. 'How do you know him?'

'I don't, you idiot!' Afzal laughed. 'Have you never seen a hundred-rupee note? The Reserve Bank governor's signature is on it. That is what it means when you tell someone that you have a letter from Rangarajan Sahib.'

In Delhi, Afzal left the Outer Ring Road just after the Chirag Dilli flyover and moved into the narrower road leading into the colony. Despite the precise directions it took him almost half an hour to negotiate the heavy Delhi traffic and reach the Aftab Cyber Café located in one of the many nondescript lanes between Malviya Nagar and Khirki Gaon. The cyber café had closed for the night, but when he knocked, a well-built man in his thirties answered the door instantly, almost as though he had been laying in wait. Afzal recognized him from the photograph that he had been sent, but he still said: 'I am looking for the owner.'

'You've found him.' The man crooked a finger at himself. He too had recognized Afzal from the picture of his that had been uploaded on a profile in a harmless matchmaking website, used by them to exchange data and messages for this particular operation. With dozens of intelligence agencies keeping a sharp lookout on cyber space even emails were no longer a safe medium. That's why he had suggested the use of a profile planted on one of the several matchmaking sites on the net. The idea had earned him the approval of Salim Sahib himself. 'You got my quilts?' The cyber café owner, who these days went by the name 'Furkan Sheikh', asked.

Afzal nodded at the truck parked a little distance away. 'Come and help me unload them.'

The two men swiftly unloaded the neatly wrapped packages and brought them into the cyber café while the nephew kept an eye on the truck. There were a handful of people around who may have seen the two men working but it is doubtful that any of them would have recalled doing so the next morning.

Driving away from the cyber café, Afzal headed for the nearest telephone booth. 'Keep an eye on the truck,' he told his helper as he darted into the tiny wooden booth and dialled the phone number he had been told to memorize.

Afzal did not know it but the number belonged to a Thuraya satellite phone registered to a small export company based in Dubai. The phone, however, was nowhere near Dubai at that time. In fact, almost from the day it had been purchased and activated it had spent most of its time in Pakistan. Right at that moment it lay on a table in a plush office on the outskirts of the Lahore Army cantonment. The phone was answered almost immediately.

SALIM

Had Afzal ever met the man he had just spoken to he would have been genuinely surprised. A short stocky man with a balding pate and an easy smile he was the prototype of the genial old gent taking his grandchildren to the park. His grandfatherly air had deceived many an adversary when they'd first set eyes on him. But then not many people had. It is said that one of the first things Salim did when he arrived at a position of sufficient power was to have all photographs of himself removed from service records and files. He seldom appeared in any public gathering and never in any place where media of any sort was present. Most people who met him casually did not know who he really was nor what he did for a living. The story goes that his wife (now late and not much lamented) had once asked him about his job. 'If I told you that, my dear, I'd have to kill you,' he is said to have replied, only half joking.

Brigadier Murad Salim of the dreaded ISI (Inter Services Intelligence), the rogue Pakistani intelligence service, had been instrumental in implementing countless covert missions all over the world. His crowning achievement had been the Talibanization of Afghanistan and the setting up of a number of training camps all over Pakistan Occupied Kashmir and Afghanistan to feed the global terror factory. He had been responsible for sending more kafirs off to the happy hunting grounds than almost all the Al-Qaida leadership put together.

The Brigadier was one of the few people the General banked on to keep the fires of jihad alive in the minds of people, at home and overseas. This state of unrest gave the Pakistan Armed Forces the perfect reason for retaining a stranglehold over the nation's economy and its body politic. Indeed, few people realized that the last thing the Pakistani Army feared were the fundamentalist political parties. Headed mostly by zealots who had little idea of governance, these parties had virtually no political, social or economic agenda and scarcely any support at the grassroots level. They were ideally suited to allow the Pakistani Armed Forces to ensure that a perennial state of fear haunted the nation, thus keeping the real political parties in the wilderness, and retaining a firm hold on the reins of power. This was vital because there was just so much at stake. The drugs, weapons and sale of nuclear technology generated millions of dollars. Most of which found its way into the countless numbered accounts of the Generals in power and the handful of Pakistani politicians who toed their line.

Not many people were aware of the huge sacrifices Salim had made for the cause, or his contribution to the jihad espoused by his country. Not that he minded, since he had his own personal agenda:

a deep, almost pathological, hatred of everything even remotely Indian. The millions of American dollars he had diligently siphoned out of the narco-terror trail, of which he was an important cog, helped him fund his passion. Salim hated the Americans almost as much as he hated the Indians. Was it his fault they were so recklessly stupid about what they spent their money on? 'How smart is it to launch missiles worth thousands of dollars to destroy broken-down ruins worth nothing?' Salim would often ask his aide-de-camp as he railed against the American actions in Afghanistan and Iraq. 'And can you beat this? They actually call it a smart bomb. The dumb shits!'

As far as Salim was concerned, the jihad began on 16 Dec 1971 when, as the recently commissioned Lieutenant Murad Salim, he had watched the Pakistani Eastern Army Commander, General Niazi, surrender to the Indian Army General in Dhaka. The humiliation of that defeat had seared his soul so deeply that Salim knew he would carry the scars to his grave. 'No matter what the cost, I will make these bastard Indians pay,' he swore to himself. He opted for a transfer to the ISI at the first opportunity that came his way; a decision thoroughly vindicated by the passage of time.

By the time a Brigadier's stars found themselves on his shoulder boards, Salim had acquired an impeccable reputation. As part of the core team of the Pakistan High Command he had discussed the debacles of Operation Gibraltar, which was launched in August 1965 to infiltrate fighters into Jammu and

Kashmir and start a rebellion with local support, and Operation Grand Slam, which a panicked Pakistani High Command had unleashed to try and contain the situation. However, both these boomeranged and led to the 1965 Indo–Pak war.

That is when the Pakistani dictator General Zia decided to inflict the festering wound of insurgency on India. Salim was part of the key leadership team that spearheaded the operation. 'We must ensure that the Valley is always in flames; make it an international example of the despicable kafir violating human rights and international agreements by denying the Kashmiris plebiscite.'

The presentation that General Zia had made to the ISI leadership team on that fateful day in April 1988 was indelibly embedded in Salim's mind:

1045 hours, 17 April 1988, Central Briefing Room, ISI Headquarters, Islamabad.

The General was a fluent and polished speaker. He chose his words with care and delivered them with conviction:

'Gentlemen, I have spoken on this subject at length before, so I will skip the details. Due to our pre-occupation with Afghanistan, in the service of Islam, I have not been able to put these plans before you earlier. Let there be no mistake however that our aim still remains clear – the liberation of the Kashmir Valley. In the past we had opted for ham-handed military options and subsequently failed in our mission.

We will now keep the military option for the last, as a coup de grace, if and when necessary.

'Our Kashmiri brethren, though with us in their hearts and minds, are simple-minded folk who do not easily take to the type of warfare against foreign domination that say, a Punjabi or an Afghan is naturally inclined towards. The Kashmiri however has a few qualities, which we can exploit. First is his shrewdness and intelligence; second, his power to persevere under pressure; and third, if I may say so, is the fact that he is a master of political intrigue. If we provide him the means by which he can best utilize these qualities he will deliver the goods. We must adopt those methods of combat that the Kashmiri mind can cope with. In other words, a coordinated use of moral and physical means other than military operations, which will destroy the will of the enemy, damage his political capacity and expose him to the world as an oppressor. This aim, gentlemen, shall be achieved in the initial phases.

'In the first phase, which could last a couple of years, we will assist our Kashmiri brethren to get hold of the power apparatus of the State by political subversion and intrigue. I would like to mention here that as no government can survive in Occupied Kashmir unless it has the tacit approval of Delhi, it would be unrealistic to believe that the Muslim United Front or any other such organization can seize power through democratic or other means. In view of this, power must apparently remain with those whom New

Delhi favours. We must therefore ensure that certain favoured politicians from the ruling elite are selected to collaborate with us in subverting all effective organs of the State.'

There was a dramatic pause. The General used it to take a sip of water from the glass on the podium.

'In brief, our plan for Kashmir, which will be codenamed Operation Topac, will be as follows' – the General nodded to his aide who flicked on the first slide and projected it on the huge screen mounted across the podium – 'Phase 1. A low-level insurgency against the regime, so that it is under siege but does not collapse; after all, we don't want central rule imposed by Delhi at this stage.

'We will plant our chosen men in all key positions; they will subvert the police force, financial institutions, the communication network and other important organizations.

'We will whip up anti-India feelings amongst the students and peasants, preferably on religious issues, and enlist their active support for rioting and anti-government demonstrations. Then we will organize and train subversive elements and armed groups that have the capability, initially at least, to deal with paramilitary forces located in the Valley.

'Without recourse to force we must develop means to stealthily cut off the lines of communication between Jammu and Kashmir and within Kashmir and Ladakh. The road from Srinagar to Kargil over Zojila and the road over Khardungla will receive special attention.

'In collaboration with Sikh extremists we will create chaos and terror in Jammu and divert attention from the Valley at a critical juncture and discredit the regime even in the Hindu mind.

'We will establish virtual control in those parts of the Kashmir Valley where the Indian Army is not located or deployed. The southern Kashmir Valley may be one such region.'

There was a slight pause as the projector blanked out and the next set of slides were readied for the screen. The General resumed:

'Phase 2. Exert maximum pressure on Siachen, Kargil and Rajouri–Poonch sectors to force the Indian Army to deploy reserve formations outside the main Kashmir Valley.

'Attack and destroy base depots and HQs located in Srinagar, Pattan, Kupwara, Baramulla and Chowkiwala by covert action. Afghan mujahideen, by then settled in Azad Kashmir, will infiltrate into the pockets with a view to extending areas of our influence. This aspect will require detailed and ingenious planning. The fiasco of Operation Gibraltar holds many lessons for us here.

'Finally, a Special Force under selected retired officers belonging to Azad Kashmir, with the core consisting of Afghans, will be readied to attack and destroy airfields and radio stations, block the Banihal Tunnel and the Kargil–Leh Highway.

'At a certain stage of the operations, Punjab and adjacent areas of Jammu and Kashmir will be put under maximum pressure internally by our offensive posture.'

As the third set of slides came up on the projector the General triumphantly concluded his presentation: 'Phase 3: Detailed plans for the liberation of the Kashmir Valley and the establishment of an independent Islamic State.'

The aide turned off the projector and the General walked briskly across to the centre of the room to look his audience squarely in the eye. 'Please remember, we do not have much time. Maximum pressure must be exerted before the general elections in India and before the Indian Army reserves, which are still bogged down in Sri Lanka, become available. By the grace of Allah, we have managed to accumulate large stocks of modern arms and ammunition from the US consignments intended for the Afghan mujahideen. This will help our Kashmiri brethren achieve their goals. Even if we create a kind of Azad Kashmir in some remote parts of Occupied Kashmir as a beginning, the next step may not be as difficult as it appears today.'

The General paused, trying to gauge the effect of his words on those around him. When he resumed, it was with a note of caution: 'On the other hand, it should also be noted that a part of the Indian Army, particularly the Infantry, will be well trained by now, especially after their experience in north-eastern India and more recently in Sri Lanka. But the situation in Kashmir will be somewhat different; more like the

Intifada of Palestinians in towns, and on the pattern of mujahideen in the countryside to attack hard targets. A period of chaos in the state is essential in the circumstances.

'And what about our Chinese friends? Our Chinese friends will help us by ensuring that the Indian forces deployed against them are not moved out; if at all, this will be required only in the third or final stage of our operations. Of course, if we are in serious trouble, the Chinese and our other powerful friends will come to our rescue; they will ensure that even if we do not win – we don't lose.

'But, remember, it will be disastrous to believe that we can take on India in a straight contest. We must be careful to maintain a low military profile so that the Indians do not find an excuse to pre-empt us, by attacking at a time and at a point of their own choosing, at least before Phase I and 2 of the operation are over. I need not emphasize any further that a deliberate and objective assessment of the situation must be ensured at each stage, otherwise a stalemate will follow that will not be good for Pakistan.'

The General paused dramatically before pumping his right hand in the air –

'Pakistan Paindabad!'

An hour later the General addressed a much smaller gathering of the key leadership team of the ISI. There was no one in the room who sported anything less than a Brigadier's stars. 'Operation Topac does not concern J&K alone,' he said. 'Let me assure you, gentlemen, it is going to be one of the most innovative and audacious covert actions launched by any intelligence agency in history. It is designed to eventually balkanize India by unleashing a low-intensity conflict that, with assistance from the ISI, will snowball into civil war. Considering the inherent contradictions of the Indian polity, this is a very feasible option and the ISI is eminently capable of executing it.'

After the General departed from the headquarters there was a massive uproar; there were many in that room who felt Pakistan was biting off more than it could chew.

Salim was not one of them.

Salim had no doubt in his mind about what Pakistan was going to do. After all, he was one of the first to advocate switching support from the Khalistani militants and focusing their energies on Kashmir at one of the quarterly review meetings of the India Strategy think tank.

'Why? What is wrong with the Khalistani militants?' The Director had asked Salim when he proposed it the first time. He did not like ideas that did not originate, or at least seem to originate, from him: 'They are doing a good job by tying up thousands of troops in Punjab...not to mention the huge economic impact that the Khalistani militancy is having on India.'

'I am not saying there is anything wrong with them. They are dedicated fighters and yes, I agree, they are inflicting huge losses on the Indian security forces.' The fire that burned deep in Salim was not evident in the measured tone he used.

'So what is the problem?'

'The major problem is that we have nothing to bond us together.'

'Bond us together? We don't have to marry them...just use them.' A dutiful titter ran through the officers attending the meeting; even the General cracked a rare smile.

'That is the problem.' Salim ignored the crude attempt to rile him. 'They know we are using them. They may be stupid, but they are not that stupid.'

The General was watching Salim carefully. So far he had not spoken a word. 'The other problem,' Salim continued, now a little wary of the General's scrutiny, 'is that it is so hard to raise funds for the Khalistani militancy, whereas in the case of Kashmir it is so easy for us to play the Islamic card. The religious bond makes it very easy for us to raise funds for them from all over the Islamic world.'

'Are you suggesting we withdraw support from the Punjab area?' The General finally spoke up.

'No, sir, not at all.' Salim turned to face the General. 'I think we should turn it down a bit and support them only as much as it does not hurt us financially or diplomatically. Our main focus area should always be Kashmir.'

IQBAL

0001 hours, 30 October 2005, Pakistan Army Post Chakoti along the LOC, POK.

The newly-trained jihadi infiltrators left the Pakistan Army Chakoti Post half an hour after midnight. There were fourteen of them: the twelve boys who had trained together and the two instructors who had trained them. Iqbal's friend, Abu Khan, was leading the way. Iqbal had taken an instant liking to him when they'd first met. Something about Abu's quiet demeanour and determination had attracted him. He was easily the star of the class – the best shot, the best navigator and the most versatile in field craft. Omar was present too, despite a fever that was raging through his skinny body. The only concession made to his condition was being spared the added torture of carrying extra ammunition. At the training camp the previous night Fazlur Rehman had given Omar the once-over and pronounced him fit to travel. 'You are Allah's soldier, what is a little fever, boy? You!'– he had suddenly barked at Iqbal who had unfortunately been standing beside Omar – 'you stay with him and help him along. Make sure he doesn't lag behind.' That was how Iqbal was designated to wet-nurse Omar.

It also explained why Omar and Iqbal were right at the end of the column that was moving in single file towards a gap in the Indian Army posts strung along the LOC. One of the instructors, Wahid Ali, was at the tail of the column with Omar and Iqbal ensuring no stragglers. The other led the column along with Abu Khan.

About ten minutes after the patrol had left Chakoti Post the instructor at the head signalled the column to a silent halt. They all stood around in silence for a good five minutes till a scruffy, battle-hardened man suddenly appeared from the flanks. 'Salaam!' the man whispered to the instructor, who acknowledged his greeting with a brief nod.

'You're late.'

'Something came up at the last minute.' The man had a guttural voice and a very pronounced Afghan accent. He took up position right at the head of the column, ahead of Abu Khan. Clearly he was their guide for the night. They set off again. The pace was slower and more deliberate. The strong current of tension in the air was palpable in the stillness of the night. It showed on the grim faces of the instructors. Only the rugged Afghan seemed impervious. All of them knew that the Indian Army was on high alert despite the recent earthquake in Muzaffarabad which had devastated a large part of that area. Infiltrating into India was becoming increasingly tough and, if Indian news channels and newspapers were to be believed, the mujahideen casualty rate during this phase of the operation had become shockingly high. During their training, the instructors had repeatedly warned the trainees about the new battlefield surveillance radars that the Indian Army was using; capable of picking out a small group of men moving six kilometres away despite the broken terrain. And those fucking Russian Dragunov sniper rifles, they'd cautioned, were certain death: 'A good man can take out a guy with a clean head-shot from over 600 metres away – day or night!'

Just how effective these devices were and how well-trained the Indian soldier was, became abundantly clear barely forty minutes later, when the infiltration party was about 300 metres across the LOC. One moment there was total silence broken only by the sound of heavy breathing as the fifteen men trudged stealthily up the rugged mountain path. Then two shots rang out and immediately dozens of flares illuminated the sky. The first two shots killed the Afghan and Abu Khan. Immediately, hundreds of glowing bullets arced through the darkness like fireflies. The ear-shattering din of the fusillade that followed was a combination of the harsh chatter of machine-gun fire and the tortured screams of the young jihadis. A few of the trainees managed to get their weapons out and return fire. Iqbal saw a couple of his friends try to rush the ambush, as they had been taught, but luck was not on their side that night. In a matter of minutes, the silence of death lay heavy around him. The merciless hail of bullets that tore through the undergrowth and blanketed the trail cut down the entire patrol, barring the three who lagged behind.

Watching his companions of six months die before his eyes Iqbal felt a liquid warmth spread down his legs. Iqbal did not even realize he had pissed in his pants as he frantically stumbled in the treacherous darkness. Wahid Ali pulled Omar and him down to the ground, fiercely motioning for them to fall back. 'Get down! *Down!*' The instructor's strident whisper was more effective than the loudest scream. 'Get down and move back down the trail.... stay low, you fools.' Maybe the sound of gunfire had deadened the ears of the ambush party. Maybe Allah was watching over them and did not want them to die that night.

A classic ambush comprises scouts or stops on all routes that lead out from the kill zone, an ambush party that is sited to deliver the maximum possible firepower on the kill zone and a small reserve party to cater for unforeseen contingencies. The Indian Army ambush was well sited. The kill zone had been totally saturated with firepower. However it had obviously been set up in a hurry to take out a suddenly emerging target of opportunity because the tail of the infiltrating party was not covered. Obviously the Indian ambush party stops were not even aware of the three people trailing about eighty feet behind the tail of the column since no shots came anywhere near them.

Twenty minutes later the three of them were back on the trail, moving stealthily, when all of a sudden

Wahid Ali stumbled and fell. As Iqbal rushed to help him up, he saw him tentatively touch his stomach and holding up bloodied fingers say, 'Crap! I think I've been hit.'

'Janab, do you think you can go on?' Iqbal asked, desperately trying to sound calm, while inside his head he was going berserk. *Please don't die on me. What the hell will I do alone with Omar? I don't want to die in the wilderness here…*

'Don't panic, boy, I'm not done for yet.' Wahid Ali seemed to read his thoughts. 'Pull out one of those field dressings from your pack…and some painkillers.'

Iqbal's hands trembled as he shrugged off his pack and pulled out the first-aid kit. Omar, sitting on a rock a few feet away, held his head in his hands. From time to time he shuddered and a low moan escaped him. He was in shock.

Iqbal watched the instructor down a painkiller and stanch the bleeding with the field dressing. Then, grimacing in pain, he wrapped a bandage tightly around his abdomen. A few minutes later, the instructor staggered to his feet and took up his weapon again. But for the fact that he clutched the right side of his stomach it was hard to tell that he had been hit. 'It must have been a ricochet that got lucky,' he said.

'Is it hurting?' It seemed an absurdly dumb question to ask. Then again, Iqbal could hardly ask him if he was going to die, though in fact that was all he was interested in knowing. Wahid Ali had to live because his own survival depended on him.

'It seems manageable right now,' the instructor spoke through gritted teeth, 'but the bullet is lodged inside. I can feel it. I need to have it looked at…or else…' he broke off; he did not want to pursue that chain of thought.

'Should we head back then?'

'We cannot go back to Chakoti,' Wahid Ali said grimly. 'The Indians will be expecting us to do that. Chakoti is the closest of our posts so they will know we must have started out from there. By now they will definitely have another ambush waiting for us on that route. We have to loop around the ambush site and head for the camp we were going to.'

'How much further is it?'

'About an hour and a half…maybe a little more if I am not able to maintain the pace.'

'Do you think you will be able to manage such a long walk with that wound?' Iqbal asked. 'And what about him?' Iqbal jerked his thumb at Omar who was now moving only when they prodded him and collapsed to the ground when they stopped for a minute.

'There is no choice.' Wahid Ali seemed determined enough. But as they stumbled and groped their way through the forest he seemed to lose focus. He halted frequently and his breathing grew heavier. The blood loss was telling on him. Once or twice he cried out sharply in pain. The sound rang out in the stillness of the rapidly receding night. Iqbal froze when that happened; his body bracing itself for the barrage of gunfire that he was sure would shoot out at them from the darkness around in response to the sound.

'Is it getting worse? You want to rest a while?' Iqbal asked after the instructor stumbled and fell yet again.

'No!' The instructor leveraged himself up slowly. 'We have to keep moving. If I stop now I will not be able to get moving again.' He licked his dry lips. 'Don't worry...I can do this...I've seen worse.' He was speaking more to convince himself than Iqbal. 'See that peak there?' He pointed to a slightly crooked peak towering over them. 'We have to take the saddle to the right of it. The path runs almost along the base. Just in case...' his voice faltered and then trailed off. Then he lifted himself up slowly and they stumbled after him again.

Dawn had started to break when they staggered upon the small camp in the thick pine-laden forest just north of the Indian village of Hari. No one who had not been here before could possibly have known of its existence. A light snow began to fall just as they approached. The sentry who emerged like a ghost from the tree-laden shadows was expecting them. He seemed to recognize the instructor because he waved him on into the small clearing where the camp was sited.

'Only three of you?' he asked.

The instructor nodded. He was too far gone to be able to talk.

'That firing last night?' The sentry raised a quizzical eyebrow. 'Was that your party?'

Wahid Ali didn't answer. He had collapsed in a ragged heap to the ground.

SALIM

It was about two weeks after that spectacular quarterly review meeting on India Strategy that Salim received a curt phone call from the General's aide. 'The President has requested your presence at the Central Command Headquarters at 1100 hours tomorrow.' Despite the way it was worded there was nothing remotely resembling a request in the order; these simple summons had led to many more important men than him vanishing without trace.

The next day Salim arrived outside the Presidential office dressed in full military regalia. Excluding the two heavily-armed guards who watched him from under hooded eyes, the plush office was vacant. He was still contemplating the implications inherent in this when the door flew open and the General strode in. 'Salim!' The General's tone was full of jovial bluster. 'Come...' The General gestured to the plush leather sofas arrayed on one side of the huge office. Two hours later, armed with explicit instructions and a very free hand, Salim's life in the ISI had hit the fast track.

It was at Salim's initiative that Pakistan began to focus attention on Nepal and Bangladesh. They proved ideal for getting at India at virtually no cost to Pakistan. 'Isn't it strange,' Salim mused to his Adjutant in a rare moment of introspection, 'how easy it is to foment hatred and violence?'

The passage of years proved how right Salim had been in the strategy he'd selected. The Indians were bled white for over two decades in a low-intensity, constantly simmering conflict that cost them millions of rupees and tied down thousands of troops and security forces in the Kashmir Valley. The Pakistanis spent scarcely a dime; simply using the poppy fields of Afghanistan to fund their war.

Salim's mind swept over the years, his thoughts dwelling briefly on all the plans of his that had drawn Indian blood. *Even when I saw our boys being thrown back from the heights of Kargil and retreating shamefully I did not feel let down because I knew we had made the Indians pay for it. I know how many body bags they shipped down from Kargil. Each Indian dead body is one more victory for us.*

Salim had ensured that the ISI exploited every possible opportunity to breed hatred, discontent and violence in India. The assassination of Rajiv Gandhi, the demolition of the Babri Masjid, Ram Janam Bhoomi, the general elections, the Mandal riots, the Godhara train burning. Even so, not many were aware of just how deeply the ISI had sunk its tentacles into every aspect of Indian society and polity. It was Salim who had almost single-handedly choreographed the hijacking of the Indian Airlines flight from

Kathmandu, forcing the damn Indians to hand over a few diehard loyalists to the Taliban. He had even ensured the buggers paid in hard currency to free the hostages. It was his ingenuity and deviousness that helped extricate scores of Pakistani soldiers, paramilitaries and irregulars from Herat and Kandahar from right under the noses of the American forces that had closed in on them when they'd attacked Afghanistan after 9/11.

'Can you imagine, those fools have the temerity to codename the Afghan invasion Operation Infinite Justice? Don't they know that it is only Allah who metes out infinite justice?' the General had said to Salim. As far as he was concerned, the American invasion of Afghanistan spelt the end of years of Pakistani domination of Afghanistan's internal affairs. The exceedingly radical and simple-minded Taliban never even realized how totally it had always been manipulated by the ISI; those of its members who had shown the slightest signs of intelligence, more often than not, finding themselves dead.

'What else can we expect from those idiots, sir?' Salim guessed what was going on in his General's mind and nodded sympathetically.

'Right, especially from that idiot who sits at the helm of America's affairs. I really wonder how he managed to get elected twice. Inshahallah, we shall see the downfall of this arrogant white Satan soon. See what those slimy buggers have done to us now.' The General tossed a sheaf of newspapers towards him. The news of the nuclear agreement coming up for discussion between India and America hogged the headlines in most of them.

Salim did not even bother to pick them up. 'The Indians have been working on this for years now.'

'True. That kafir President will try to ensure the agreement goes through before the American elections due at the end of next year. That way, no matter who wins, he will go down in history as the one who put Indo–American relations on the fast track.'

'More than that, he desperately needs something to divert the attention of his public from the American body bags that are being flown in from Afghanistan and Iraq. Of course, it is also no great secret that the Americans are always salivating for a bigger share of the huge Indian market.'

'The bastards will do anything to ingratiate themselves with these damn kafirs,' the General said harshly.

'Undoubtedly,' Salim nodded. 'Why else are they running around offering the F-16s and F-18s to the Indians? They are dying to do that despite the fact that they denied us the same planes because of the nuclear tests we conducted. They are treacherous bastards. The American dogs will jeopardize Pakistan's security without giving it a second thought. This is nothing new for them. They used our Afghan brothers and us against the Russians when they needed to do so. Then they tossed us aside like used toilet paper when the Russians withdrew from

Afghanistan. They are now happily using Pakistan to bring Afghanistan to heel since there is no way in hell they could do it on their own.'

'Can you imagine, they have about 12,000 soldiers in Afghanistan? 12,000?' The General's harsh laugh rent the air: 'There are more than 12,000 cops in New York alone and I don't have to tell you how safe New York is.'

'Who cares!' Salim retorted. 'It is not as though we are doing anything much beyond feeding their propaganda machine. Our top brass is savvy enough to throw them the middling, meaningless foot soldier once in a while so that they can trumpet to the world that they have taken out another Al-Qaida commander and are winning their war on terror. That keeps the fools happy and as long as they are happy the dollars won't stop. It is a foregone conclusion that as long as Sheikh Sahib is not found the dollars will keep flowing in.'

The Americans had no clue that the man they were spending millions of dollars trying to find was safe and sound, right under their very noses. On any given day Salim could have strolled down to the safe house the ISI had placed him in and have tea with him. In fact, very often that is precisely what Salim did. He had tremendous respect for the man's dedication to the holy cause, not to mention the lethal forces and incredible wealth that lay at his beck and call.

There was another longish pause as random thoughts skewered through the minds of both men.

Yet again it was the General who broke the silence.'In fact, I often wish we could teach them a nice lesson about what happens to people who stab their friends in the back. Unfortunately, this is not the time...the diplomatic consequences and economic fallout would be too high. We need those dollars right now if we have to salvage our economy and get back on our feet.' There was another pause. The General gave Salim a long look. 'Of course, there would be no such problems with punishing the Indian bastards.'

When the meeting ended a few minutes later and Salim strode out of the office his leader's unspoken command lay clear in his mind. He had only three months to retire and in this short period of time he had to do something that would make the General proud of him. Salim knew the time had come to deliver one last major strike against the kafirs.

No matter what the political rhetoric, everyone in the ISI knew that the hunting season on India was always open. In any case, their pussyfooting leadership, full of eunuchs, just begged to be hit. The General would be thrilled; so long as the strike could not be traced back to them overtly. Plausible deniability. That was the name of the game. *Whether we do it or not is not the issue, as long as we are not seen to be doing it.* That was the mantra of the times they lived in. Salim laughed at the thought.

'I am going to be taking direct charge of every aspect of the operation,' Salim told Maulana Fazlur Rehman when they met to discuss the final plans in August 2005. Rehman did not seem very pleased but then what choice did he really have? He and his terror clansmen were almost totally at the mercy of the ISI.

On his part, Salim was beyond caring what anyone else thought about it. He had seen these dim-witted jihadis mess up one mission after another with their ham-handed approach and was quite fed up with it all. *They are motivated and ready to die, but they lack the perception and creativity to actually strike a lethal blow. This time I am going to ensure that things go exactly as planned. This is my final mission; there cannot be any mess-up.*

Salim carefully picked each man himself and took personal charge of every little detail; he wanted his final mission to be a memorable one, a fitting end to an eventful career. As Salim went over the minutiae of the operation for the hundredth time in his mind he wished he had more time to plan and execute the hit. Unfortunately, the day of the strike was predetermined. If the damage had to be both to Indian morale and material, there could be no better day for it.

IQBAL

December 2004, New Delhi, India.
It was the feeling that something was missing from his life that had made Iqbal first accompany his uncle Rashid to the mosque. Six months had passed since Iqbal had moved to Delhi from Lucknow to join a diploma course in engineering and work with his uncle in his spare parts shop. But the impersonal monotony of life in the metro had begun to get to him. 'You don't seem very happy these days, son,' Rashid mamu said to him one day. His uncle was a perceptive man, quite sensitive to the feelings of others.

'I'm fine, mamu jaan,' Iqbal replied with a polite smile. But the truth is that he wasn't. He missed his friends and family back home. The day scholars in the engineering college he had enrolled at had all grown up in Delhi and had their own cliques. The out-of-towners were all in the hostel and stuck together because of that. The long evenings he spent tinkering in his uncle's shop were becoming less the pursuit of an enjoyable hobby and more a refuge from loneliness.

Rashid waved his hand expansively at the shop – 'I could never have imagined that my little shop would turn into such a goldmine. All the credit goes to you of course, my boy. But you need a break. Maybe I can introduce you to some of the neighbourhood boys at the mosque?'

'Yes, mamu,' Iqbal said, not wanting to offend his uncle.

The only religious experience that Iqbal had hitherto been exposed to had been the morning chapel service at La Martiniere, his school in Lucknow. Despite the tranquil beauty of the school chapel and the soothing cadence of the hymns, the service had never been an exceptionally moving experience for him. Iqbal only attended because it was mandatory. In any case, Iqbal always made sure he blended in as much as possible. He was only too aware of the fact that he would never have been admitted to such a fancy school had his father not been a staff member; something the rich brats in his class seldom let him forget.

Unlike the strangely sterile chapel service, Iqbal's first visit to the mosque left him disturbed and confused. The serene, softly-lit, incense-laden school chapel contrasted starkly with the densely-packed mosque that smelt of sweat and toil – a smell Iqbal associated with the workers in the garage. And the angry talk of harsh realities that the Maulavi gave later was so unlike the namby-pamby teachings of his school. He thought of the soft, well-fed, self-absorbed boys at school and college and was surprised at the bitterness he suddenly felt.

Iqbal was not sure why he returned to the mosque again, but return he did. On his second visit to the mosque Iqbal found himself listening closely to the Maulavi's sermon. Something in the man's words touched his own barely articulated feelings of persecution. He was completely engrossed in the sermon the Maulavi gave that day. Possibly that is why Maulavi Sahib noticed him and stopped him as he was leaving the mosque. 'You are new around here, aren't you?'

'Yes, sir. I have just moved here from Lucknow.' Iqbal lied instinctively, knowing that the Maulavi would not be pleased to learn that Iqbal had not been coming for prayers all these days. 'I stay with my uncle, Rashid.'

'And what do you do, young man?'

'I am studying engineering, sir.'

'Good, good. We need educated people. Engineers, mechanics, doctors, surgeons – all men of science and all believers.' He patted Iqbal on his shoulder. 'May Allah watch over you.' The Maulavi was old and frail looking but his eyes were straight and clear and his demeanour conveyed unmistakable strength. There was something deeply mesmerizing in the way he communicated his ideas to the congregation. Iqbal felt flattered that he had singled him out.

Thereafter it became customary for Iqbal to go to the mosque every day and to stay on after the evening prayers to spend time with the Maulavi. Iqbal was not the only one whom Maulavi Sahib spoke to. There were always a few young men hanging around, most of them in their late teens. Almost all of them were starting their careers, pursuing a higher education or doing some technical course. Barring the rare exception, most of these young men were small-towners who had recently moved to Delhi. This struck none of them as strange; in fact their rootlessness bound them together. The youths in the group changed constantly. Every once in a while one or two of them would abruptly stop coming and literally vanish from the city; then other young men would take their place.

It was perhaps three months after Iqbal became a part of this group that the Maulavi took him aside. 'Why don't you stay on after the others leave today, I want to have a talk with you.'

Iqbal instinctively sensed that something cataclysmic was going to happen to him. Maybe, deep down, Iqbal even knew what it was because he was not in the least surprised when the Maulavi began to talk. That was the day the frail man with the steely eyes recruited Iqbal into the dreaded militant organization – the Lashkar-e-Toiba. 'The kafirs have never accepted us...not then and not now. We have always been outsiders for them. They tried to wipe us out at the time of Partition.' There was such hatred in the old man's words that for a moment Iqbal forgot he was a man of god. 'What they are doing today is even worse. They are trying to subjugate our very spirit. Remember, as a devout Muslim it is your fundamental duty to stand up and fight when your religion and community are threatened.'

Two weeks later when Iqbal was about to leave after the evening prayers, the Maulavi beckoned to him again. 'Meet me in my room in fifteen minutes.' Iqbal slowly made his way to the room just behind the mosque where the Maulavi lived. When Iqbal reached the room there were two other young men waiting by the locked door. Both were about his age. In fact, Iqbal even knew one of them since he, Omar, a pale skinny guy, one of the few originally from Delhi, was also one of the regulars who stayed back after evening prayers every day.

When the Maulavi Sahib arrived a short while later they all stood up to greet him. He unlocked his room, ushered them in and went straight to a small metal box placed in a corner to empty the contents of his pockets. Iqbal saw several bundles of crisp currency-notes stashed in the box.

The three boys spent a couple of hours with the Maulavi that evening and he spoke about the huge struggle that Islam was facing to overthrow the dominance of the kafir and how they could all be a part of the victorious army that would stride forth in the footsteps of the Prophet (Peace be upon Him). 'I think all three of you are ready to stand up and be counted.' The Maulavi gave them an assessing look: 'It is time you three went for higher training...'

'What kind of training, Maulavi Sahib?' Omar asked.

'My boy, you are going to wage a tough and dangerous war against a well-trained enemy. To do so you must be trained equally well. We will be sending you out of the country for the required training.'

The very thought of going abroad to train to fight the kafir in exotic battlefields the world over sent the blood coursing through Iqbal's veins and thrilled him more deeply than words could express; he shivered with excitement as the Maulavi continued: 'We understand that all of you are family people and cannot just run away from your basic responsibilities. You will all be handsomely compensated. In fact, just before we leave for training you shall receive one lakh rupees each.' The generous amount took the youngsters by surprise. 'There will be more once your training is over. We will take good care of you at all times,' the Maulavi smiled.

Iqbal's mind was in a whirl. He was unable to focus on anything except the glorious visions that were described to them. He imagined himself firing guns, handling explosives and radio sets...like they did in the movies. The only problem was that he could not talk about it to his family or to anyone else for that matter.

Still, Rashid did not look shocked when Iqbal handed over the money that the Maulavi had given to him. 'Please have a bank draft made and send it to Ammi.' Iqbal was smart enough to know that his mother would ask too many questions if he called her himself. Sure enough, she phoned the next day.

'Where on earth did you get so much money from, Iqbal?'

'This is the training stipend they have given us, Ammi.'

'Training stipend? Who gives out so much money in advance to people they have barely hired?' Hamida felt a little sick. 'Iqbal, are you sure you know what you're doing?'

'Come on, Ammi! Do you think I will do anything dumb?' Iqbal went into a long spiel about a company in the Middle-East that had come to the college to recruit students and send them abroad for training.

Then Rashid mamu took the phone from Iqbal and gently persuaded his sister that all was fine. Her son was doing well in college, he assured her. With his diligence and dedication it was no wonder that the Middle-East company had picked him out. One day her son would be famous all over the world.

And so Iqbal found himself a few days later, en route to Nepal along with Omar and Akram.

Two weeks later the three boys got off the bus at Bahraich on the Indo–Nepal border just as the sun was coming up over the horizon. There were not too many people about at that hour and the bus-stand wore a deserted look. They walked over to the telephone booth in the corner and called the number they had been given. It was snatched up: 'Go towards the exit gate. To the right of the gate is a bookstall. I will be there in ten minutes. Don't wander off, I can't go looking for you all over the damn place,' a voice said curtly before banging down the phone.

The three young men did as they were told. About twenty minutes later a stocky, hard-looking man in his late thirties walked into the bus station. He loitered around for a few minutes, pretending to be waiting for someone before walking up to them. 'You have something for me?'

For a moment they were all nonplussed; then Omar's face brightened. 'Yes, yes. We do.' Reaching into his pocket he pulled out the postcard that the Maulavi had given him the day they were leaving. All three of them had read the brief message on it a dozen times, but it had communicated nothing to them. Apparently it did make sense to the man who stood before them now. 'I'm Khurram. I will be taking you across.' The way he said his name Iqbal knew that it was not his real one.

'Hullo.' Omar couldn't help being himself; he extended his hand, 'I'm Omar.'

'Enchanted,' Khurram's voice dripped sarcasm. 'Alas, I have no wish to socialize with you. I suggest we communicate as little as required.' Khurram led them to a battered-looking Maruti Gypsy parked outside. A man waited behind the wheel. He started the engine when he saw them approach. Iqbal had heard enough engines in Rashid's garage to figure that the powerful, well-maintained engine belied the dented exterior of the vehicle.

Half an hour out of the town the driver abruptly drove off the road and swerved onto a scarcely visible dirt track. The hardened mud track ran through a forest that became progressively thicker as time passed. The bumpy ride was made more uncomfortable by the tense silence that pervaded the jeep and the clouds of dust that streamed in from the windows. No one said a word to the three of them, but they knew for sure that they were in the middle of an illegal border crossing.

Abruptly, the Gypsy came to a screeching halt in the middle of nowhere. The man who called himself Khurram got off and vanished into the thick undergrowth. The three lads from Delhi sat in the stifling jeep watching the dust slowly settle around them. About ten minutes later Khurram reappeared as suddenly as he had vanished. 'Get off,' he whispered. 'We go on foot from here. No noise, understand?' He waited till all three of them had disembarked and then strode off into the undergrowth.

'I hope there are no snakes around,' Iqbal heard Omar say softly.

Khurram turned around immediately and glared at him: 'Shut up, you dumb fuck,' he hissed. 'One sound from you can get us all killed. I won't warn you again.'

Though Iqbal could not see them himself, he knew Khurram was following some markings on the ground as he stopped every so often to check and get his bearings.

Twice during that hour-long walk Khurram came to an abrupt halt. Both times he froze and urgently gestured to the others to follow suit. Mouths went dry and hearts raced as the three young men waited, tense with anxiety. Both times Khurram waited for a good five to ten minutes before he resumed the journey.

The thick foliage ended abruptly and they came to a clearing. A man lolled in the grass on its outer edge. 'Ah! There you are!' The obviously Nepalese man clad in faded jeans and a dark brown jacket jumped to his feet when he saw them. He gave a hearty laugh. Startled by the sudden loud sound they looked around nervously, but there seemed to be no further need for silence since the new man and Khurram were conversing in normal tones. Iqbal followed only the occasional word as they were talking in Nepalese. Khurram seemed amazingly fluent in the language. When the Nepalese man turned to walk away his jacket unfurled slightly revealing a pistol stuck in his waistband. It was Iqbal's first sighting of a real gun and it sent the adrenaline pumping into his system; he could not wait to feel the cold metal of a gun in his own hand.

A few minutes later the small group moved on again. The jungle soon gave way to sparsely cultivated bits of land on the edge of which stood a desolate looking hut with a dilapidated station wagon parked next to it. Though the vehicle was definitely worse than the Gypsy they had left behind, the road ahead was a marked improvement. Thirty minutes later they stopped at a house on the outskirts of a small village. 'Any idea where we are?' Omar asked.

'The signboards are all in Nepalese,' Iqbal whispered back. 'But I saw one in English. It said Kathmandu on one side and Nepalganj on the other. I guess we are on the highway from Nepalganj to Kathmandu.'

'You three have fifteen minutes to freshen up and grab a bite. Then we leave,' Khurram announced before going across to meet the other nine recruits who had been waiting for them in the house. 'While they wash up, you guys get your stuff loaded.' He jerked his thumb at a bus parked outside.

Twenty minutes later they were speeding towards Kathmandu. This time the bus was new and well-maintained. The twelve boys in it exchanged curious glances with each other, but Khurram's presence went a long way in curtailing any conversation. They halted only twice when bladder pressures threatened to get out of control.

It was just after Pokhara that they took the second proper halt. Another safe house organized specially for transients like them. There was an indifferent but hot meal waiting. After they had eaten, Khurram gathered them around the table and pulled out a bunch of passports. He flipped open each, checked the photograph and particulars, and handed them out. Iqbal's passport was made out to a Wasim Khan. It had been issued in Karachi a week ago.

'The passports are genuine; no immigrations authority anywhere will be able to find any flaws,'

Khurram said. 'I want all of you to memorize the personal details mentioned in the passport. Go through the brief history of your life on the piece of paper in the passport. These are your official legends. If you're questioned by anyone that is the story you will give out and no matter what happens, you stick to that story.' He looked around authoritatively. 'Once you have memorized the details return the paper to me. You have fifteen minutes before we leave for the airport.'

The actual check-in at Kathmandu airport was an anti-climax. The people manning the customs and immigrations counters were busy chatting with each other. The twelve trainees collected their boarding passes after being expertly hustled through immigrations by Khurram, who was obviously more than a little well-known; everyone seemed to have a polite nod for him. Then they breezed past security, seeing that none of them had any carry-on baggage.

Khurram walked away from them even as the last of the twelve recruits was being cleared through security.

Once he disappeared from sight, the twelve recruits were on their own. Only then did they actually start talking to each other. The flight from Kathmandu to Karachi was still over an hour away; enough time to catch up on their real life stories.

Though Iqbal didn't particularly care for Omar, they had started out together on this long journey and they were together when Abu Khan walked up to talk to them. In the months that followed the three of them were to become good friends. Maybe because all three had similar backgrounds as far as their schooling went. Omar and Abu Khan were also from English-medium schools. Omar had just dropped out of law college and Abu Khan had enrolled for a computer course when Allah put them on this path. By the time they reached Karachi they each had a reasonable idea of what the other was about. Over the months they spent together Iqbal would learn a lot more about his new friends. Omar was a skinny, soft-looking guy but he was rock-solid in the head. Sometimes Iqbal had a tough time believing Omar had actually got into law college but, then again, he had yet to meet another person his age who knew the Koran Shareef better than Omar did; the guy could quote it chapter and verse.

Abu Khan, on the other hand, was quiet and dignified with a strong athletic build and rock-star looks. He excelled effortlessly at whatever he did. In all the months they trained together Iqbal never saw him seriously apply himself to anything. It was almost as though he just absorbed stuff he saw happening around him. None of the others in their group felt any shame in admitting that they envied Abu Khan. Possibly the only thing that Iqbal did better than him was handling explosives. It must have been his training with Rashid that gave Iqbal the edge in this department.

All that came much later. The flight to Karachi was short and sweet. It was the first air trip that Omar, Abu Khan and Iqbal had ever taken.

The man who met them at Karachi Airport was waiting right on the airfield when they deplaned. He stopped each of them the moment they got onto the aerobridge and took them aside.

'This guy has to be Khurram's twin,' Omar whispered to Abu and Iqbal.

Abu grinned back. 'I think he is the elder twin if his surliness is any indication.'

The man in question stood there oblivious to everything around till all twelve of them had deplaned. When they were all finally gathered around him he commanded, 'Give me all your passports.' He shoved them into the small laptop bag he was toting. 'We will leave now.'

'What about our bags?'

'They will come. Follow me.' Then he turned and walked away.

The twelve young men did not encounter a single security, customs or immigrations checkpoint all the way to the small exit on the far left of the airport terminal, where a large, white bus waited outside. They saw their bags already stowed in the boot as they boarded the bus.

The man who escorted them outside sat on the seat behind the driver. He spoke to no one. Nor did he get off the bus when it pulled up outside a large, white building with light green doors two-and-a-half hours later. If there had been a signboard with the name of the madrassa they were being put up in, it had been removed before the recruits got there. But a madrassa it definitely was; that much was obvious from the lay-out of the building, even though it was strangely devoid of people.

A large, robust looking man waited for them. 'Greetings, brothers!' His beard wagged as his voice boomed into the bus. 'Welcome. Welcome to Tatta.' It was a pleasant change to finally meet someone who did not behave as if he was perpetually sitting on a hard, sharp object.

Early next morning, after a fairly decent breakfast, they were off again. The bus was the same, as was the driver, but the pleasant guy had replaced the surly one. The atmosphere in the bus changed dramatically. Now a light, almost festive, spirit prevailed as decibel levels in the bus rose in animated chatter.

'I know exactly how you all must be feeling,' their new escort said as they sped along. 'I too felt the same way when I came here six years ago.'

'Six years ago? Wow!'

'You must have seen a lot of...'

'Don't you feel like going home?'

Almost everyone had a question to ask or an observation to make. Between sporadic bouts of sleep the chatter continued as Hyderabad, Tando, Nawabshah, Moro, Khairpur, Rohri and a host of other cities and unheard of villages fell away in the dust behind them.

From Tatta onwards the road ran almost parallel to the Indus River. Every so often they crossed a small cluster of houses, very similar to those in India. The terrain on both sides of the road could easily have been mistaken for a part of Rajasthan or Haryana except for the fact that there was a lot more military presence in evidence and the starkness of poverty was more sharply visible.

Iqbal had been watching the milestones along the highway for quite some time and knew they were at Sukkur when the bus halted for the night; once again at a strangely desolate madrassa.

The Indus was left behind on the second day when they crossed it at Uch and the Chenab took over all the way up to Muzaffargarh. From the little geography Iqbal had studied he knew that the Indus still flowed alongside, flanking them, but it was not visible from the road. The madrassa they halted at that night was a much smaller one and not as well maintained. 'How come all the places we stay at are so deserted?' Omar wondered aloud.

By the time the bus reached Talagang on the fourth night, their enthusiasm was on the wane. The road from Muzaffargarh to Mianwali had been okay. Not as good as the roads they had covered but a darn sight better than the pot-holed moonwalk they hit once they crossed Mianwali. However the Talagang madrassa they halted at that night was beautiful and old. Even the food was palatable for a change.

Iqbal was not sure what disturbed his sleep but he woke suddenly in the middle of the night. There was a bright moon outside and its silvery light bathed the hall. Iqbal got up and headed out for the courtyard.

It was a clear, beautiful night. The rectangular courtyard had a small water tank almost directly in front of the dormitory. The still water sparkled in the moonlight and beckoned to him like a long lost lover. Iqbal felt an amazing sense of tranquillity as he sat on the edge of the water tank and watched the night sky.

'Not able to sleep?' The voice was soft but the suddenness of it jolted Iqbal out of his reverie. He turned to see their genial escort standing behind him.

'No...something woke me up and then I just couldn't sleep again.'

The man sat down beside him. They sat in companionable silence for a while until he asked, 'Where are you from, my friend?'

'Lucknow.' It was the first time he'd been asked a personal question in Pakistan. 'My name is Iqbal. What is yours?'

'Wasim.' Then noticing the smile on Iqbal's face, he asked, 'Did I say something funny?'

'That is the name I am travelling under from Kathmandu to Karachi. Strange coincidence, isn't it?'

Wasim smiled. 'I am from Aligarh.'

'I have never been to Aligarh but my folks are originally from there.'

'Really?' Wasim laughed softly. 'Another strange coincidence. You know, it has been almost six years since I have been to Aligarh...Sometimes I really miss my home... but I cannot go back now.' He took a deep breath: 'Not that I mind...it is a small sacrifice to make for the cause. There are others who have given up so much more. But then things seldom turn out the way we think they would. True, isn't it?'

Iqbal shrugged. 'Tell me, Wasim, how come all the places that we are staying in are totally deserted? Where is everyone?'

The man gave Iqbal a long look before he replied, 'They're not abandoned or empty. It is just that we have to be careful and ensure external trainees don't mix with the others...Salim Sahib is very strict about that.'

'I don't understand...what others?'

'The locals, primarily.'

'Why?'

'Not every one here supports the jihad. There are some who feel that Pakistan should worry more about itself and its economy rather than expend time, energy and resources on external problems.'

That is not what they have been telling us. 'I thought the people of Pakistan were solidly behind us...behind the jihad?'

'The people of Pakistan?' Wasim shrugged. 'People are people...when push comes to shove they tend to worry about basic things like food, shelter and clothing. Everything else is secondary.'

They sat in silence for a minute. Then Iqbal asked, 'Who is this Salim you just mentioned?'

'Salim Sahib?' Wasim suddenly looked uncomfortable. 'You will come to know in good time. I am sure you will run into him sooner or later...'

'He runs the camp where we are going?' Iqbal prodded him.

Suddenly Wasim was not in the mood to talk any longer. He got up abruptly. 'I need to get some sleep. Why don't you try to rest too…it is going to be a long day tomorrow.'

Iqbal could not see the expression on Wasim's face in the dark. Even so the turmoil within him reached out to Iqbal across the silvery moonlight. He stood there for a very long time after Wasim had gone, until the chill of the night began to add to the disquiet Wasim had stirred in him.

The tranquillity of the night had been disturbed.

The terrain started to change and the air grew distinctly colder as they crossed Rawalpindi and Islamabad late the next evening. They saw hills appear in the distance; small at first and then higher and more rugged. The winding road began to climb steeply. The sun had almost set when the bus finally came to a halt half-an-hour after crossing Muzaffarabad.

A cluster of silent huts and tents greeted the young recruits as they scrambled off the bus. There was not a soul visible anywhere. A frisson of fear ran through Iqbal.

Then the doors of one of the huts opened and two men walked out towards them. Everything about them screamed 'army'. Iqbal felt another stirring of apprehension as the duo strode up to the recruits. 'This is the Muzaffarabad training camp. I am...'

The men were neither welcoming nor warm. *Rather like the grumpy sergeants in the old war movies that I used to watch in school,* thought Iqbal.

SALIM

2210 hours, 27 October 2005, ISI Office, Lahore Army Cantonment, Pakistan.

'Allah be praised! That Afzal guy has delivered. See, sir, I told you he would.' Captain Azam Cheema gave a satisfied smile; Afzal had been his discovery.

'I still don't trust him,' replied Brigadier Salim. 'He is the only one in this mission who is here just for the money. If he can sell out his country for cash he can as easily sell us out to the Indians for more.'

'Don't worry, sir, he will continue to deliver. I have him well under control.' In the five years that he had served as Salim's aide, Cheema had never let him down. Somehow, deep inside, Salim knew he would rather die than let that happen.

'Well, Cheema, just make sure he is out of Delhi ASAP and in position for his next task.' Salim shelved further thought on Afzal for the moment; he had more important things to worry about. Picking up the satellite phone he dialled a number that was stored in the phone's memory. A moment later he was talking to the old Maulavi in Delhi. 'Are the boys ready?'

'Of course.' As usual the old man sounded supremely confident.

The Maulavi was one of the few Indians whom Salim did trust. Over the years he had regularly delivered a stream of young motivated men to the training camps run by the ISI. Many of these men had gone on to achieve great things in the Valley and inflicted terrible losses on the Indian security forces. This time too, it was the pick of Maulavi's recruits who had constituted the Lashkar. He had personally handpicked nine of them for this assignment. One had gotten injured during the training, but that was not a problem since only seven were needed for the actual operation. Even if they had taken one more hit the mission would not have been jeopardized. After all, reserves were the lifeblood of any operation. Wars were never won without cannon fodder.

'Excellent. Then let us begin.'

Ten minutes later, Salim's Lashkar swung into action.

The prelude to the dance of death had begun.

THE STRIKE

0520 hours, 28 October 2005, Aftab Cyber Café, Khirki Gaon, New Delhi.

The cyber café was a deep cover implant that had been established by the ISI several months ago and was to be activated only for a priority assignment, after clearance from the very highest quarters. Brigadier Murad Salim was definitely high up enough in the ISI hierarchy to ensure it was made available to him without a fuss.

The café, located in one of the several narrow lanes that radiated into Khirki Gaon colony opposite the small temple on the main road, was sited in a carefully reconnoitred and selected building. This particular lane was almost always deserted since it dead-ended just two houses beyond the cyber café. Both houses behind the cyber café were occupied by mid-level workers employed in the host of small factories and offices that crowded the colony. Since most of them were out-of-town migrants, residents were quite used to all kinds of people coming and going at odd hours; new faces drew no special attention here.

The first man arrived just before daybreak. The other five men arrived separately at irregular intervals of ten to twenty minutes. With the exception of one who looked as though he was barely out of his teens, all of them were in their late twenties or early thirties. There was nothing exceptional about any of them except that they were all physically much more fit than the average man on the streets and that they seemed to have a lot more money on them. All of them were clean-shaven and wore nothing that gave any indication of the god they worshipped.

'We will be working in this room. This is where I stay.' Furkan, the cyber café owner, pointed to the inner room. 'No one ever goes in there and the room has enough space for us to work comfortably.'

Unlike the outer room with the gleaming Pentium 4 machines the inner room was Spartan. The only modern thing in it was the small television set in a corner. In the other corner stood a small worktable with an assortment of tools stacked neatly on it.

'The packages are in the cupboard. Don't be in a hurry. One small screw-up, and we all get blown to bits,' Furkan cautioned needlessly.

'You two unpack and clean out the weapons,' the oldest member of the team said. He had an aura of authority and was clearly the designated mission leader. He was also the only one among them who had been in active operations before, although this was his first mission on Indian soil.

'You two,' he indicated Furkan and the youngest man in the team. 'Stay in the outer room and keep an eye open. No one is to wander in by mistake. Try and discourage people from using the cyber café today. Just don't get jumpy and do anything stupid.'

The youngest member and Furkan did as they were told. The youngest member was also the most tech savvy of them all. The two of them fiddled with the computers as they kept careful watch. The few customers who walked in during the day hung around for a few minutes and then left when they showed no sign of moving. Only one persistent young fellow tarried for almost twenty minutes before Furkan told him it was futile to wait. 'We are upgrading the machines and changing the Internet services provider,' he said apologetically.

For the rest of the day the three men worked without interruption, carefully assembling the bombs. There was not much by way of conversation as they all went about their carefully rehearsed tasks.

When the muezzin called the faithful for the Asr (afternoon) prayer, the team leader who had just finished cleaning all the weapons looked up. 'It is time for the namaz. After that I want you three,' he pointed to the men who had handed in the vehicles for servicing, 'to get the vehicles from the service stations. Make sure you check them out properly. Take a trial run and if you feel anything is even slightly amiss get it sorted out. We don't want any breakdowns tomorrow.'

As soon as they finished praying, the designated three moved out from the cyber café separately and went straight to the garages. The three stolen vehicles were collected, checked, test-driven and brought back to the cyber café. The two cars were parked at a little distance from the cyber café and dust covers were placed on them. The motorcycle was wheeled into the inner room where the men fitted used-looking metallic containers on both sides of the rear seat. As soon as the containers were fitted on, the two bomb makers moved in. The bomb itself was a simple device and took ten minutes to assemble. Wiring it up and fitting in the switch took another fifteen. When it was done, they checked the circuit with the tester. It worked fine.

After sunset the men went to work on the cars parked outside. They worked at a slow and deliberate pace and checked everything repeatedly. They worked with the precision of people who had rehearsed every action several times. The bomb that had been assembled during the day was placed in the boot of the Esteem and the wiring was connected up. A couple of old clothes were thrown over the bomb to conceal it. Next morning, by the time the muezzin called for the Fajr (morning) prayer, all the preparations were in order. Then they set to work thoroughly cleaning up the room and removing any telltale signs. All the scraps of material they had used were carefully bagged in a large garbage disposal bag.

'I'll take care of that,' Furkan said, picking up the bag. 'You guys go ahead and get some rest. We have a long day ahead.'

The six men dispersed, again in ones and twos at intervals of a few minutes each. They left the café with the satisfaction of people who had completed a difficult task properly and thoroughly. Everything was in order. Now all that remained was for the Lashkar to carry out the strike.

Death was straining to unleash.

1025 hours, 29 October 2005, M4K Multiplex, Delhi. The housekeeping and maintenance staff in the multiplex were almost done with their early-morning cleaning. Shopkeepers had arrived early, bracing themselves for the weekend rush. With Diwali and Eid just around the corner there was a note of festivity in the air. In the wake of a good harvest and a booming economy, shopkeepers and business owners were expecting a huge upswing in business.

'Jane kya hoga Rama re, jane kya hoga Maula re...' The ironically apt lyrics of a Bollywood film song floated through the air, powered by the sound system of the multiplex. The multiplex had been commissioned into service fairly recently. Its newness was evident in the fresh paint and sparkling walls. It was also evident in the manner that the staff responded to situations. Their operating procedures had yet to achieve the stability of time and experience. In fact, it was one of the reasons why this multiplex had been chosen as a target for the strike.

At ten-thirty the stolen Tata Indica turned off the main road and drove into the mall. The parking lot outside the mall was almost empty, as was the one in the basement. The man behind the wheel collected his parking token right at the entrance and started to drive in. The security guard standing just beyond the barrier gestured to him as the car approached. He tapped the window when he saw that the man driving the car was looking the other way. 'Sir, you can park right here.' He pointed at the empty parking lot.

'That's okay,' the man replied. 'I would rather park inside.'

Suit yourself, weirdo. I was just trying to help. As the guard shrugged and walked away the man at the wheel of the Indica heaved a sigh of relief. Engaging gears, he drove into the basement and headed straight for the parking slot nearest to the huge electricity transformer installed there. 'Allah be praised!' The slot was empty.

He had picked out two other suitable alternatives during the dry run earlier, but neither of them was half as effective as this one. He carefully reversed into the slot and locking up the car made his way towards the ticketing window. 'What are the show timings?' he asked the youngster manning the counter.

The eager lad handed over a beautifully printed brochure. 'These are the movies and their timings. You can check out availability on that screen there,' he pointed at the monitor installed above the counter. Almost all the morning shows had a small green light glowing in front of them, but the afternoon and evening ones mostly had red dots, indicating a full house. *Good! The more the merrier.*

'Thanks.' The man spent the next few minutes casually wandering about the multiplex. The crowd had started to build up and the parking lot had a fair number of vehicles in it.

Leaving the multiplex he made his way out to the main road and flagged down a taxi. As the cab pulled away he tossed the movie brochure out of the window. It was irrelevant now. Show-timings were about to be rudely interrupted.

1400 hours, 29 October 2005, behind Savita Nagar Mosque, New Delhi.

'Surely Allah has bought of the believers their persons and their property for this, that they shall have the garden; they fight in Allah's way, so they slay and are slain...'

The Maulavi had deliberately chosen verse 9: 111 of the Koran to remind them of the heroic battle against the white Satan. As the prayer drew to a close, the Maulavi looked up and studied the seven men gathered in the small room. They were no different from all the other young men he had personally recruited for the jihad and sent to Salim. *I wonder how many of them are still alive*? The Maulavi smiled at the men. *How many of these boys will be alive today when the sun sets?* He was experienced enough to know that despite the most thorough planning anything could go wrong. There were simply too many variables to be able to factor them all in. *So be it. After all, men must fall in battle. Their sacrifice will not go waste.*

The youngest of the men was totally impervious to the tension that hung in the room like a naked wire. The other six men were more seasoned. They were tight-lipped and avoided looking at or talking to each other. *He is too young and inexperienced to know about the fear that comes as a precursor to battle. The fear that keeps men alert and alive.* For a moment the Maulavi thought he should speak to the youngster. Then he decided against it. *This is not the time to raise doubts in his head.* Instead the Maulavi sent up a silent, special prayer for Allah to watch over him. Then he looked at the men clustered before him and nodded. 'It is time.'

The men left the room in pairs at irregular intervals of five to ten minutes. Only Furkan waited for almost twenty minutes after the third pair had left. Pausing at the door he nodded to the Maulavi and said in a soft undertone, 'I will keep you informed. Keep your phone on. Khuda Hafiz!'

IQBAL

Life in training camp was the typical bittersweet experience that most military type trainings are – more bitter than sweet, with the sheer buggery of relentless physical exercise ensuring a constantly aching body sweetened by the occasional thrill of weapon-handling and bomb-making that appeals to young male minds as nothing else does.

In the first week itself Omar, Abu Khan and Iqbal got dubbed the 'English school types'. The instructors took a special delight in what they called 'sorting out their wrong notions'. 'We are going to make men out of you, boys,' the instructors told the recruits gleefully each morning till they began to dread the gruelling pre-dawn runs, the mind-numbing physical training and the forced marches with heavy weights on their backs and dummy rifles in their hands.

The instructors were better tolerated when the recruits moved on to weapon-handling, firing and bomb-making, from the third month of their training. Iqbal loved the thrill and excitement of bomb-making. In fact, he became so adept at it that even the explosives instructor acknowledged his mastery. But this was not much solace when they lay on their cots at night with every bone aching from the rigours of the day.

'These thick-headed Army clods are complete masochists. They thrive on torturing themselves and us,' said Abu Khan.

Omar was silent for a moment. 'You think they are from the Pakistan Army?'

'Well, they definitely don't look like Salvation Army types to me. Of course they are Army. Can't you tell from their haircuts, the way they walk and talk to each other?'Abu Khan answered.

It was an open secret that the instructors were junior and non-commissioned officers from the regular Pakistan Army. Though no one spoke openly about its support, the Pakistan Army's involvement was clearly evident in every aspect of the training camp; from the vehicles that ferried them about to the weapons and ammunition the jihadis used; but mostly in the manner in which people from the villages around avoided coming near the camp.

'I want the camp spotless and shining today,' they heard Maulana Fazlur Rehman tell the instructors during the morning parade, one day in their fourth month of training. 'Salim Sahib is going to be visiting us.'

The tall, heavily-bearded Fazlur Rehman was not only the camp commander, but also the founder of the group that sponsored this particular camp. He was a mesmerizing man. His deep commanding tone and bottomless eyes signalled the fire in his belly and the passion that jihad generated in him. He was a much-respected man and his group had the honour of being responsible for the highest number of successful strikes against the Indians, not just in Kashmir Valley but all the way down to the Akshardham Temple in Gujarat and the Indian Parliament in the heart of Delhi itself.

'Who is Salim Sahib?' Iqbal heard Omar ask one of the instructors as they were being put to work on cleaning up the camp.

'Shut up and do what you have been told,' the man replied irritably as he walked away.

'Don't you know better than to ask such dumb questions?' Abu Khan said to him after the instructor had moved out of earshot. 'Salim Sahib is Brigadier Murad Salim of the ISI. He is the one who provides our group with the support and money we need.'

'How do you know all this?'

'My cousin told me.'

'How does he know?'

'He trained here a year back. He is the one who motivated me to join.' Abu Khan paused. 'He was martyred in the Valley last month.'

Brigadier Salim came to the camp often in the last five or six weeks of their training. He spent most of his time with Fazlur Rehman. A tall, hard-looking man in his early thirties accompanied the Brigadier; he was like Salim's shadow.

On the last three days that the Brigadier was at the training camp a group of eleven men joined him. They spent all their time closeted in the large hut where radio, tactics and explosives theory classes were taught. The newcomers aroused a lot of curiosity amongst the other trainees, especially when it became clear that Brigadier Salim himself was spending a fair amount of time with them. But despite the endless debates their presence generated, no one was any the wiser about their identity. And then, one afternoon when the trainees returned from the firing range, the men were gone. So was Brigadier Murad Salim.

Their sudden disappearance would have surely led to another round of extensive debate if nature had not stepped in the way.

It was the eighth of October 2005. The twelve recruits were returning from the firing range when suddenly the earth began to move. At first Iqbal thought he was feeling giddy but then there was a deafening roar and the whole world started to buck and sway, shiver and tear up. Just as suddenly as it had started the frenzied shaking stopped and a harsh silence slammed down on the mountains. By the time he understood what was happening the earthquake was over. There was no time to be afraid; that came later.

The trainees ran up to the crest of the last hill overlooking the camp; the horrific sight below took their breath away.

The town of Muzaffarabad had been totalled. It was as if a herd of marauding elephants had trampled it to the ground. Even as they watched, weakened walls and buildings crumpled to the ground in softly billowing clouds of dust and debris. From the distance one could not hear the screams but it was not hard to imagine the death and destruction that had decimated the town.

The camp remained miraculously intact barring the hut that stored the arms and ammunition and the communications hut where the radio set was installed. The other huts had weathered the quake reasonably well, being temporary and lightweight structures.

The next two days were like a surreal nightmare; Fazlur Rehman was kind enough to immediately volunteer the services of the trainees for rescue work. It was obvious that Rehman's decision was more to do with propaganda than any feeling of goodwill. 'Double the guard on the camp,' Rehman ordered the senior instructor after sending out the trainees to Muzaffarabad for rescue work. 'Make sure no one gets at our supplies.'

Screams of anguish and pain met Iqbal as he and his colleagues walked into the devastated town. Bodies and body parts were everywhere, bleeding bewildered people stumbled about with dazed expressions looking for those they had lost, little kids wounded and traumatized with no one left to console them wailed into the wilderness. Iqbal knew he would carry the memories of this horrific nightmare to his grave.

'Allah is merciful!' Omar whispered as they started digging through the rubble. 'Had it been snowing who knows how many more would have died?'

Iqbal himself was witness to five huge heaps of mangled bodies that they recovered from the debris on the first day. By evening their minds and bodies had been pushed to the threshold. Stomachs and throats ached horribly from the constant retching and throwing up.

When darkness finally forced rescue efforts to a halt, the tired beaten men who stumbled back to camp that night had nothing in common with the enthusiastic young boys in search of adventure and a cause to believe in. The thrill and excitement of bombs and beliefs receded into the gaunt futility of death. *If this is how life can be brought to a sudden wrenching halt then what is the point of it all? What meaning does the jihad have...does anything have?*

The next morning again found them headed for the devastated town, sombrely shouldering their picks and shovels. The pieces of cloth tied around their mouths and noses did not smother the stink of death. They split up in pairs as they entered the town and reluctantly began to make their way into the desolation. Iqbal and Omar came up to the ruins of a small settlement. The silence was deathly. Suddenly Iqbal heard a dull thud and a muffled cry. Quickening his pace he walked around the collapsed wall of the hut.

A plump, thickset woman in her early forties lay in the rubble of what was once her home. Iqbal's heart lurched when he saw her. It was as if Hamida, his mother, was lying before him. The same kindly face, the same hennaed hair. The right side of her face was badly bloodied. The lower half of her body was buried in the debris. A thick wooden log lying across her body pinned her down. Iqbal could see her straining to raise the log and free herself.

Frantic hope flooded the woman's face when she saw Iqbal. 'My daughter is still buried under,' she flailed a hand. 'Please get her out of there. She is terrified of the dark.' The women's voice broke: 'Please, son ...please...my little girl.'

'Don't worry, Ammi.' The word eluded Iqbal's control; he looked away. 'We will, but let us get you out first.'

'Please!' she begged. 'Get her out first. She has been calling out to me and crying the whole night.' The woman's voice broke into a crazed sob. 'I have not heard her crying for sometime now,' she whispered after a long pause. 'She must be hurt.' There was a dogged hope in her words; words that resolutely denied the other reason for her daughter's silence.

'We will help you first.' Raising his voice Iqbal hailed Omar. Together the two of them managed to move the log away. And then he wished they hadn't. The lower half of the woman was pulp. Blood surged out as the pressure of the log lifted away. 'How is she still alive?' Omar whispered harshly. He too was struggling to retain control over himself.

'Zeenat...my daughter...' the woman seemed oblivious to her own pain. Or maybe the hurt in her heart overrode everything else. 'Please get her out.'

She pointed again towards the huge heap in the centre of the hut.

Omar and Iqbal exchanged a long look. Then they both went to work with their shovels. Minutes bled away. As did life from the lady lying on the hard cold floor of the place that had once been her home. She watched them with an unblinking gaze; the hope in her eyes glazing over into death as Iqbal and Omar pulled out the lifeless corpse of her daughter from the rubble. It was as though she had willed herself to stay alive only for her daughter.

Iqbal could not bring himself to abandon the dead woman and her teenage daughter. 'I want to bury them,' he finally told Omar.

'Let's get them to the…to where the other bodies are…'

'No, Omar, I want to bury them here…where they lived…' He looked away. 'She looks like my mother,' he finally whispered softly…reluctantly.

The two men began to dig. Iqbal felt his head explode with pain as he gently lowered the woman who reminded him of his mother into the shallow grave they had dug. He then placed her beloved daughter in her arms.

Religion? War? Guns? Bombs? Jihad? Was there any point to it all? How much more futile can Man make life?

Iqbal wished he could close his eyes and then open them and find himself home with his family. By the side of his near and dear ones to whom his life was precious. Nature kills so ruthlessly, without a thought to the suffering she inflicts. Nature had made her callousness clear. To her life was of little consequence.

Iqbal stood among the debris of the countless dead and thought of the training he had undergone. To kill without compassion in the interest of a larger cause. Maybe Nature's cause is larger than mine, Iqbal thought with a twisted smile.

They finally managed to get the camp radio set fixed on the morning of the third day after the quake. Minutes later, the radio operator came rushing out to call Fazlur Rehman. Immediately the trainees were rounded up by the instructors and assembled in the centre of the camp. 'Get ready to move out at once,' the Maulana told them. 'We move to another campsite within the hour.'

'Apparently some international aid agencies are reaching the area,' Abu Khan whispered. 'It would not be politically correct for the training camp to be seen by any one of them.'

No, obviously it would not, Iqbal thought to himself. *Considering the fact that Pakistan expends so much breath and energy denying that any such training camps exist in their country.*

'Who cares as long as we can get out of here,' he whispered back as they hurried off to gather their stuff.

The move to the new camp was a painful, time-consuming exercise. Most of the roads and tracks had been badly damaged, some totally severed. The new campsite was located just a dozen miles from the Pakistan Army post at Chakoti along the LOC. They only reached there on the evening of the second day. The site was on coarse and jagged turf with no habitation of any kind close by. The settling in took up the three remaining weeks of their training period as everything in the camp had to be built from scratch. By now, all twelve recruits were looking forward to the end of training. This, despite the fact that they spent a lot of time worrying about the reality that awaited them on their return to India.

Iqbal knew that the stress of their move back across the LOC overshadowed every other thought in all the trainees' minds. Despite the danger of the trip Iqbal looked forward to going back home. He vowed to focus only on that and gloss over the gauntlet of cold steel, hot lead, barbed wires and mines that lay between home and him.

1600 hours, 29 October 2005, Malviya Nagar Bus Stop, New Delhi.

The two men comprising Team One of the Lashkar caught the bus plying on route 535 that was headed for Rajender Nagar via the Shivaji Stadium. They were both carrying almost identical-sized, but differently coloured canvas bags. Both bags had been lined with cardboard to give them a distinct shape. Both men handled their bags with extreme caution.

Malviya Nagar being a popular and cheap market, the bus was overflowing and no one paid any heed to either of the men. In any case, people were carrying all kinds of baggage. When the ticket-collector came by both men bought their tickets separately.

It took almost an hour for the bus to reach Shivaji Stadium, their final destination. Both men got off on the road and walked into the crowded terminus. Pausing briefly at the entrance the older man nodded to the youngster. 'Go with God,' he said softly.

The youngster nodded. '*Inshahallah fateh hamari hogi*...I will see you later.' Then he turned and walked away towards the right of the bus station. The older man watched him for a while then turned and headed into the bus station in the opposite direction.

*

1708 hours, 29 October 2005, Shivaji Stadium Bus Terminus, New Delhi.

Despite the fact that it was a Saturday and quite a few offices were closed in view of the impending Diwali and Eid festivals, there was a huge crowd at the bus station. Everyone was rushing to get home before nightfall. Almost every bus leaving the terminus was filled over capacity. The two men moved slowly through the crowd; they were on the look-out for buses that started from the station.

'Generally all buses refuel before they start a fresh run.' The older man remembered their agent-handler briefing them.

'That means they will have filled fuel tanks...good for us,' one of the Lashkar had commented with a smirk. *'The more the diesel the bigger the impact of the explosion, right?'*

The handler had given the man a contemplative look. *'Good thinking, except for the fact that for quite some time now all public transport vehicles in Delhi run on CNG (Compressed Natural Gas). The older type of buses have six CNG tanks, two on either side of the bus towards the rear section and two fitted right at the back of the bus. All of them are fitted on the underside. See...'* He had pointed out the positions of the CNG cylinders on the photograph of a bus he was holding up. *'The new buses are longer...they have a higher capacity and these ones have eight CNG tanks fitted on them. Here.'* He pointed them out on the same photograph. *'There are three on either side and two at the rear. The long distance ones have three at the rear, but you're not likely to encounter these at any intra-city bus station. You must try to target the bigger buses and try to place the bag under any of these seats.'* He had pulled out another photograph of the inside of a bus and pointed out some seats. *'Remember, you must try for the aisle seats. They are the ones where you have the maximum chances of detonating the CNG cylinders...not the window seats.'*

'Why? What's wrong with the window seats?' The same man who had spoken earlier asked again; he was trying to retrieve some lost face and feel a little less stupid.

'A large part of the blast gets wasted on the outer walls. In any case you want the explosion right in the thick of the crowd...not to the side.'

The older of the two men, the one who had moved to the right flank of the bus station, saw a new model Delhi Transport Corporation (DTC) bus heading his way. It was empty and seemed about to be getting ready for a fresh run. He was right. The bus scheduled to ply on route number 505 pulled into an empty slot a few feet away from him and people started boarding it even before the bus conductor got on.

The older man was one of the first to get onto the bus. He made his way unerringly to the seat directly above the CNG tanks fitted on the left side of the centre of the bus. It was one of the seats recommended by the agent-handler and also the one closest to the exit door. Despite the fact that the entire seat was empty the man took the aisle seat. Before sitting down he carefully eased his bag under the seat, taking care to push it as far out of sight as he could.

Within minutes the bus had filled up. Soon all seats were taken and the aisle was packed with standing passengers. As if on cue the driver and bus conductor hopped on. Almost instantly he heard the familiar thumping sound on the side of the bus and the loud, 'chalo, chalo...ticket, ticket...' as the conductor gave the driver the all-clear. The bus juddered to a start as the driver gunned the engine and with a loud meshing of gears began to edge it out of the heavily-packed terminus.

Barely had the bus begun to move when the terrorist casually leaned forward. Reaching down, his fingers found the side of the bag and located the small lever recessed in a cup that shielded it from accidentally being pressed. He pressed the lever till his fingers registered a faint but distinct click. He waited for a few seconds then he abruptly got up and muttering vague apologies pushed his way down the aisle to the rear exit. He managed to get off just as the bus was pulling out of the terminus, before it had picked up speed.

The middle-aged man who had been standing in the aisle near him eagerly grabbed the newly-vacated seat. He felt as tired as he looked. His rumpled clothing betrayed the long sleepless night and hectic day he had spent at the hospital waiting for his wife to give birth to their second child. She had finally done so a few hours ago and was resting comfortably with her newborn son nestled beside her when he left the hospital. Now he was on his way home to see how their ten-year-old firstborn was faring on her own. He blessed the man who had vacated his seat not knowing that he had just ensured his newborn son would never get to know his father.

It was precisely seventeen minutes past five when the bus left the terminus carrying its lethal cargo and over fifty passengers blissfully unaware of the ugly death they were hurtling toward. From now on till the time the bomb finally exploded the bus would stop at least eleven times. Some lucky people would get off. Some unlucky ones would get on.

The man who had instigated their death walked calmly towards the main road outside the bus station. He crossed the road and went up to the first autorickshaw in the queue outside. '*Nai Dilli railway station chaloge*?' he asked him and climbed in when the man nodded. 'I'm in a bit of a hurry. My train is due to leave in twenty-five minutes.'

'Don't worry, sahib. I will get you there,' the enthusiastic, beardless youth replied with a wide grin. He swerved his autorickshaw out of the bus station with one hand pressed firmly on the horn and joined the shrill cacophony of Delhi traffic. The man sitting in the back held tightly on to the metal rail in front of his seat as they careened through the traffic. 'Hey, ease up, will you. You don't just have to get me there, you have to get me there alive.'

He was well out of the station when shouts of confusion were heard from the other side of the bus terminus.

Things were not going well for his younger team-mate.

The younger Lashkar man had also spotted a bus coming into the station barely a few minutes after the older man had sited his target. 'Thank God!' he mumbled to himself as he hurried to board it. 'Here goes.'

Now that he was alone his bravado had deserted him. Despite all the training, briefing and rehearsals he was deeply nervous. He tried to dissipate his anxiety by talking to himself; a coping behaviour amateurs routinely use to deal with combat stress. Hefting his bag he headed for the bus.

The bus scheduled to run on route 982 was headed for Model Town. There was a huge crowd waiting to board it when it pulled into its allocated slot at 1715 hours. Due to the sheer press of human beings trying to get on the bus the young terrorist took a while to get on board. By the time he finally managed, there were just a couple of seats left. He rushed forward, squeezed into the first vacant aisle seat and pushed his bag under it. To his surprise there was already something under the seat and the bag he was trying to push in jutted out. *'Shit!'*

He looked around for another seat, but they had all been taken. Left with no alternative he tried to push his bag in further under the seat and get it out of sight when his co-passenger nudged him gently. 'Bhaisahib, please be careful, there is glassware in my bag. Gift items, you see.' The man sitting on the window seat gave an apologetic smile, 'If you push too hard something in my bag might break.'

His co-passenger had barely finished speaking when the bus engine revved to a start and the bus got ready to commence its journey. That is when the young inexperienced terror merchant made his first mistake. He should have simply taken his bag, left the bus and tried again on any one of the other buses that were moving out of the station at regular intervals. Instead, the young man reached down, armed the timer device of the bomb, and getting up hurriedly tried to disembark. 'Excuse me, excuse me,' he shouted as he began to push his way down the crowded aisle. 'I need to get off, excuse me.'

The man who had been worried about his glassware was staring mindlessly out of the window. He heard him vaguely and turned around out of idle curiosity. He saw the man pushing his way towards the door. He happened to look down and saw the bag still under the seat. 'Hey! You! Bhaisahib, you have forgotten your bag.'

The young terrorist heard himself being called and glanced back involuntarily. It must have been something in his face that gave him away.

'Oye! You! Bhaisahib, you have forgotten your bag. Stop. Come back and take your bag.'

A better trained and more hardened man would possibly have just gone back and brazened his way out of the mess by pretending he had forgotten his bag. The tactic might have worked and he would have lived to fight another day. However the young terror merchant was new to the game. He lacked the mental mobility that comes with experience and his sleep-deprived brain was not coping well with the stress. He panicked. That is when he made his second and fatal mistake. 'Move! Move! *Let me off!*'

Frantically pushing his way through the last two or three people who stood in the aisle between him and the door the man jumped off the bus and began to run through the crowds towards the nearest exit. Some stupid, knee-jerk instinct in him made him pull out his pistol from under his jacket.

The man who had been worried about his glassware saw him jump off the bus in a rush and his panic deepened. He did not see the pistol but by now he knew for sure that something was seriously wrong. That is when, somewhere in the recesses of his mind, the hundreds of advertisements released by a terror-sensitized Delhi Police kicked in and he raised the alarm: 'Oye! That man has left a bag in the bus. Stop the bus! *He has abandoned his bag in the bus!*' He was pointing bug-eyed at the bag under the seat imagining all kinds of things jumping out from it. He suddenly unfroze and leaping up began scrambling towards the door, his gift items long forgotten.

The sound of the man shouting inside the bus attracted the attention of his fellow passengers, the conductor and the bus driver. The bus driver heard the words 'abandoned bag' and brought the bus to a screeching halt right in the middle of the busy terminus. The passengers vacated the bus faster than rats abandoning a sinking ship. There were quite a few cuts and bruises as people literally jumped over each other in their hurry to get off. But the injuries were nothing compared to the catastrophe that would have occurred had the bomb gone off inside a bus full of passengers.

Seeing a bus come to a screeching halt right in the middle of the terminus and a horde of screaming people beginning to jump out of it, the two policemen on duty at the bus station were intrigued. They automatically altered course to head for the bus to investigate. At this point they were more annoyed at having their peaceful routine disturbed than unduly alarmed. They were still a few metres away from the bus when they saw a young man rushing straight at them brandishing a firearm. Alarm replaced annoyance in the blink of an eye. 'Shit on a stick!' the younger cop swore. He was new on the beat and had never experienced anything like this before. 'He's got a bloody gun!'

'I can see that, you idiot.' The senior cop, a blue-blooded product of the Jat hinterland, was a man of action, not much given to fancy things like thinking. He saw a man running towards him with a lethal weapon. Behind him he saw a bunch of people yelling and screaming as they tried to jump off a bus. Deciding the scenario could prove potentially injurious to his health he pulled out his pistol and without much ado fired at the man running towards him.

The running terrorist saw the two cops suddenly appear right in front of him. He saw the older cop draw his weapon. He should just have taken aim with the weapon in his hand and fired. At that range it was unlikely he would have missed. However he had never fired at anything other than paper targets and shooting a man did not come naturally to him. By the time he primed his mind and started bringing up the weapon his body had instinctively begun to duck in a reflexive survival act and he was also starting to veer away from the cops. This coincided with the cop pulling the trigger of his pistol.

The cop may not have been much of a thinker, but he was an excellent shot. The terrorist was just ducking and beginning to turn away when the bullet completed its short journey and reached him. Because he was ducking, the bullet caught him high on his left cheekbone instead of the upper torso at which it had been aimed.

The .38 calibre slug passed almost clean through his face and exited the other side leaving a huge gaping hole that spewed blood, bone and bits of teeth onto the people he was running past. The shattered jaw stifled the shrill shriek of pain that erupted as he was thrown backwards by the impact of the bullet. Even if he had screamed it would have been lost in the cacophony of screams that erupted from the terrified crowd around. The terrorist was still clutching the pistol in his wildly flailing hand as he fell. The younger cop ducked and weaved, desperately trying to stay out of the line of the constantly moving gun.

'Shoot, sir…shoot. He's still alive. Shoot him again! Look…'

The senior cop, who had his eye fixed firmly on the pistol as it wavered in all directions, decided his younger colleague was right for a change. He also concluded that there still was a clear and present threat to the people in general and his precious self in particular.

'*Behenchod*!' Yelling loudly he rushed forward and fired again. At point-blank range the second shot smashed through the terrorist's breastplate. It hammered into his heart killing him instantaneously.

This was the first tragic mistake that occurred that evening. Had the terrorist lived to tell the details of the plot so many others would not have died.

The second tragedy took place almost at the same time as life left the hapless young terrorist's body. Having brought the bus to a halt the over-zealous driver, a diehard Rajnikant fan, decided to take matters in his own hands. 'Call the cops!' he ordered the conductor. 'Let me have a look at what is going on back there.' Before anyone could react he darted to the rear of the bus and picked up the abandoned bag.

'You idiot! What are you doing with the bag? Leave the fucking thing alone!' a frantic passenger who was still trying to get off the bus yelled as he saw the driver pull out the bag from below the seat and place it on top. 'It might be a bomb. Leave the damn thing alone.' He literally threw himself off the bus, gibbering in panic.

The driver was not to be deterred. In any case he knew he led a charmed life. 'Don't worry. *Main hoon na...*' He unzipped the bag to see what it contained. As the zipper slid open it activated the crude but effective booby trap that bypassed the timer device and set off the detonator embedded snugly in the RDX. In the confined space the bomb exploded with incredible ferocity. Small unrecognizable parts of the driver's body merged with a hailstorm of shredded metal. One moment, he was alive. Then *Boom!* He had ceased to exist.

Luckily the bomb was on the seat when it exploded. The seat absorbed a part of the impact and saved the CNG tanks from blowing up. Had they exploded simultaneously it would have added to the mayhem and carnage. Even so the bomb wreaked a terrible toll. No one would ever be sure how many people died in the explosion. The official body count that evening was twenty-nine dead and scores wounded, some of whom succumbed to their injuries later.

In the confusion that reigned at the bus terminus it was a while before anyone thought of the possibility of another bomb on another bus. Then all hell broke loose as people rushed out of the bus terminus and frantic transport supervisors ran for their phones. 'Which buses have left the station in the last ten or fifteen minutes? Get them on the phone and warn them immediately,' the Duty Officer commanded the supervisors maintaining the vehicle logs.

A series of phones came into play and airwaves burned as calls went out to the drivers or conductors of the buses that had left the terminus. Anyone and everyone who had a mobile phone was called. Amongst the ones not carrying phones were the driver and conductor of the bus running on route 505.

The bus plying on route 505 had just reached the end of Tughlak Road and slowed down at the crowded traffic roundabout when, at 1735 hours, the 2558 Sapt Kranti Express pulled out of the New Delhi Railway station, seventeen minutes behind its scheduled time.

The older man of Team One of the Lashkar was on board the train when it pulled out from platform No. 7. He was in a second-class sleeper compartment, lying in the uppermost berth that he had deliberately chosen when he had booked the ticket a few days back. He had no desire to interact with the other passengers. In any case he had every intention of catching up on the sleep that he had missed the previous night.

The leader of Team One of the Lashkar had no way of knowing that his team-mate was neither on the train nor in this world. Even if he had lived and boarded the train he would still not have been aware of this since both their tickets had deliberately been booked at different times for different compartments.

By about 1800 hours the train had cleared the city and was gathering speed when the ill-fated bus running on route 505 started going down the flyover spanning the small run way of the Safdarjung Airport. It was on the slightly deserted patch just before the densely-populated INA Market area that the bomb exploded.

The explosion triggered off not just the CNG tanks directly below the bomb but also, seconds later, the ones on the opposite side of the bus. Coming hard on the heels of each other the three successive explosions not only decimated the bus but also sent a couple of cars driving past flying into the air. The out-of-control bus slammed into the crash barrier on the outer side of the flyover. It smashed through the barrier and toppled over the edge landing on the concrete ten metres below with a horrific thump.

In Delhi, in fact in most of this part of the world, no one ever keeps track of how many people get on to a bus. That is why it will never be known for sure how many people died on that bus or what religion or belief they belonged to. What is certain is that no one on board survived.

The news of the bomb blasts spread like wildfire. All over the city hundreds of buses ground to a halt and panic-stricken passengers rushed out as the buses were scanned for abandoned packages. The speed with which the terrified passengers fled the crowded buses ensured there were plenty of abandoned packages. Each had to be carefully checked and declared safe before any bus could move again. Almost all over the city traffic ground to a halt.

The terror was escalating.

TEAM TWO

1605 hours, 29 October 2005, Malviya Nagar, New Delhi.

The two men of Team Two drove the dark blue Maruti Esteem carefully through the heavy late afternoon traffic. *Always maintain a safe and constant speed. Leave well in time to ensure you don't have to rush. It would be absolutely disastrous to get stopped for a dumb thing like jumping a traffic light or speeding.* The words of the ISI agent who had given them basic field craft training ensured that the car was driven at normal speed.

It would not do to get pulled over by the cops. They will check everything thoroughly. There is no way your documents or that of any stolen vehicle will stand up to a close scrutiny.

At about the time when Team One was arriving at the Shivaji Stadium Bus Stop, Team Two drove into the M4K multiplex in the stolen Maruti Esteem. By now there was heavy traffic. It took them a while to drive the car down to the basement parking. The man driving the car collected the parking token and then drove straight to the parking slot where the Tata Indica had been parked by his team-mate earlier that morning. He stopped a couple of cars short of the Indica and gestured to the other man. 'Get it out fast! There will be a traffic pile-up behind us otherwise.'

'Give me a second.'

The man moved rapidly and getting into the Indica started it. The engine caught once and then died away. By now there were already three cars lining up behind the Esteem halted in the middle. One or two horns tooted impatiently. The security guard started walking towards them. It was his job to keep the traffic flowing.

'Hurry up, godammit.' The man driving the Esteem cursed under his breath as he watched the guard approach in his rear-view mirror.

'Shit! Not now!' The man breathed in panic as he turned the ignition key again. This time the Indica engine fired and settled down to a regular rhythm. He reversed it out of the parking slot and drove off a little ahead.

Seeing the Indica finally pull out, the man driving the Esteem quickly drove into the now vacant slot. The cars behind him began to move past. The security guard saw the line of cars begin to move again and lost interest in the situation. His job was to ensure that the flow of traffic was not impeded. As long it flowed smoothly he was fine. He began to amble back towards the entrance where he normally positioned himself. The man driving the Esteem waited till there was a slight break in the cars moving out. Then he quickly drove the Esteem out a bit, drove it forward a little and reversed it back into the vacant slot. He needed to ensure that the boot of the car was as close to the transformer as possible.

Retrieving another of the trademark canvas bags from the rear seat of the Esteem, he threw the timer switch arming the bomb in the boot, carefully locked up the car and moved to the Indica that had pulled over to one side a little ahead. It was drawing some angry stares from people driving past, but there still was adequate space for vehicles to get through. Squeezing himself into the passenger seat he said, 'Let's get out of here.'

The security guard who now stood some distance away did not notice them leave. There was nothing amiss to be seen anyway since there was no way he could have noticed the bomb placed inside the boot of the Esteem. Packed tightly between two newly-filled LPG cylinders lay seventy kilograms of RDX.

Team Two came out of the multiplex in the Indica and drove swiftly but still very carefully to the Inter State Bus Terminus. They left the Indica in a paid parking slot in the Kashmiri Gate car parking. Just before he got out the terrorist who had earlier been driving the Esteem activated the timer of the device kept in the bag on the floor mat below the rear seat. While he was doing so the other man paid the parking fees and collected the parking token. Exiting the parking lot the two men walked across the road.

One of them hailed a three-wheeler passing nearby. 'Old Delhi Railway Station?' he asked when the autorickshaw driver brought the vehicle to a stop near them. The driver nodded and clanged down the meter with a flourish. 'Get in, sahib.'

About thirty minutes later they entered the railway station separately. Both handed in their tokens and collected a suitcase each from the left-luggage counter at an interval of about ten minutes. They used the second-class restrooms and changed into the casual attire of typical small town businessmen taking a trip. The restrooms were crowded as usual. No one paid much attention to the two men who came and went their separate ways.

The two men did not know it of course but they had been driving out of M4K complex when the bus driver had probed the first bomb at the Shivaji Bus Terminus causing it to explode. Of course they were generally able to time the other explosions since those went off precisely as planned. In fact one of them had been looking at his watch when the bomb on board the second bus exploded. A few seconds after that the bomb in the boot of the Esteem parked in the M4K multiplex ripped through the parking lot.

Luckily the transformer at M4K survived the blast reasonably well. Even so, the effect of seventy kilograms of RDX and the two LPG cylinders that exploded with it was absolutely devastating in the close confines of the basement parking lot. The effect was compounded when the fuel tanks of a couple of other cars also exploded due to the fire that broke out after the primary explosion.

A lot of the people who had come to the M4K multiplex that evening to watch the antics of Saif Ali

Khan and Preity Zinta in *Salaam Namaste,* the latest Bollywood pot-boiler, did not live to enjoy the movie. 93 died and over 280 were injured when the car bomb took out half the densely-crowded basement parking lot.

The people flowing through the Kashmiri Gate car parking were a lot luckier. The bomb inside the Indica was a much smaller one and did not have any thing else that exploded with it. It had been planted more to add to the terror and confusion than to the death toll.

This bomb went off just a couple of minutes after the one at the M4K multiplex. Around a dozen people died along with the hapless parking lot attendant who happened to be leaning against the Indica when the bomb detonated.

Both men of Team Two watched the carnage on television screens in different parts of the railway station some time later.

They were the first to come to know that one of the Lashkar had fallen. A twinge of alarm ran through them until they saw the detailed coverage of the episode and knew for sure that he had gone to Allah before he could open his mouth and spill the beans.

Even so, as planned, they did not approach each other. Neither did they join in any of the several heated and panicky debates that erupted all over the platforms.

All trains departed a bit late that night since the police swept through the railway station and checked every compartment. However the 4001 Attari Express was one of the luckier ones. It left the platform at 2115 hours and was soon hurtling through the night across the plains of Haryana and Punjab, on its way to Attari in Pakistan. The two men of Team Two of the Lashkar were in different compartments. They wolfed down the hot, but plastic-smelling dinner handed over to them by the enthusiastic coach attendant and then slept through the night.

The stress of the past few days had finally caught up with them.

TEAM THREE

1625 hours, 29 October 2005, Khirki Gaon, New Delhi.

When the bus carrying Team One was turning right on the road going under the IIT (Indian Institute of Technology) flyover and the Maruti Esteem with Team Two was going over it, the Bajaj Caliber motorcycle carrying the two men of Team Three left Aftab Cyber Café.

Team Three had the shortest distance to cover to their target and so was the last to leave. The man on the pillion of the motorcycle carried another cardboard-lined, dirty-looking canvas bag with its lethal cargo.

Twenty-five minutes later, the two men of Team Three reached Sarojini Nagar and parked their motorcycle about fifty metres away, in one of the numerous lanes that radiated into the colony surrounding the market. The man riding the motorcycle remained seated as the pillion rider got off and handed the canvas bag to him. 'Hold it carefully,' he told the rider who remained seated on the parked motorcycle. Then he walked into the market.

A slight chill, the advance guard of a rapidly approaching winter, was perceptible in the air despite the dense crowds. The man walking towards the market did not seem to feel the cold. In fact he was sweating slightly. Despite the tension he felt he made sure he walked calmly.

The mass of humanity surging through the market place,which was bedecked like a bride for the festive season, was so large that it took him almost six minutes to reach the corner where three roads converged at the edge of the market. Here, traffic from all sides blended in splendidly chaotic harmony. It was a perfect, natural bottleneck. The two traffic policemen on duty were fighting a perennial and constantly losing battle to keep the traffic flowing in all directions. 'Keep moving! Keep moving, behenchods!' They shouted in frustration; their harassment manifest in the rough manner in which they occasionally shoved the wayward pedestrian out of the way or spewed abuse at an errant driver.

The man stood around for about five minutes, leaning against the trunk of one of the many trees that lined the pavement. He surveyed the scene carefully, spending a few extra minutes to make doubly sure that no unscheduled activity waited to surprise them. Then he walked back to the man waiting on the motorcycle. 'All clear. Just the normal rush. Let's go.'

The other man was relieved to hear this. 'Good. Let's go.' He handed back the bag to the scout and kick-started the motorcycle. The scout waited for the engine to settle to a steady beat and then carefully got on, securing the bag in his lap. Only then did he nudge the rider. 'Carefully now.'

It was almost 1715 hours when the two men finally managed to navigate through the impossibly crowded market and bring the motorcycle to a halt near the pushcart selling chai and samosas at the place where the three roads converged. A huge crowd swirled all around them. They squeezed the motorcycle in between the other scooters and motorcycles already parked there. Collecting the parking token from the harried attendant they walked up to the samosa-seller about fourteen feet away and joined the hungry crowd around his pushcart.

It took a few minutes before they managed to attract the attention of the samosa-wallah and get him to serve them. The man carrying the canvas bag took it off his shoulder and put it down casually on the ground before taking the samosas from the vendor. It was a perfectly natural action and would not have drawn any attention even if someone had been watching. As he paid the man he used his foot to push the bag as far out of sight behind the wheel of the pushcart as possible.

The younger man's wrist-watch showed 1725 hours when they walked away from the pushcart. The canvas bag rested unnoticed against the wheel of the pushcart at the feet of the hungry shoppers thronging around the cart.

As they walked the man who had been riding the motorcycle took a short detour and stopped by his bike. Pretending to check that it was properly locked he bent down and flicked a small hidden switch under the metallic boxes fitted on either side of the rear of the bike. Then he swiftly rejoined his team-mate and they walked away from the marketplace at a steady pace. They finished eating their samosas as they walked.

IQBAL

Hamida knew that there was something special about her son the moment she set eyes on Iqbal. 'You feel like that just because he is our firstborn,' Nawab would always tell her, but she noticed that her husband too had that special look in his eyes when Iqbal was around. Hamida never saw him look quite the same way at Ashraf who was born three years later, and even less so at their daughter Navaz who was born after another five. In fact, though she never said so aloud, it bothered Hamida deeply to see that her husband was totally unable to relate to his daughter in the way he did to the boys. That is why it gave her tremendous pleasure to see the special bond that Iqbal and Navaz shared. Despite the eight-year difference between them they were inseparable. 'That girl will never feel the lack of a father as long as Iqbal is around,' Hamida would often think when she saw the two siblings playing or studying together.

Hamida was born in Aligarh twelve years after the partition of India and Pakistan, which claimed the lives of untold numbers of innocents who happened to be caught on the wrong side of the border. Of course her siblings and she were subjected to all the gory stories. Not that they were overtly troubled by them. They were, after all, only children and their inherent innocence had not yet been corrupted by the rigid notions of adulthood. Most times, they even found it hard to remember which kids they could play with and which ones they were not allowed even to talk to.

'Why can't we play with them, Ammi?'

'They're kafirs, that is why.'

'What's a kafir?'

'A kafir is a person who does not believe in the true God, child.'

'Who is the true God?'

'Haven't I told you that a hundred times already? We worship the true God.'

'What God do they pray to?'

'I'm not too sure...they have dozens of them...'

'And all of them are not real Gods?'

'Hush!' An exasperated cluck. 'Don't ask so many questions, Hamida. You will understand as you grow up.'

But no matter how much she grew, Hamida didn't understand. Her mother had no time to explain anything to her. As for her father, Zafar, a librarian's assistant at the local university; his family and career had been destroyed by the Partition. He needed someone to blame for his woes. For this the kafir Hindu was a convenient and logical target. Hamida remembered vividly this constantly festering and seething cauldron of hatred, crime and poverty which they grew up in. Her father's hatred turned her off religion. After all, how can a God in whose name one could hate, kill and maim so easily ever inspire faith and love in a child whose life was not mangled by riots and killings and who knew her Hindu neighbours as children like herself, as classmates and friends?

There was also, of course, the undeniable fact that they all had many other, far more pressing problems than religion to deal with in those days, with survival being paramount. Just the simple act of surviving from one day to another took up most of their life and energy.

Hamida had barely crossed her teens when her marriage was arranged to Nawab, the carefree and sports-loving youngest son of the neighbourhood butcher with a simple, 'No matter how hard times are, they will always have something to put on the table.'

Three months before her twentieth birthday she moved to her husband's home, where her father-in-law indulged his younger daughter-in-law with the same affection that he indulged his youngest son – letting him skip off from work to play cricket with the neighbourhood boys. Unfortunately the bubble lasted six months. It burst on the day Nawab's father returned from the jumma prayers and suddenly keeled over. They rushed him to the hospital but he was already with Allah. 'It was a massive heart attack,' the doctor said. 'He never had much of a chance.'

His death was the harbinger of change. The relatives who had gathered to mourn had not even begun to depart when Mansoor, Nawab's elder brother, laid claim to the butcher's shop and asked Nawab to look for a job for himself claiming the family business was not doing too well.

'Really? *Why*? I think it is doing pretty much the way it always did.' Nawab was a little puzzled. 'Abbu never said anything about it doing badly.'

'Well, it is,' Mansoor retorted curtly. 'It is doing quite badly. In any case it is time you started doing something other than hanging aimlessly around the shop.'

'Hanging around?' Nawab's face started to redden.

It was pretty clear that Mansoor wanted him out. 'Nawab miyan, you are a married man now with a family of your own. It is high time you stood on your own feet.'

Watching the stand-off between the brothers, Nawab's uncle Shafiq, who had come down from Lucknow, took Nawab aside and had a long talk with him.

'He has been working at the same school in Lucknow for as long as I can remember. If he says he can get me a job I'm confident he can,' Nawab told Hamida later that night. And so, two weeks after his father died, Nawab moved to Lucknow with his wife of not quite seven months. Nawab's uncle had got him a job as an assistant to the physical training instructor in La Martiniere College and it wasn't long before Nawab and Hamida settled into a quiet but happy life on the school campus in the small house allotted to them in the Staff Colony.

As a member of the staff, Nawab's children were allowed access to what would otherwise have been an education well beyond his means. And he was thrilled when Iqbal more than proved himself as a good scholar and an outstanding sports player. 'He is my son after all,' Nawab would proudly proclaim.

'Of course he is. I was just a sleeping partner in the whole thing,' Hamida would chuckle, barely concealing her pride.

Though Iqbal did well in school he had few friends; he couldn't compete with the other boys' socio-economic status and so maintained a distance. He took to spending his spare time at a small auto-repair workshop on the edge of the school campus. He had gone there to get his cycle fixed one day and fallen in love with the sights, sounds and smell of machinery. Shukla Sahib the owner of the workshop took an immense liking to him and spent hours teaching him whatever he knew. Soon Iqbal was getting under the hood of all sorts of vehicles and fixing engines himself.

'I tell you, madam,' Shuklaji would jokingly complain to Hamida, 'the way he is going, very soon this boy of yours will ensure I am jobless and hungry.'

Nawab on the other hand would grumble whenever Iqbal arrived home covered with grease and oil. 'What is the point giving this boy an education? You don't need to study if you just want to be a motor mechanic.'

As things turned out, Shuklaji and his garage were to have a profound influence on Iqbal's life. It was his love for engines that made Iqbal decide that he wanted to be a mechanical engineer. It was this quest that had led Iqbal to Delhi to join engineering college and look after the business of Uncle Rashid's spare parts shop.

Iqbal's move from Lucknow was a highly traumatic experience for all of them, but especially so for Hamida and Navaz. Hamida's grief at parting with her firstborn was enhanced by the fear and worry that she felt for him. All of them had heard such horror stories of life in Delhi that she was petrified at the thought of his having to brave the evils of a large city on his own. 'How will you manage? You are so fussy about your food. Are you sure you will be all right?'

'I will be fine, Ammi. I have to move out one day and learn to manage on my own.'

Hamida understood this but that did not mean she liked it. She put on a brave front as they got ready to drop Iqbal off at the railway station. 'Come on, Ammi, all of you don't need to come to the railway station to see me off.'

'If your Ammi had her way she would go all the way to Delhi to see you off,' Nawab quipped. They all laughed at that; Hamida did too. The laughter helped dispel the tears that were crowding her eyes.

Rashid's spare parts shop was located just opposite the small mosque in Savita Nagar. Iqbal used his exhaustive knowledge of cars to expand the shop's scope of activities to include repairs and modifications.

Rashid could not stop singing Iqbal's praises whenever he spoke to Hamida or Nawab. Hamida was so proud of her son. Maybe that's why she was not surprised when a year after moving to Delhi she got a phone call from Iqbal. 'Ammi, guess what?' He seemed really thrilled and excited. 'I have got a fantastic job in the Middle-East.'

'But, bete...'

'I have said yes to them, Ammi.'

Her heart sank.

'I will soon be leaving to take up this assignment. In fact I have to leave for training in a few days...'

Iqbal seemed so thrilled that Hamida was sure he had not thought things over in detail. It bothered Hamida but he was so excited about it that she didn't have the heart to say anything to him. If Nawab had any misgivings they were swept away when he received Iqbal's letter and a banker's draft for seventy-five thousand rupees in the mail a week later.

Iqbal called a day later to check if we had received his letter and the bank draft. 'That was just the first instalment, Ammi.'

'Bless you, my child. May Allah shower many more successes and happiness on you.' Hamida was more moved by the pride in her son's voice than by the money. She didn't tell him that of course. 'So tell me more about this job. What company is it? Where are they sending you?'

'Oh Ammi, I'll call you once I get there. Now I have to go. We are leaving tomorrow. I will call again soon, Ammi.'

But he didn't.

Barring those two phone calls there was no word from Iqbal for the next five months. Hamida was starting to get worried when the second bank draft and another short letter from him arrived.

'My training is almost over. All going well. I should be in Delhi in a month or so. I will make sure I take some time off to come to Lucknow before I join duty. We will have lots of fun. Give my love to everyone. Tell Navaz I think of her all the time. Miss you loads. I will be back soon.'

It was at Navaz's behest that the two of them took the train to Delhi the week before Eid. 'Come on, Ammi. It will be such fun. Iqbal bhaijaan will also be coming back soon. Won't it be great if we are there in Delhi to surprise him?'

Nawab was unable to accompany them since school holidays had not yet begun. While Ashraf dismissed the whole idea with a disdainful, 'All you will do is drag me from one shop to the other.' So, in the end it was just Navaz and Hamida who found themselves on the train to Delhi with Eid and Diwali less than a week away. It was the first trip the two of them were taking on their own and both were totally excited. Navaz was a bundle of energy throughout the journey. 'You don't need to keep peering out of the window at every station, child. Delhi is the last halt. We will be sure to know when it arrives.' But nothing Hamida said convinced that girl to stay away from the window. Navaz did not sleep a wink that night.

When the train pulled into the New Delhi Railway Station early next morning the two of them could not stop gawking and exclaiming at everything. Despite the early hour the station throbbed with energy.

The first few days passed in a blur as they visited the Jama Masjid, the Red Fort, Qutab Minar, some dargahs, the Lotus Temple and India Gate. Despite the crowds and the rush Hamida and Navaz could not get enough of sightseeing. When they weren't touring the city, they ate and chatted ceaselessly with Rashid's wife and kids. Even though Navaz had never met them before, she got on famously with all her cousins.

Time flew the way it does when one is on holiday.

That morning Hamida was quite surprised when Navaz said, 'Ammi, do you realize Eid is just four days away? We have to go back to Lucknow the day after that. When exactly are you planning to take me shopping?'

Hamida was amazed by the speed with which time had passed. She immediately got after Rashid. 'We need to go shopping, bhaijaan. Will you take us please?'

'There is no way I am going shopping with you, Hamida. I have no desire to run from shop to shop looking at things I have no intention of buying.' Rashid had the typical male lack of enthusiasm for shopping. 'But I can drop you off and pick you up.'

'Sarojini Nagar is the cheapest market around here; you can get just about anything,' Rashid said as he drove them down to the market. 'But it is always very crowded. You need to be very careful about pickpockets...and don't buy anything without bargaining first. They will rob you blind otherwise.'

On entering the market he stopped at the first parking junction. A veritable sea of cars, scooters and motorcycles were parked every which way. The thin sliver of road that ran between the market and the parking lot teemed with people. 'Be sure you return to this spot by 6.30.' Rashid wagged a stern finger at them. 'Don't keep me waiting in this hell-hole.'

The next few hours were pure heaven. Navaz and Hamida picked happily through the marketplace full of hawkers and colourful shops crammed with the most amazing stuff. Lucknow was a big city full of markets but it had nothing to compare with the sheer size and exuberance of Sarojini Nagar.

After a couple of hours of shopping, Navaz was famished. She looked around and spotted a samosa vendor. She was pulling her mother towards the samosa-wallah when the old man selling tablecloths on the pavement opposite caught her mother's eye. In the pile was a bright red table cover with small mirrors embroidered on it. It beckoned to her like a spark of life, shining enticingly among the other drab pieces in the heap. The vendor, a toothless old man, squatted beside the heap picking his nose and ogling the women going by.

Navaz pulled harder. 'Those samosas look so yummy.'

'It will only take a minute, child...now listen, we must not let him know we like it so much because then he is sure to hike the price,' Hamida whispered conspiratorially as she dragged her reluctant daughter to the stall. That is why Hamida first picked up two or three other covers and haggled over the price of each before she even turned to acknowledge the existence of the red tablecloth that had so caught her fancy.

She was bending to pick it up when from the corner of her eye she sensed more than saw a bright yellow spark looming larger and larger.

And then there was nothing.

1815 hours, 29 October 2005, Shivaji Stadium Bus Terminus, New Delhi.

The first television camera and news-team reached the Shivaji Stadium Bus Terminus about eighteen minutes after the bus driver set off the first bomb. The television crews responded much faster to the subsequent explosions that ripped through the city with horrifying speed. By 1825 hours a shocked world watched as blood-soaked images of the Delhi blasts beamed into millions of homes across the globe.

The firestorm of metal and miscellaneous debris that was unleashed by the two bombs and the LPG cylinder scythed through the dense crowd of shoppers and shopkeepers gathered around. The official estimate was that forty-seven of them died on the spot. Another twenty-nine succumbed to their injuries in the days that were to follow. Over a hundred more were injured. Quite a few of them were handicapped for life.

The Team Three men did not hear the explosion or see the devastation. They only got confirmed news of the blasts when they arrived at the Cantonment Railway Station. By that time the television cameras and crew had reached the sites of most of the bomb blasts. The platform was abuzz with the shock of the blasts that were decimating the city. Knots of people clustered around the television sets positioned on the platform.

*

'The blast at Sarojini Nagar seems to have caused almost as many casualties as the March 1993 blast at Century Market in Mumbai. The police are still trying to ascertain the number of dead ...' The camera cut away from the fear-stricken reporter trying to make some sense of the terrible mayhem and moved on to another grim-faced reporter at the Shivaji Nagar Bus Terminus. 'This is where the first blast took place.' The camera panned to the shattered bus. 'It is still not clear how many more buses have been affected. So far we only have confirmation of one more blast onboard the bus that was operating on route No 505. No one has so far claimed responsibility for these blasts, but one of the suspects was gunned down by...'

At 2136 hours, when the 4791 Bikaner Mail left the platform of the Delhi Cantonment Railway Station both men of Team Three were safely on board. Like the men of Team Two, they also were in different compartments. Once again, the ticket-checker did not notice anything untoward or suspicious about either of them.

Team Three boarded the train and left behind a city torn apart with fear, death and destruction.

And a nation seething in anger.

1820 hours, 29 October 2005, Aftab Cyber Café, New Delhi.

Sitting in the rear room of the Aftab Cyber Café Furkan watched the coverage on television with keen interest. Like the rest of the Lashkar he too was saddened by the death of his young colleague. 'Thank God he was martyred instantly and the operation was not compromised,' he consoled himself. When Furkan had watched enough he muted the television. By now it was pitch dark outside. Erratic blue, yellow, red and black images from the television screen flashed through the otherwise darkened room. Squinting slightly in the darkness he stared at the screen of his mobile phone and carefully dialled a pre-stored number. When he spoke into it there was a distinct pride in his voice. And rightly so. After all, all the men of the Lashkar had been recruited and trained by him. When he finally depressed the disconnect button his phone informed him that the call had lasted ninety-seven seconds. Then he went back to the television and turned up the volume.

But, unable to contain his excitement, and despite being warned to do no such thing, an hour after his exhilarating talk with Maulana Fazlur Rehman, he picked up the mobile phone again. This time he dialled a number that had been added to his phone book fairly recently. 'Is this the Aaj Tak news channel?'

The stunned Aaj Tak staffer who took the call was speechless with horror when she answered the phone. Luckily she did not have to do much except listen. By now it was the norm for all calls coming into any television network to be recorded automatically. The calling line identification facility on the telephone of the news channel duly noted the number of the mobile phone the call was originating from.

The young Aaj Tak staffer called up her boss as soon as the call ended. 'What? Say that again!' The senior editor had just parked his car outside his house when he took the call. His mind raced. A slow day had suddenly been converted into a major news exclusive. Cutting the call he jumped back into his car and gunned the engine as he reversed out. His rear fender hit his wife's car parked by the side, but for once he didn't care. His hands were busy dialling another number. The Deputy Commissioner of Police for South Delhi was well known to him. Consequently the police were informed within minutes of the call made by Furkan claiming responsibility for the bombings.

Furkan was a trained and highly motivated terrorist but there were obvious gaps in his knowledge of technology. He had little idea what mobile telephone companies were capable of doing. Not only did they maintain extensive records of who owned which phone, they could almost instantly track down the location of the owner by following the electronic trace left by his mobile phone. By making this phone call the seventh man had just signed his own death warrant.

It took a few minutes for the Deputy Commissioner of Police to rouse the senior operational staff of the cellular service provider that Furkan was using. In this day and age of terrorism all cellular companies have to function within strict operational and security guidelines. Most governments have mandated that all operators instal the technology required to track and monitor all their subscribers on real-time basis. Unknown to most people this technology is put to use almost every day for a host of reasons.

Each mobile phone handset has a unique ESN (Electronic Serial Number). Whenever a mobile phone is switched on the handset periodically broadcasts the ESN to let the cellular company know where it is located. This is how the cellular phone company knows where to route a call received for a particular phone. That is why they always know where each phone user is. The cellular operator can also ping any phone and then use overlapping signal monitors to triangulate and give its most likely global positioning coordinates. This tower triangulation method enables them to pin down the precise location of any mobile phone to within a few feet.

Had Furkan switched off his mobile phone after

calling Aaj Tak it is possible that he may have lived a little longer. Unfortunately, he didn't.

Within a few minutes of the request, the Vice President, Operations, of the concerned mobile phone company called up the Deputy Commissioner of Police who headed the Anti-Terrorist Cell. 'The phone is registered to a Furkan Sheikh and the billing address is of a cyber café in Khirki Gaon.' He read out the address. 'In fact, that is where the phone is located right now.'

'Keep tracking the phone and let me know immediately if it changes location.' The cop disconnected the call and dialled again. 'Mathur, move the strike team out immediately. What? Yes, of course I want them loaded for bear. Tell them to meet me in front of Panchsheel Rendezvous...and listen, call up the Saket people and tell them to keep a team ready...just in case.'

As his vehicle sped through the traffic the DCP called the Delhi Police Commissioner and briefed him. He had barely finished when Mathur's name flashed on the screen of his mobile phone: 'Our strike team is on its way and Saket's is standing by, sir. The team should be at the Rendezvous in five minutes...max seven, sir.'

Clearly, sitting in the control room, Mathur had no clue what hell had broken loose on the streets. The strike team took much longer to reach simply because traffic was in complete chaos. The city was in turmoil over news of the horrific blasts and the news channels were doing nothing to dissipate the panic. People swamped the streets as they fled their workplaces and rushed to the apparent and elusive safety of their homes. Consequently it was almost 2200 hours by the time the anti-terrorist team finally moved into place. Fortunately, this was the only glitch.

The strike team surrounded the cyber café deftly in a slickly choreographed manoeuvre. They moved in so fast and so unobtrusively that passers-by barely noticed them.

The operation was over almost before it had begun.

2201 hours, 29 October 2005, Aftab Cyber Café, Khirki Gaon, New Delhi.

'Now!'

The Bikaner Mail was still pulling out of Delhi Cantonment Railway Station with the Team Three men on board when the first police commando braced himself to kick in the door of the cyber café. The flimsy door crashed open and hit the wall. Furkan was sitting behind a computer, lost in thought, when the commandos burst in.

'Son of a bitch! *How...?*' Furkan's mind was still adjusting to the stunning reality of the two helmeted figures in black bullet-proof jackets as his hand reflexively freed the small Chinese automatic pistol from his belt.

'Police! Raise your hands in the air!' one of the commandos shouted.

Furkan's mind was screaming into overdrive. He heard the call but it did not really register. He sprung to his feet and was raising his pistol to take aim at the black figure racing towards him when the second commando, who stood near the door with his weapon already raised, fired. The tiny 9 mm lead slug slashed through the air. It was travelling at sub-sonic speed. Even so it spanned the scant seven feet between them almost instantly and reached Furkan as his finger groped for the trigger. The blunt, soft-nosed slug hit Furkan high on the chest and flung him backward. The first commando pounced on him and wrested the pistol away. Furkan never even managed to get off a shot.

In retrospect, that single shot fired by the second police commando proved a serious error in an otherwise perfect operation. Had that shot not been fired they would have taken the seventh man alive. If they had taken him alive the Indian Government would have been able to unravel the conspiracy much faster and they'd have been able to produce walking-talking proof of the terror strike to the world.

Not that anyone could find much fault with the shot. The commando had been working on a highly-keyed-up adrenaline response. He'd fired only when he saw there was no other way to prevent the terrorist from using his weapon on his buddy.

*

The man named Furkan was unconscious when the police ambulance carrying him raced into Modi Hospital in nearby Saket. The ambulance entered the hospital gate at almost the same time as the Bikaner Mail cleared the city limits on its way to Bikaner.

'We need this bastard alive,' the cop told the doctor on duty. 'He is one of the men involved in today's bomb blasts.' The hospital activated its best medical team to stabilize the injured terrorist who had lost a lot of blood. The head injury was far more critical than it looked. The police was so keen to revive the man and question him that they had a Deputy Commissioner of Police from the Crisis Management Team sitting right outside the door of the ICU. However, it was to be a long and agonizing wait.

It was almost two hours after midnight when Furkan regained consciousness and spoke his first word since he had been hit. 'Water.' The croaked whisper was barely audible but everyone was so keyed up that the sound electrified the atmosphere. The news that he had spoken swept through the hospital and within seconds a cabal of khaki descended on the room he was in.

'You will definitely kill him if you start questioning him right now,' Manish, the doctor who had taken charge of the wounded man said. 'Give us some time to stabilize him first.' He had to literally fight off the police but was not able to do it for long; too much rode on the man talking. Around 0230 hours Dr Manish finally came out of the room with a resigned expression on his face. He nodded to the cops waiting impatiently outside. 'Question him now. He won't last much longer.'

By 0300 hours the man known to the world as Furkan Sheikh had told the police the whole story, chapter and verse. The only thing he did not disclose was the role of the Maulavi from the Savita Nagar mosque. Whether he did not wish to involve a man of God or did not consider it important to do so, no one will ever know, because he succumbed to his wounds just as he was coming to the end of his story. Whirring video and audio recorders captured every last thing he said, right to his rasping last breaths.

Within minutes, copies of the tape were rushed to the Crisis Management Committee. The tapes had complete details of the Lashkar team members who had carried out the strike, their escape routes, details of the training camp in Muzaffarabad where the strike had been planned and the Lashkar had trained and information about Maulana Fazlur Rehman and Brigadier Murad Salim who had masterminded, coordinated and executed the strike.

'Send a copy to the PMO,' the Task Force Commander told his assistant.

'At this time of the night?' The man looked up incredulously.

'The Headman had said he wanted to be in the loop at all times.'

The Task Force Commander was right; twenty minutes later the Indian Prime Minister was listening to the recording. Despite the late hour he was wide awake.

Soon a lot of other people would be too.

The Indian Government was well aware of the location of the terrorist training camp that Furkan had referred to, as it was one of seventeen other similar camps that dotted the landscape of Pakistan and the POK. So were the Chinese, the Russians, the Americans, the Israelis, the British, the French, the Germans, the Somalis, the Guatemalans and anyone else who cared to know. It was an open international secret.

Almost every nation was aware that the Pakistani General's claim that he had curbed all terrorist activity in his country was a blatant lie. The whole world knew about it yet refused to acknowledge it. The Americans even went about applauding the General and praising him for his help in hunting down the Al-Qaida. But the time for beating about the bush was over. Every successive terrorist strike was shortening the global fuse.

IQBAL

1950 hours, 30 October 2005, Terrorist Camp in Jungle above Hari, Kashmir.

Even through the thick fog of sleep shrouding him Iqbal heard the scream and felt a hand grip his shoulder. A panic-stricken scream erupted uncontrollably from his own mouth as the horror of the night gone by returned. Once again, the ricochet of gunfire shattered his mind. He saw the illuminating rounds flare up in the dark sky with harsh metallic clicks. Psychedelic flashes of guns firing tracer rounds, bullets arcing through the night like fireflies, and the images of writhing men falling lifelessly to the ground suffused his mind. Literally gibbering with fear he pushed away the hand clutching his shoulder and forced his eyes to open. There was no one there. That is when another moan of pain broke through the fog of his nightmare and Iqbal realized that it was only Wahid, the instructor, crying out in pain.

Reality returned like a cold shock.

Except for a few smouldering embers, the fire in the angeethi in the centre of the hut was dead. However it was obvious that someone had fed the fire at some point in the night or it would have gone cold by now. Iqbal could hear the wind hissing in the trees around. He guessed night had fallen many hours ago because his body told him that he had been asleep for a long time; it felt painfully stiff and ached from countless sores and bruises. But the hunger pangs gnawing at his stomach reassured him. *If you're hungry you're okay.* The voice of the instructor conducting the first-aid class at the training camp came back to him. He suddenly realized the same man now lay a few feet from him; and he was far from okay.

Iqbal forced himself to go across to him. When he knelt down beside him a sickly sweet smell assaulted his senses. He felt more than saw the pool of blood the instructor lay in. Wahid Ali was slipping in and out of consciousness and was obviously in tremendous pain. Lying restlessly on the cold, hard floor, he still clutched his side as though desperate to keep life from flowing out of him. Blood seeped from between his fingers.

'He is going to die.'

Iqbal gave a half scream as he turned with a start and saw the sentry who had met them at the outskirts of the camp. 'There is nothing we can do for him here. Maybe if you all had returned to Chakoti last night he might have made it. Maybe...' The sentry spoke in a dryly matter-of-fact manner. Almost as though he was discussing the weather.

'There must be something we can do.'

The sentry had been hardened to the realities of life by almost three years as a jihadi. He had seen his contemporaries fall to the bullets of the Indian security forces. Some, he had even seen felled by other jihadi groups. He knew it all. The reality of life on the run. Living in hellish camps such as this one. Then dying the death of an animal without even the courtesy of a proper burial.

He looked bemused by Iqbal's innocence, as though unable to fathom how Iqbal was missing the obvious. 'Look around you. There is nothing here. Nothing except a few bandages and some basic medication for headaches, fever, loose motions and shit like that. This bugger,' he pointed at the gut-shot instructor, 'needs to be taken to hospital. That's not going to happen, you know.' He sighed wearily and shook his head in disgust. 'Inshahallah, he will go soon and not be tormented by the pain much longer.'

How can he be so damn cold-blooded? How can he not care for his own comrades?

The sentry saw the shocked look on Iqbal's face. It seemed to arouse something inside him and for one brief moment he wanted to reach out and speak to him: *Don't judge me, my young friend. You don't know what it is like to live in perennial fear of betrayal by villagers who are sick of the constant turmoil and killing that plagues their lives, of colleagues who are disillusioned by the futility of the fight, of our own treacherous masters sitting in Pakistan who have their own agenda that has nothing to do with Islam, the liberation of Kashmir or the jihad.*

Instead he said harshly: 'Don't you know this is how it ends for most of us? Barely a handful of people who enter the mujahideen mill that flourishes in the

Kashmir Valley live to see the end of the first year. As for those who live out the second year, you can count them on your bloody fingers.'

At twenty-six years of age the sentry was already a bitter old man. 'Come,' he said to Iqbal a shade more gently, 'look after this one instead.' He pointed to Omar who lay as still as a corpse on the other side of the hut. 'I'll go out and get some wood.'

Iqbal tried to turn his attention to Omar and tend to him but the instructor's screams of pain began again a few minutes later. Every successive scream was like a spear jabbed into his head. Then, abruptly, the screaming stopped. It took him a while to register that something had changed. Sudden, illogical and childish hope lit up in him. *Maybe the bleeding has stopped!*

Hope died abruptly when he saw the darkness of death settled on the instructor's face. It was drained white; the pool of blood around him had spread all over the floor. A fearful sob escaped unbidden from him as he stared at the dead man. Iqbal stumbled out of the hut and collided with the sentry who was now returning with a pile of wood chips in his arms.

'Where do you think you are going?' The tone was not unkind, but the steel of command was unmistakable.

Conditioned to six months of unflinchingly obeying orders it brought Iqbal to a dead halt. 'I'm...he is...so much blood...' Iqbal fumbled, barely coherent.

'Here...' said the sentry as he dumped the

woodchips in Iqbal's arms and nudged him back inside. 'Throw some into the fire. Let's have a little more light.'

Back inside, the sentry took in the dead man lying in a pool of blood. He did not bother to check his breath or pulse. The sentry had seen too many dead men not to be able to recognize death when he saw it. 'Come on. We need to bury him. Come and help me.'

'Bury him? Isn't he from the Pakistan Army? Do you think it is okay to bury him here?' Even as he spoke Iqbal realized it was not a very smart remark and his voice trailed off.

The sentry gave a short mirthless laugh. More like a bark. 'What do you think we should do? Take him back to Chakoti, hain? You think those buggers care?' He waved a vague hand in the direction of POK. 'They refused to collect their dead even when the Indian Army was handing their bodies over at Kargil. Because that would have meant acknowledging that they were Pakistanis.' The anger he felt came through loud and clear.

'Why do you say that? Why are you so cynical about them? You know they are helping us. They train us, give us money, weapons and...'

The sentry's bitter laugh shocked Iqbal. 'You think they are doing it for us? You silly fuck!' He hawked loudly and spat in the corner of the hut. 'They just don't have the balls for a fair fight. They have lost every damn war with India, that is why they have inflicted this endless, aimless jihad on India. They are trying to bleed India by forcing it to fight this constant low-intensity war.'

Standing there in the cold mountain air the sentry jabbed a finger at him, his anger evident even in the darkness. 'For the college guy that you seem to be, you are quite a fucking moron. Can't you do some simple maths? They didn't hire you for money, but they know you need it to live so they give you…what? A few thousand bucks, right? What do they give you if you die? Bugger all, right?' He made another vehement gesture. 'But what happens when one of their own regular army soldiers dies? They have to pay hundreds of thousands as insurance, gratuity and pension to his family, right?'

He gave Iqbal a long angry glare: 'Twenty dead jihadis like us cost them less than one dead Pakistani soldier. Plus they have the comfort of denying that they are the ones who train us and task us to fight their war. They get to fight a cheap war at almost no cost to them. Even the few bucks they throw at us we earn for them by bringing out their drugs.'

'Drugs?' There was an incredulous look on Iqbal's face.

'How do you think the drugs from Afghanistan reach America and Europe? Do you have any idea how many millions of dollars those shit-eaters earn from drugs? Most of it fills the coffers of those fancy ISI Generals, CIA agents and our great fearless leaders…a few paltry pieces are also thrown at us to buy arms and ammunitions.'

'I don't believe that,' Iqbal answered with angry vehemence.

'Really? You want to go and take a look at the backpack of that guy? Go on!' He gestured angrily toward the dead man lying between them. 'You want to come with me to the main camp in the next valley and have a look? Damn you!' he shouted. 'I know what you are feeling. Exactly how I felt when I came to know how I had been used and abused...'

The sentry stopped suddenly. He threw up his hands in a weary gesture as though the futility of it all had gotten to him.

'They are ruthless bastards. We are just pawns in their great game. Irrelevant. Expendable. They don't fucking care who lives or who dies...' He looked away. The pain and confusion starkly etched on his face reached out to Iqbal, overwhelming his mind with confusion. Suddenly the sentry shook himself and returned to reality. 'Come, let us bury the poor bugger before he begins to stink.'

'Then why do you still accept their support if you know all this?' Iqbal finally mustered the gall to ask as they carried the body towards the forest. 'Why do you continue fighting if you think all this is futile?'

The sentry didn't answer for a long time. When he finally did, he spoke softly, almost as though he was talking more to himself than answering Iqbal's question:

'What choice do I have now?' His voice was almost lost in the wind and Iqbal had to strain to hear what he was saying. 'Back in those days...when the blood ran hot and the cause burned bright I killed many Indian soldiers. Seventeen...you know...I have taken part in seventeen operations. My rifle has accounted for many of them. They know about me...' for a fleeting moment his face shone with a deeply buried, long-forgotten pride before it grew dark again – 'Do you know what they will do if they catch me?'

He didn't speak again till they were putting down the body to start digging: 'The Indian soldiers have become hard today. Much harder than they were when the jihad began. These days, they are far more willing and ready to pull the trigger than they used to be.' He paused. 'I guess their patience is running thin. Maybe they are tired of waiting to be shot at...'

The silence returned as they started to dig. The ground was cold and hard. The chilling cold only made it tougher to dig. 'Do you know what happened once?' The sentry spoke again. 'We had gone to pick up rations and stores from Srinagar when Indian soldiers suddenly started a cordon-and-search of the area. I was standing right there, barely ten feet away, when one of our guys panicked and tried to run. He was a young kid barely out of his teens...a new recruit who had just gotten back from training. They shot him down like a dog. They must have pumped him at least a dozen times. He was still alive...trying desperately to crawl away when one of the Indian soldiers walked right up to him and put one last bullet through his head. Can you imagine...just walked up to him and...*Bang!*.. right between the bloody eyes.' The sentry snorted. 'Do you know what I heard the soldier say when he was walking away from the boy he had shot?' The sentry looked at Iqbal, as though he expected him to know. '"Motherfucking Pakis...the only good ones are dead ones."'

The fire had almost died down when they re-entered the hut. Despite this, the warmth inside was heavenly after the bone-chilling wind in the jungle outside. Omar was awake and watching the two men in wary silence. The sentry seemed to unnerve him.

'We need to get some food into you,' Iqbal said going up to him and touching his forehead to check his temperature. It felt normal.

'I appreciate all the trouble you are taking of me, Iqbal,' Omar smiled weakly. 'I would not be alive if it wasn't for you.'

'You'd have done the same for me, I am sure.' Iqbal gave him some of the thick broth the sentry had made. Having ensured he had eaten enough of the broth Iqbal then gave Omar the last of the pills. 'Try and get as much rest as you can, we have a long journey ahead,' he said as he stepped away and sat down to eat his own food.

Surprisingly, the sentry joined him. After they had consumed their meal in silence, the sentry looked him straight in the eye. 'When do you two plan to move out?' he asked pointedly. 'I have very limited provisions here, you know. I cannot feed you two much longer.'

Iqbal turned to look at Omar who returned his gaze worriedly. 'Is something the matter?' he asked.

'Are you feeling well enough to move out now?'

'*Now?*' An expression of dismay crossed Omar's face. 'You want to move right away?'

Iqbal did, but he could see that Omar was not up to it. 'I mean, are you up to travelling tomorrow morning?'

'I guess so.'

In fact it was Omar who shook him awake the next morning. The sentry was hunkered down by the fire, watching them with narrowed eyes. He did not say anything as Omar handed a bowl of broth to Iqbal, but the minute they'd finished eating he took them to the edge of the jungle. 'Do you see that?' The sentry pointed to a thin sliver of road twisting away in the distance at the foot of the mountain. 'Get to that road and hitch a ride. Try to get hold of a truck or bus. Avoid private cars and government vehicles. They tend to ask too many questions. If you stop the wrong one you may well end up in prison...or dead. Understand?'

Both men nodded wordlessly at him.

'Good! If you head that way,' he said, 'you will get to Srinagar. Catch a bus from there to Jammu or Pathankot. From there you can get a train to wherever it is you have to go.'

When they went back to the hut to pick up their backpacks the sentry stopped them. He pointed to a thick polythene sheet, slick with oil, in a corner of the hut. 'Wrap your weapons in this sheet and bury them.' He handed them a pick and shovel. 'Here...use these.'

Omar and Iqbal looked at him uncomprehendingly so he explained, 'Bury the weapons here. You don't need them. They won't help you. In fact, if you are caught with them on your person by Indian soldiers you are more likely to be killed by them.'

The sentry led them to a small cluster of rocks on the edge of a ravine that ran down the side of the mountain, about four hundred metres from the hut. Working quickly, Iqbal dug a shallow hole and Omar placed the weapons, wrapped in the polythene to prevent them being spoiled, into the crevice. On the other lip of the ravine was the spot where they had buried the instructor.

An hour later the two young jihadis descended the mountain and skirting Hari village hit the road a little ahead of it; they lay hidden by the side of the road till a truck drove by some time later. Iqbal ran forward to flag it down but it did not stop. As it rattled past dangerously close to him Iqbal caught a glimpse of the angry grimace on the driver's face. The second truck did not stop either. Nor did the third.

'Maybe we should stand in the middle of the road and force it to stop?'

'Be my guest, Omar...please. You're welcome to give it a try,' said Iqbal sarcastically, only to follow it up with, 'Why didn't you think of it earlier?' when twenty minutes later, the fourth truck screeched to a noisy halt.

'Can you give us a lift to Srinagar?'

The man behind the wheel gave them a long, dubious look.

'We can pay,' Iqbal added hurriedly. 'My friend here is unwell and we really need to get him to a doctor.'

The mention of money brought a flicker of interest to the man's face. He reached out and took the two crisp five-hundred-rupee notes that Iqbal held out. 'Get in at the back.'

Neither of the three knew it but the notes were fake. They had been printed at an ISI-sponsored, illicit printing press operating deep in the alleys of Multan. As a forgery it was excellent and would have passed anything but a detailed scrutiny at a bank. The note was an integral part of the ISI strategy to destabilize the Indian economy by pumping in fake currency.

Iqbal helped Omar into the rear of the truck and then climbed over the tailboard. He patted his rucksack into a kind of seat and was sitting down when he felt something hard in it. A little puzzled he opened the rucksack to see two grenades nestled at the bottom of the bag. He had wrapped them in the spare trousers he had carried in his rucksack when they were leaving Chakoti and then forgotten all about them. 'If you are caught with weapons you will surely die or, at the very least, you will rot in some

Indian prison for a very long time.' The sentry's words came back to him. He toyed with the thought of throwing them out of the truck. The grenades were the typical fragmentation types that splintered into thirty odd bits of shrapnel when thrown. The feel of cold knobby metal spread a chill in him. Iqbal shivered.

In the end he held on to them. Reaching inside the rucksack he re-wrapped them in his clothing and pushed them to the bottom of his bag.

'You need to get off here.' The truck was parked on the side of the road. There was no other vehicle in sight. However, some evidence of human habitation was starting to reveal itself in the distance. 'The town is just ahead.' The trucker looked at the two men as they jumped off: 'I can't take you further. There are security checkpoints all over.' He looked away for a moment. 'I don't know who you are but I strongly suggest you avoid the main roads. Stick to the back alleys and you will be safe. Inshahallah.' He gave a short wave and engaged the gear. 'By the way, in case you are stopped, don't try to run.' Another short pause. 'Nobody hesitates to shoot these days.'

The roar of the engine escalated and the truck moved off in a cloud of dust leaving the two men standing there with confusion in their minds and fear in their hearts.

Iqbal and Omar gave each other a long look.

'Have you ever been to Srinagar before?'

Omar answered with a shake of his head.

'Me neither.'

'Inshahallah, we will be fine.'

'Let's take that lane.' Iqbal nodded at the dirtiest, narrowest lane leading away from them towards the town.

The two men hefted their packs and started to walk.

30 October 2005, BBC Television Studio, London.
'Your administration calls Pakistan a key ally in the war against terror,' Jack Robbins, the anchor said to the American Secretary of State during the popular television show, *Brasstacks*. This particular episode was a much-publicized one. Not only were the recent Delhi blasts on everyone's minds, it was also a huge casting coup since the British Foreign Secretary and Pakistani Foreign Minister were also present in the studio and the Indian External Affairs Minister was in attendance via a video conference link from Delhi.

'Yes, we do,' the Secretary of State conceded. 'They are a frontline state in our war against terror.' The Pakistani Minister nodded vehemently. The Indian one managed to look simultaneously pained and amused. The British Foreign Secretary was quite aware of Jack's reputation as a journalist who asked uncomfortable questions; he looked apprehensive.

'I'm glad to hear that,' Jack replied. 'Well, then, you may like to enlighten me on this, Madam. How is it that in the last ten years whenever there is a terrorist attack anywhere in the world it seems to have some link to Pakistan?'

'I don't think that is a fair assessment, Jack,' the Secretary of State replied gravely.

Jack gave her a long look before reaching for a small sheaf of papers on the table before him. He handed them out to the panellists as the camera zoomed into the paper he was holding up for the benefit of the Indian Minister and the audience. 'You might like to take a look at this. It is a list of recent terrorist attacks carried out all over the globe. In front of each is the list of people apprehended or suspected of these attacks. You will note that in almost every case a fair number are either Pakistanis, people of Pakistani origin, or have visited Pakistan and spent a couple of months there at some point in the twelve months preceding the attack.'

The American Secretary of State took a while to reply; she was still fumbling for an answer when the Pakistani Minister butted in: 'I think this is a most irresponsible statement for you to make. You must really check your sources.'

'I am so glad you brought this up, Minister. The sources I have used are freely available to anyone who chooses to make the effort. I suggest you simply log on to the Internet and check out these websites.' He handed over another sheet of paper to the Pakistani External Affairs Minister.

'You are right, Jack.' The Indian Minister could no longer contain his irritation. 'Our government has provided detailed proof of Pakistani involvement in almost all the terror strikes that have taken place on Indian soil. If you want names I can give them to you right now.' He pointed to a thick file on a table in front of him.

'Websites? What hogwash!' The Pakistani Minister's face was red with anger. He totally ignored his Indian counterpart and focused his attention on Jack. 'Anyone can write whatever he wants on a website.'

'I agree with you, sir. That is why I suggest you stick to the websites of various governments and organizations that have a reputation for being neutral. Please feel free to do your own research and yes, we would be more than happy if you shared the data with us for the benefit of our viewers.' Jack gave a helpful smile that was in sharp contrast with the tension palpable on the screen. He knew when he had his man and could afford to be gracious. 'And since you have brought up this point, sir, I would like to point out to you that out of the 65 religious terrorist organizations listed on almost any search engine on the Internet you will note that...' His ever-helpful cameraman flashed another table on the screen as Jack read off:

Religious Terrorist Organizations:

Christian:	07
Hindu:	04
Muslim:	40
Jewish:	03
Sikh:	10
Others:	01

The slide dominated a million television screens across the world backed with Jack's voice over.

There was a pause as the camera cut back to the men sitting around the table. 'You will also be interested to note that out of the forty Muslim and ten Sikh organizations listed here seven of the Muslim ones and almost all the Sikh ones have been founded in or are based in and functioning from Pakistani soil,' Jack pointed out.

There was a marked absence of sound bytes as silence descended on the panellists. Then the Pakistani minister decided that volume was the better part of valour and the show degenerated into an uncontrollable slanging match, which contributed significantly to the channel's TRPs.

Outraged by the massive carnage and the huge public outcry that this and other such television programmes unleashed even the Americans were forced to sit up and take note. There were too many Americans in the body bags flying in from Afghanistan and Iraq for them to be able to ignore this strike. Each body bag was a rude reminder of what it felt like to be at the receiving end. Each body bag drove home the hard truth that the Indians had been crying hoarse about for all these years.

For the Indian leadership too, this time it was a totally different ball game. The festering wounds of the Mumbai blasts, the Akshardham outrage and the attack on the Indian Parliament were not far from public memory. They were ripped wide open by this latest and most horrendous outrage. The Indian public wanted blood and they wanted justice. And this time they wanted it fast.

The normally soft-spoken and urbane Indian Prime Minister radiated a grim determination as he called for the Crisis Management Committee to present full details of the terror strike to an emergency session of the Cabinet at 1030 hours the next day. 'Our countrymen have shown tremendous fortitude and patience. The patience of this nation has been repeatedly and severely tested. It is high time we put an end to this and send out a clear and unequivocal message to the terrorists and the rogue states that continue to support them. This time the guilty must be made to pay.' He added, 'We have to ensure that those responsible for these bombings are brought to book even if it means sending out more people in harm's way. That is going to be the sole and immediate priority of this administration now...and at any time in the immediate future.'

As the magnitude of the crisis slowly sank in there was considerable confusion at all levels. However, the Indian Crisis Management Team was considerably battle-hardened by the constant terror attacks it had been coping with in recent years. It swung into action immediately; for once there was no dithering in the Indian response.

0335 hours, 30 October 2005, Anti-Terrorist Task Force, New Delhi.

A red alert went out to Bikaner, Gorakhpur and the Attari border to intercept the fleeing terrorists.

Unfortunately, the Attari Mail was crossing the border when the call was received. By the time the recipient put down the phone the train had already crossed the border and entered Pakistan.

At 0500 hours the Attari Express clocked in at Attari Railway Station. Getting off the train the two men headed for the nearest telephone booth and called the mobile number they had been given.

'You have reached. Good.' The man at the other end had obviously been waiting for the call. 'Just go to the refreshment counter near the exit gate and wait for me there.'

The man who strode up to them fifteen minutes later wore a black cap and leather coat that would have made the Gestapo proud. 'Follow me...and keep your mouths shut.' He flashed some kind of an identity card and they were immediately hustled through without any papers being produced or scrutinized. Two hours later, Team Two of the Lashkar was resting comfortably at the ISI safe house on the outskirts of Mari, just north of Lahore.

Team Two had eluded justice. However, the other members of the Lashkar were still within grasp of the Indian security forces.

'I don't want the trains to Bikaner and Gorakhpur intercepted at night,' the Task Force Commander told the strike team leaders. 'We will be giving the terrorists an unacceptably high chance of slipping away in the darkness.'

'True, sir,' one of them nodded in agreement. 'There are also too many chances of collateral damage and innocents getting hurt.'

'But what if they get off en route...for some reason or the other?' the second one broke in.

'Absolutely correct,' the Task Force Commander said. 'That's why all railways stations en route, where the two trains halt, are being placed under a heavy security blanket and everyone getting off will be subjected to detailed scrutiny. I want you guys to meet the two trains at their final destinations. Your teams should be in place at least an hour before the trains reach. Try and take the buggers alive.'

The team leaders nodded and headed out for the helicopters waiting to whisk them away to Gorakhpur and Bikaner. Then the Task Force Commander got on to the phone again and activated all the police stations on both the routes the trains were running on. It caused a lot of discomfort to a lot of security men and passengers, but it was nowhere near what lay in store for those present at Gorakhpur Railway Station at 0715 hours when the Sapt Kranti Express rolled in.

0715 hours, 30 October 2005, Gorakhpur Railway Station.

The bomber from the Shivaji Stadium Bus Terminus only realized that something was amiss when he failed to spot his team-mate at the platform. He got off the train and walked briskly to the prearranged spot near the exit gate where he waited for five minutes before he started getting uneasy. Not knowing what else to do, he decided to move out of the station and resume his journey. Perhaps it was this worry that preoccupied him because he failed to take note of the extra precautions being taken by the security men until he was almost at the gate.

That is when, like his team-mate the previous evening at Shivaji Stadium, he made a fatal mistake. He tried to break out of the line at the exit gate and get back onto the platform. The anti-terrorist cop watching the gate from the flank spotted the sudden movement and immediately closed in on the man trying to break out of the queue. 'Oye, you there! One second...' the cop said gruffly as he placed a firm hand on the man's shoulder. 'Let us have a look at some identification.'

The terrorist panicked; he tried to free himself, and pull out his weapon at the same time. The man had barely managed to get the pistol out when the cop hammered him hard on the temple with his rifle butt. The blow brought the terrorist to his knees. The pistol he had managed to free from his belt fired as the terrorist's fingers clenched reflexively from the blow to his temple.

The first bullet blew off the heel of a man walking past. The second slammed into the ankle of the lady just beside him. Suddenly there was chaos all around. Everyone tried to run at the same time. Luckily there was no third shot fired because by then the cop had slammed his rifle butt into the terrorist's head again and the man had slumped down unconscious.

'We've got the bugger!' The team leader could not keep the pride out of his voice as he reported to the Task Force Commander.

'Excellent work!' The Task Force Commander complimented him. 'Now just make sure you handle him with kid gloves. Check him out for suicide pills. No matter what happens I want him alive. Remember he is the first living proof of the strike that we have in our hands.'

0845 hours, 30 October 2005, Bikaner Railway Station.

The terrorist captured at Gorakhpur Railway Station was carted off to a small isolated room in the rear of the police station. He had just started to sing when the Bikaner Mail pulled into the Bikaner Railway Station at 0845 hours. It was delayed first because it started late from Delhi and second because it was halted just outside town for a few minutes to let through another train that was running even later.

The place where the train halted for those few moments was about three hundred metres short of the railway station, adjacent to a small marketplace located on the road running parallel to the tracks. The market was a cluster of about fifty shops selling all kinds of odds and ends. It was just beginning to stir to life.

It was during this halt that both the Lashkar men got off the train They got off not because they suspected anything. They did so simply because the halt was close to the market where they had to meet their conduit, Afzal. They had both seen the train slow down as it came up alongside the marketplace. Both recognized the market as the designated rendezvous point. They had seen it a few days earlier during the dry run. To them the aggravation of walking across the shit-streaked rail tracks was preferable to walking all the way around the station and then coming back to the market. The two men linked up near the tracks and walked across.

That is why the cops manning the Bikaner Railway Station came back empty-handed. They did take seven young men into custody, but detailed interrogations proved each of them innocent. 'They were not on the train,' the Anti-Terrorism Cell Team leader told his boss in the Crisis Management Team.

'You're sure about that?'

'Positive, sir. We detained everyone who could have even remotely been them,' the cop assured him. 'They either got off en route or never got on the train at all.'

'OK, listen, we got the other guy at Gorakhpur. He's told us the whole story so we know where those two fuckers are headed and have an idea of how they plan to reach there. You get your boys back to Delhi. I'll take care of it from here.'

Then the Crisis Management Team got down to managing the crisis: 'Those two will be linking up with someone called Afzal at Bikaner and then make the crossing to Fort Abbas.'

'Hang on,' the Army Liaison Officer flipped open the map of that area on his laptop. 'In that case these are the logical jump-off points.' He swivelled the laptop towards the cop and pointed at the area between Pugal and Anupgarh. Fort Abbas in Pakistan lay almost between them, directly to the north.

The cop pondered it for a moment. 'Right...that seems logical. That is where the hunt has to be concentrated.' He mulled some more over the map. 'It is a huge area to cover.'

'You have no clue, pal,' the Army LO laughed dryly. 'I have served there...the terrain is bloody rugged. You can put a thousand men down in that area and still not see a soul.'

'Shit!' The cop looked disgruntled. 'Anyway what has to be done has to be done. Let me speak to the DGP there and get things moving. What do you Army guys have available in that area?'

'Let me find out.' The Army LO reached for the nearest phone and dialled the Division Headquarters at Bikaner.

'We need to move fast.' The cop looked at the map again and did some mental calculations. 'They can reach there in four to five hours if they have a vehicle available to them.'

'Right! We assume they do have a vehicle, but I am sure we still have till tonight,' the Army LO replied as he waited for the phone to be picked up at the other end. 'They're not stupid enough to try the border crossing by daylight.'

Both tried to fight down the sense of urgency assailing them. They knew that in another few hours the two terrorists would be out of reach of the Indian authorities and would just become two more names on the list of people wanted for terrorist and criminal activities in India who were hiding in Pakistan.

During his telecast to the nation the Indian Prime Minister did not talk about the terrorists who had been captured by the security forces. Thanks to the message left behind by Furkan on the tapes of Aaj Tak the world already knew who was responsible for the Delhi blasts. The tapes had been repeatedly played by the news channel and quoted relentlessly by the print media. None of the revelations came as any real surprise to anyone. Maulana Fazlur Rehman and his organization were already a designated terrorist organization and banned in almost every responsible nation in the world. Likewise, Brigadier Murad Salim and the ISI's involvement in terrorist activity raised no eyebrows anywhere.

Other than this, the Indian Government clamped down on all news. As decided by the Crisis Management Committee, all real-time information about the ongoing investigations was being kept strictly under wraps and no news regarding the case was being released to the press. It had been decided at the highest possible level that no information would be released till such time as the guilty had been dealt with.

'No further comments, please,' was the PRO's constant refrain. 'We have already released all the information we have.'

'What about the shoot-out at Gorakhpur Railway Station this morning, sir?'

'What about it?'

'Did it have anything to do with the bomb blasts?'

'To the best of my knowledge, it didn't,' the PRO handling the conference replied. He was being quite truthful too, since his knowledge was reasonably out-of- date and likely to remain so for quite some time; 'What he doesn't know he can't let slip,' is what the Crisis Management Committee had decreed.

1150 hours, 30 October 2005, Indo–Pakistan Border, Rajasthan Sector.

The first set of orders going out from Army Headquarters unleashed an avalanche of security forces along the Rajasthan border. The orders were simple and clear – the terrorists who had eluded the anti-terrorist team at Bikaner should not to be allowed to cross over to their safe haven in Pakistan.

Even though the Indians had a clear idea of who they were looking for and where these men were headed, the desert was not an easy place to go looking for three men, specially in the Khajewala sector where the terrain was really rugged and scores of little-known, scarcely-marked trails crisscrossed the borders between India and Pakistan. Monitoring each one of them required massive resources not available under normal circumstances.

Luckily for the Indians, at that time, one of their desert brigades was carrying out induction training in the area between Khajewala and Anupgarh. The Brigade was immediately diverted for this task.

'Take them down or take them out,' the Brigade Commander was told. 'No matter what happens no one crosses that damn border. And listen,' the GOC stressed, ' make damn sure that your boys keep things quiet and low-key. I don't want those buggers getting spooked and hightailing it from there. We may not get another fix on them again.'

'Three men. We are looking for three men heading for Fort Abbas. They are most likely to be using the Khajewala–Fort Abbas axis.' That was the simple message that went out from the Brigade Major to all three units of the brigade. 'Stop everyone and everything moving along the border and bring them in. The terrorists must not be allowed to get across.'

Within hours, the Army and Border Security Force posts all along the international border had been placed on high alert and scores of patrols from the brigade under training were scouring the desert. An unseen array of battlefield surveillance radars lit up every inch of ground along the border between the border outposts. Senses were honed and gun sights gleamed darkly in the night.

The two terrorists who had gotten lucky at Bikaner Railway Station had an early dinner with

Afzal. Then as shadows lengthened and darkness overcame the light the three men set off for the Indo–Pakistan border. The three merchants of death were blissfully unaware of the ring of steel and fire that was coming into place between them and the ISI safe house at Fort Abbas in Pakistan towards which they were headed.

Over seven thousand men with loaded guns and bristling bayonets eagerly sought the honour of bringing them down – dead or alive. Each one of them was aching to avenge those hundreds of innocents Delhi-ites who had fallen to the bombs of these subhuman bastards.

2240 hours, 30 October 2005, Indo–Pakistan Border, Khajewala Sector, Rajasthan.

As it turned out, the honour eventually went to the platoon commanded by the young Sikh Light Infantry officer who was patrolling the dunes directly to the north of Khajewala, covering the ancient smuggling routes between Khajewala in India and Fort Abbas in Pakistan.

'Sir, No. 2 Section is reporting some movement,' the patrol Second-in-Command informed him.

'I'm on my way.' No.2 Section was the one on the right flank. The Captain moved to it rapidly. 'Show me,' he said to the soldier manning the battlefield surveillance radar.

A relatively new development of the Indian Defence Research and Development Organization, the all-weather-capable BFSR-SR Mark III man portable battlefield surveillance radar had been recently inducted into service by the Indian Armed Forces and other paramilitary organizations manning the border. It was a highly improved version of the radar that had been used by most Indian Army units till recently. The battery-powered radar weighed barely 22 kilograms and could be brought into action in less than four minutes. The radar had an inbuilt Global Position System to facilitate self-location, could track up to 50 targets simultaneously and classified targets based on the Audio Doppler signature. The portable colour PC display presented the viewer with an easy-to-read, high-resolution, coloured, north-oriented radar picture. User trials had confirmed that it could detect a crawling man 800 metres away, a walking man 2600 metres away, a group of men up to 6000 metres away and a vehicle or helicopter over 9000 metres away.

The three men walking on the unmarked desert trail that night were precisely 2017 metres away when the radar picked them up with startling clarity.

The Captain tracked the movement of the three men for a few moments, got a fix on the direction they were moving in and then cross-checked it with his map. They were headed almost directly for the Pakistani BOP (Border Out Post) at Ranabhana along the international border. 'Papa Six for Tiger One. I have three people moving just north of Temple Hill. They are moving on the old Sugar Four trail. Likely bearing indicates they are most probably heading towards Romeo Bravo. Over.'

His battalion commander took a minute to make the mental placements on the battle board hung on the wall before him. He took note of Old Sugar (Smuggler) Trail Four. The winding trail led right past the border and crossed into Pakistan barely 300 metres to the east of Romeo Bravo (the Ranabhana BOP).

'Tiger One for Papa Six. What's your assessment?'

'Tiger One, at this time and place? Can't be anyone but smugglers or ANEs. May well be the ones we are looking for.'

'Papa Six, I concur, but be careful...Make sure you keep the boys on a tight leash and there is no collateral damage.'

'Roger that Tiger One.'

'I want them alive. This is what I suggest you do...' he rattled off concise orders concluding with, 'Maintain radio contact. Papa Six Out.'

The young Sikh Light Infantry Captain tossed the radio handset back to his radio operator and started forward purposefully towards the dune where his patrol headquarters was deployed. A large whack of adrenaline thumped into his system and his mind slammed into overdrive.

The Sikh Light Infantry finds its origins in the Sikh Pioneers raised by the British in 1857. The Pioneers were disbanded in 1933 but revived as the Sikh Light Infantry during the Second World War. It was on the

Burmese front that they first tasted blood and won their first battle honours. Known as redoubtable fighting men the Sikh Light Infantry occupies a special place of honour in the Indian Army for courage, resource and ingenuity. They are ferocious warriors who require minimal orders and direction.

Reaching the dune behind which his patrol headquarter was sited the Captain gestured to his three Section Commanders to gather around him. 'Keep your eager beavers in strict control. The old man wants these buggers alive. No firing unless they fire first. And if you have to fire then aim low.'

The patrol moved out to set up the ambush. By the time the three moving figures were 400 metres away the opportunity ambush was firmly in place. Weapons had already been cocked to ensure there were no giveaway snicks. The two-inch mortar and the rocket launcher had been loaded with illuminating rounds.

Afzal the smuggler was in the lead when the three men entered the small gap between the two sand dunes. 50 metres away the young Captain controlled his mounting excitement as he watched the three men walk straight into the kill zone.

When they were exactly where he wanted them to be he raised his right hand and fired the pencil flare straight up in the air. The mortar and the rocket launcher fired illuminating rounds into the air even as the pencil flare was breaking out into light. All at once the desert night was bathed in light. *'Freeze! Hands in the air!'*

Like a deer caught in the headlights of a hunter's jeep, Afzal froze. He did not even bother to think of putting up a fight or attempting to flee. He just stood with his raised hands shaking in the air. So did the terrorist immediately behind him. But the third man thought differently. He turned and made a run for it, hurtling down the dune into the darkness. He was fast, but not fast enough, stumbling at the first shot and crumpling to the ground at the second.

Within seconds a storm of dark camouflaged figures had surrounded them. The two men who had frozen with their hands in the air were unceremoniously knocked down. Rough hands disarmed them and then slapped on handcuffs before subjecting them to a more thorough second search to check for any other concealed weapons.

The third man who had been stupid enough to try and run was alive, but barely. Both bullets had been aimed low. The first had hit him in the upper thigh causing him to fall. The second, fired a split second later, had been aimed for his lower body but had caught him in the throat as he fell. The field dressing applied to him by the patrol medic stanched the bleeding but was unable to stop life seeping out from him. The 5.56 mm full metal jacket slug fired at that range wreaks substantial havoc to the human body. He died midway to the one-ton truck parked a few hundred yards away when he was being carried to it on a field stretcher.

'Inshahallah!' the Captain shrugged. 'Anyway, let us find out who they are and why they are wandering around here at this time of the night.' It took the Captain just five minutes, a couple of slaps and one kick before Afzal decided to blab. The man he was escorting out of India listened in mounting horror as he spilled his guts out to the Indian Army Captain.

'It is them all right, Tiger One.'

'Excellent job, Papa Six. Bring them in fast.'

'Roger that, Tiger One, we are on our way. Oh, by the way, one of them didn't make it. He tried to make a run for it...we had to stop him.'

There was a short pause. 'Shit happens, Papa Six. You did what you had to do. Don't worry about it. Get moving now. These guys need to be interrogated ASAP.'

The relieved Captain tossed the handset back to the radio operator and turned to the patrol. 'Hurry up and get the buggers moving. You,' he addressed the Section Commander escorting the terrorists, 'keep a sharp eye on them. These behenchods are treacherous. If they try anything...anything...even if they breathe too hard just blow their bloody heads off, okay?'

The NCO nodded vigorously, enthusiastically landing a resounding thump on the head of the terrorist closest to him. 'Don't worry, sir.' He looked as though he couldn't wait for the terrorists to try something.

A dozen miles to the north, the ISI agent waiting at the Ranabhana BOP for Afzal and his two charges to show up did not start to worry almost till daybreak. He finally decided to call his superior at Fort Abbas when the three men did not reach the post even an hour after daybreak.

'I just hope those assholes have not been taken alive by the Indians,' was the first thing his superior said, then he added, 'Maybe they missed their train...or had a breakdown en route...or some such thing.' He mused some more. 'Hang in there for another day and let's see.'

The ISI Agent put down the phone and went back to the command hut the Company Commander had so proudly offered to share with him. 'Life is a such a bitch,' he thought to himself as he tried to shut out the constant whining of the Company Commander about life in the desert. He fervently hoped that the three lost morons would fetch up soon so he could get his sorry butt back home.

1000 hours, 30 October 2005, South Block, New Delhi.

Dr Singh, the Indian Prime Minister looked sombre but composed when he addressed the nation. However he did not in mince his words when he assured the nation that justice would be ensured and the guilty made to pay.

All television channels interrupted their normal telecasts to carry the Prime Minister's address. Almost every household across the country had already turned on their TV sets when he started to speak. Those who were en route or caught in their cars were not denied the Prime Minister's words since almost every radio station also carried the broadcast. And not just in India, despite the time zone differences, a lot of people in a lot of countries watched and listened. The Prime Minister spent the first few minutes recapitulating the horror that the terrorist bombs had unleashed on the Indian capital before he actually touched upon the meat of the matter:

'For over two decades now India has withstood the scourge of this menace. We have repeatedly produced undeniable proof to the world of the people responsible for these cowardly and reprehensible acts, but the world has chosen to do nothing about it. Well, this time the comity of nations must take note that India will not take this heinous act of cowardice as anything other than an act of war. We shall bring the guilty to book. No matter what the cost and what the means this time justice will be meted out. I have mobilized the Indian Armed Forces into the highest possible state of alert and we stand ready to do whatever is required to defend ourselves and our way of life. I assure the people of India that any person or nation that stands between us and these cowardly terrorist killers shall encounter the full fury and might of the Indian Armed Forces.'

There was deadly intent and a new sense of purpose in the PM's address; made even more palpable by the calm deliberation with which it was delivered.

*

All over the world a series of high-level meetings erupted as a panicky world contemplated the threat of yet another war in the Indian subcontinent; since few had any doubt about who was behind the terror.

'Sir, the Indians are dead serious this time.' The intelligence analyst briefing the American President told him. 'We have every indication that they are not going to take this one lying down.'

'What kind of response are you talking about?'

'It is still too early to say, sir, but there is nothing to prevent them from going Israel's way and taking the chase into Pakistan; they clearly have the means. If the Indian people build up enough pressure on their politicians they may very well find the will.'

'What happens if they do that?'

The analyst chose his words carefully. 'That's anybody guess, sir,' he eventually replied. 'The Pakistanis won't take it lying down. They have too much at stake and are quite likely to up the ante. As it is, both armies are always on high alert, especially along the Kashmir border...and the strike formations of both countries are never very far from the borders.'

'You think they will go nuclear?'

'Well...' It was the question all intelligence analysts dreaded – trying to guess what they thought the other guy was going to think. He wanted to say: 'Who do you think I am, Mr President? The only balls I have are between my legs and they are definitely not crystal.' Instead he gave him a profoundly intellectual look: 'It is hard to say, sir, but logically the Pakis are dumb enough to do it. Although if they do, the Indians can literally wipe Pakistan off the map. Between the two of them only India has the strategic and physical depth to live through a nuke attack.'

The President studied the painting that hung on the wall facing his desk. 'Get the Pakistani President on the line for me.'

The aide was walking away to do his bidding when he spoke again: 'And the Indian Prime Minister too.'

A flurry of phone calls erupted, but strangely enough, let alone the Indian Prime Minister, no one even remotely senior was available for comment. The underlings who took the message were apologetic, but vague. 'Yes, we will definitely pass on the message. We will make sure they call you back ASAP.' This stonewalling was a feature of Indian diplomacy that the world had not encountered before.

The only one who did get through was the Israeli Premier. His call with the Indian PM lasted barely two minutes. The call between the Intelligence chiefs of the two countries that took place a few minutes later lasted almost half an hour.

Thirty minutes after the television address, the Prime Minister chaired an emergency Cabinet session. Despite short notice, every member was in attendance.

Indian Cabinet sessions are not noted for being calm and peaceful and this session had all the ingredients for turning into a particularly nasty one. It didn't. The PM set the tone by speaking in a calm manner: 'Let us be very clear that this time the nation must stand firm. I appeal to all parties and members, this is no time for petty politicking...We must deliver on our commitment to the people. We must ensure we present a united front and bring the guilty to book. This is what I propose to do...'

There was a stunned silence in the room when he finished. Then a storm of questions exploded.

'Gentlemen, please. You must understand and appreciate that I cannot go into operational details at this point in time. In any case, these matters are for the Armed Forces to handle and I have complete confidence in their ability to do so. What I need from all of you today is just the answer to a simple question – Is there anyone here who feels we should not act to defend ourselves?' He gave a long pause to drive home the import of his words. 'If so, this is the time to speak.'

The PM had worded his question so beautifully that it would have taken a very brave politician to answer in the negative. None did.

The PM did not meet any resistance from any quarter since even his worst political foes were solidly behind him. From this emergency session he moved straight to another meeting of the Crisis Management Committee in South Block.

The Crisis Management Committee meeting was not publicized or talked about at all. For once there was no bureaucratic bullshit or hyperbole. The PM went straight to the heart of the matter: 'We need to give an appropriate and befitting response. Such acts cannot be taken lying down any more.'

A loud and affirmative murmur met his words.

'I tell you, we must sort these buggers out once and for all!' The Defence Minister was a salty man of the soil, a direct contrast to the genteel PM. 'If Mrs G was still around our forces would be striking deep into Pakistan. I tell you, people, that lady had balls.'

The Home Minister and the External Affairs Minister exchanged horrified looks at this crassness. They were still struggling for words when the Defence Minister thumped a huge hand appreciatively on the table. 'Remember 1971? She gave those buggers something to chew on for a long time.'

'Well, sir,' the Army Chief addressed the Defence Minister; he was not a political appointee and had only about three months to go before he hung up his spurs,so he could speak with undue candour. 'In 1971 we were told to go in and liberate East Pakistan. We did it. There is no gainsaying that militarily it was an exemplary war, but otherwise, strategically speaking, how much sense did it really make?'

The Defence Minister reddened considerably. He had not expected to be contradicted, especially not from these quarters. But before he could say anything the Army Chief resumed speaking:

'East Pakistan was a festering wound for Pakistan. It was perennially facing drought or floods. It was a massive and continuous drain on the already fragile and fragmented Pakistani economy. Not only that, it was also a strategic and administrative nightmare for Pakistan to maintain forces in two such widely separated areas. By liberating East Pakistan we released them from these perpetual sorrows. We allowed them to concentrate their forces on one front...'

The External Affairs Minister quite liked the way this was going. 'But of course,' he butted in, 'that is exactly what my predecessors had pointed out. But who was listening?'

'Not only that, Minister, we have given that damn ISI a perfect and deniable base for terror activities. They now happily use Bangladeshi territory to pump in arms and militants into India without involving their own country.' The Home Minister, who belonged to the same political party as the External Affairs Minister, could not resist this opportunity to tell off the Defence Minister, who had been thrust upon them by the politics of a coalition government.

'That is exactly what they have also started doing in Nepal now. Are you aware that the Habib Bank of Pakistan is supporting 800 madrassas in Nepal? 800! Can you believe it? 800! That is almost as many as we have in India and we're talking about a country that is smaller than our smallest state. I mean, let's get real, Nepal has fewer Muslims than we have in any one of our states.'

'The Habib Bank is just a damn front for their bloody ISI. You know how these filthy Pakis are...Give the buggers an inch and there they are with their terror factories. Those bastards will never stop. The only way is to go in and just...'

'Well, sir,' the National Intelligence Chief broke in, 'you must understand that these madrassas have a key role to play in how Pakistan influences and controls terrorist organizations. Are you aware that the word Taliban literally means a group of madrassa students? Do you know that five of the Taliban's key leaders are graduates of a single madrassa?'

'Really?'

'Yes, sir. Five of them are from the Darul Uloom Haqqania, in Akora Khattak...that's near Peshawar. The Taliban are mostly Pashtun veterans of the Afghan–Soviet War. They have transformed the classical belief that jihad is a defence of Islam into a very radical, militant worldview. They are possibly the most violent face of Islamic fundamentalism and they target Muslims and non-Muslims alike. Many Muslim leaders have opposed their puritanical and intolerant doctrines as deviations from Islam.'

'I didn't know that,' it was the Defence Minister again, 'but I can believe anything about these Pakis...'

'Very true, sir. After all, barring Israel, Pakistan is the only country in the world to have been formed on the basis of a religion.' For once the External Affairs Minister agreed with him. 'If they did not have India to hate and fight what would they base their national and foreign policies on?'

'True again, sir,' the Intelligence Chief couldn't

resist the opportunity to display his intelligence. 'Do you know that it was at Peshawar that most of the hiring was done by the Pakistani Army, at the behest of the Americans, to supply mujahideen to Afghanistan to fight the Soviets? After all, the Al-Qaida is a creation of the CIA and the ISI. It is because of their short-sightedness and stupidity that the world is suffering these horrific terror attacks.'

'Bloody Al-Qaida...' the Defence Minister muttered. 'What kind of a name is that anyway?'

'Sir, Al-Qaida, literally means "the database".' The Intelligence Chief was on a roll. He seldom got such an august audience under one roof. 'It was originally the computer file of thousands of mujahideen who were recruited and trained to fight the Russians. The database was divided into two parts, the information file from where the participants in the meetings could pick up information they needed, and the decision file where the decisions made during the previous sessions were recorded. In Arabic, the files were called,"Q eidat il-Maaloomaat" and "Q eidat i-Taaleemaat". Those two files were kept in one file called "Q eidat ilmu'ti'aat", which is the exact translation of the English word "database". But the Arabs commonly used the short word Al-Qaida, which is the Arabic word for "base". For instance, the military air base of Riyadh, is called "Q eidat riyadh al askariya". "Q eida" means "a base" and "Al-Qaida" means "the base". It is an organization with the stated objective of eliminating foreign influence from

Muslim countries. Most of its prominent members are adherents of Salafism, a very fundamentalist Sunni sect.'

There was a short pause as the Intelligence Chief stopped speaking. He suddenly realized that though the information may have been new and fascinating for many of those present in the room this was definitely not the time for it.

'That is very illuminating I am sure, but right now I need to know just what the hell we plan to do.' The Home Minister looked at the PM as he spoke. The PM acknowledged the cue offered to him with a brief nod.

'Gentlemen, I am sure all of you will agree that we have soft-footed around for too long. I think it is time we learnt a thing or two from the Israelis. We must let the world know that India is not a perpetual target for any lunatic terrorist to hit upon whenever he feels like it.'

A babble of angry comments erupted. The PM held up his hand and waited till some sort of silence was reached. 'I want you all to listen carefully...This is what we are going to do...'

When he finished speaking there was a stunned silence in the room. For a good long minute no one spoke, then all at once everyone erupted almost simultaneously; barring the three Service Chiefs with whom the PM had obviously had a prior sit-down.

'The Americans will have kittens.'

'Let them. This is not their problem.'

'Don't you think we should...?'

'Why can't we just bomb all those training camps also?'

'I am sure that we should be able to...'

'Gentlemen, please.' The PM raised his hand again and waited till silence returned to the room. 'We will not worry about what anyone has to say or do. The right to defend itself is not the sole right or privilege of any single nation. We too have the right and we will exercise it...this time, and from now on, whenever we are compelled to. I have told you what needs to be done. Now you have to translate it into action.'

'I agree with you totally,' the Defence Minister rasped importantly. 'These damn Americans with all their talk of human rights and their moral high ground are absolutely full of shit. They have historically always supported dictators, drug lords and terrorists all over the world.'

'Come, come, Minister,' the Foreign Minister tried to butt it. 'Let us not get...'

'Let me speak, man. You know what I am saying is true. We all know who gave birth to the terror factories in Afghanistan and pumped in planeloads of arms into the region. We all know who supplied chemical weapons to the Middle-East so that they could be tested at no cost to those bastards themselves. We all know who is responsible for the mess in and around Israel. And Afghanistan.'

'There I agree with you, sir,' the Army Chief spoke up. 'I am sure you know that it was the ISI and the

CIA that encouraged opium cultivation in Afghanistan during the 80s. It is an established fact. They wanted the Soviet troops to get hooked on to it. Of course, once the Soviets withdrew, the ISI and the Afghan terror networks simply diverted the opium supply to America and the West. So you are right in…'

'Of course I am right!' The Defence Minister was so angry that flecks of spittle flew all around him. It was obvious that no one was going to be able to stop him. 'The kind of proof we have given those pansies about Pakistan's involvement in terror activities all over the world…. What have they done about it? They have just gone and sold them more arms and fighter planes. Whereas with one-tenth of that proof they have attacked Afghanistan and Iraq just to further their economic goals.'

'No proof is enough for the Americans when it comes to Pakistan.' It was the Army Chief again.

'Of course it is not! You think they need any proof? You think their CIA does not know what is going on in Pakistan? We all know those shit-eaters are running drugs along with the Pakis, after all if they could smuggle drugs in the body bags of their own soldiers during Vietnam why can't they do it here? What involvement or attachment do they have with this part of the world, except oil and their own goddamn economic agenda?' He paused to catch his breath. 'Do you think they have the balls to do anything to make the Pakis stop? You think they will do anything except cosy up in bed with that rabid General and give him some more tanks and planes? Who the heck are the Americans to tell us what to do?'

The Defence Minister suddenly found an unexpected ally in the External Affairs Minister: 'You can rest assured that the Americans are going to pay a very heavy price for all this Paki mollycoddling. The Pakis are going to carry out more and more terrorist strikes on the American mainland with their own money and resources.'

'Absolutely! But then that's their look-out. If they are so stupid and short-sighted then they deserve what is coming to them.' Even the normally contrary Home Minister concurred. 'Why should we worry about what they have to say or wait for them to sort out our problems?'

'That is exactly what I am saying!' The Defence Minister was half out of his chair as he shouted. 'I agree completely with the Prime Minister. There has been enough beating around the bush. This time we must act. It is our problem and we have the means to sort it out...all we need is the bloody balls.'

'Please leave it to us, sir.' The Army Chief, who was also the Chairman of the Chiefs of Staff Committee said quietly. 'We know what needs to be done...and how to do it.' His quiet, calm tone radiated confidence.

'Good!' the PM nodded. 'For a world that has become so used to taking India for granted and has always mistaken our non-alignment and love for peace as a sign of weakness the Indian response must come as a powerful and assertive warning.'

*

The world had forgotten that this was the same nation that had executed one of the most successful military campaigns in the history of modern warfare – when its Armies had raced in and liberated Bangladesh 34 years ago even as the Pakistani Army stood by, stunned and shocked, as over 95,000 of its soldiers were taken prisoner.

The world had forgotten that this was the same nation that had withstood hundreds of years of occupation and was now an economic tiger raising its head quietly and proudly.

The time had come to remind the world of the strength and resolve that lay behind this huge democracy. And, as fortune would have it, the right man was at the helm of affairs. A scholar of world renown, known for his love for peace and justice, Dr Singh was just the right face to present to the world. No one could ever accuse him of being a rabid warmonger.

In a very short time a number of orders were issued from various offices of the Indian Army, Navy, Air Force and the Home Ministry.

A series of small but lethal cogs began to move into place. A strategically planned, innovative and well-orchestrated drama was about to begin.

Justice was about to be meted out at last.

IQBAL

Srinagar, India.

Allah was clearly watching over the two newly-trained terror mechants that day. Omar and he were not stopped even once though they passed several clusters of cops and Army men as they made their way into Srinagar. They simply used the flow of traffic to guide them to the city and only started asking for directions when they were well inside it.

The walk into town took them an hour, not because of the distance but because they had to switch routes continuously to avoid the checkpoints.

They were also lucky to get on the bus for Jammu almost as soon as they reached the Srinagar bus station. Barring the interminable stops for security checks en route the journey down to Jammu was uneventful.

The wait for the train to Lucknow at Jammu was a lot longer since the next train only left at 2205 hours. 'We have more than two hours to kill,' Iqbal said checking the time on the platform clock.

'I don't mind. Not as long as I get to sit down.' Omar heaved a weary sigh as he parked himself on the hard wooden bench at the very edge of the platform. He looked totally played out.

'Well, I need to change and clean up,' Iqbal said; the smell from their unwashed bodies was getting to him.

'Come on, Iqbal.' Omar protested. 'You've managed without it so far...live with it for a bit more. We can always clean up on the train.'

'No. I am sure I smell really bad. I know you do. I can smell you long before I see you...besides we will attract too much attention if we continue like this. Come on, the shops are just outside the station... ' Iqbal pushed Omar to accompany him and they both went to the nearby market and bought themselves new clothes.

'We can bathe and change in the waiting room,' Iqbal said as he led the way back into the railway station. 'Then let's find something decent to eat. I need to get rid of the vile taste of that broth we have been surviving on.'

Two hours later, the two young men who boarded the train for Lucknow looked nothing like the scruffy jihadis who had left the camp near Hari the previous day.

'Is it okay if I come to Lucknow with you?' Omar had asked Iqbal the night before. 'I don't think I am up to travelling alone.'

'Not a problem.' Iqbal hadn't really wanted to be alone either. He still dreaded the nightmare memories of the earthquake and the sight of his comrades being killed; terrifying thoughts which clamoured to return whenever he found himself alone. Beneath the tremendous eagerness he felt to be going home, a disturbing medley of thoughts whirled tumultuously through him as the train devoured the miles and crossed the heart of the country. He tried to shrug away the fear. *Abbu and Ammi will understand and forgive me.*

Iqbal felt a sharp sense of excitement course through him as he rang the doorbell of the house in Lucknow in which he had grown up. Every memory of his childhood lay entwined with this house. *Where is everyone? They can't be sleeping at this time.*

He rapped impatiently on the door again. They seemed to be taking forever, or maybe it was just his eagerness to meet everyone that was making him unduly impatient. He could almost smell his Ammi's siwai and rogan josh and involuntarily his mouth watered. Oh yes! It was good to be home. He rang the bell again. A longer and more insistent ring.

It was his brother Ashraf who finally opened the door. 'My God! Iqbal bhaijaan! It is you!' Ashraf gave him a long disbelieving look and then hurled himself at Iqbal. Thoroughly pleased at such a stupendous welcome Iqbal hugged him back warmly.

Iqbal felt the wetness of Ashraf's tears on his neck as they hugged tightly and was a bit nonplussed. 'Hey, relax, yaar. I know you are overwhelmed, but I am coming home not going away.' All at once Iqbal was acutely aware of Omar standing a few feet behind him and for no apparent reason his presence bothered him. 'Come on, Ashraf…' He tried to gently push his brother away and enter the house. 'Stop crying and let me enter the house at least.'

But Ashraf would not stop sobbing. He clung to Iqbal as though he had no strength left to hold himself up. 'What the hell? Can't you see there is an outsider standing behind me? It's embarrassing…' Iqbal's nerves were shot to hell from the events of the past few weeks and Ashraf's apparently meaningless tears shred what was left of them. He was about to completely lose his patience when the bedroom door opened and he saw his father standing there.

One look at his father and Iqbal knew that something was seriously wrong. Nawab's strong muscular body seemed to have been drained of life. Those solid athletic shoulders drooped in a way Iqbal had never thought possible. Pulling away from Ashraf he ran up to his father and took him in his arms. 'What's wrong, Abbu?'

The sobs that racked through Nawab surprised Iqbal and, even though he declined to acknowledge it, scared him a bit. 'What has happened, Abbu? Talk to me, please, tell me…'

'Your Ammi has left us.' Nawab was speaking so softly that the words were almost lost. 'She is gone, she is gone…' Then he said it again: 'Your Ammi has left us, Iqbal. She has gone forever.'

'*How?* What happened?' Iqbal's breath whipped out of him and bands of pain tightened across his chest. His head felt heavy as his mind refused to absorb what his father was telling him. His father was sobbing brokenly. His strong, invicible father, so defeated, so pathetic. *Control yourself. Get a hold on your emotions. They need you…Abbu and Ashraf need you to be strong and take charge.* Iqbal felt his body stiffen and some measure of control return. He knew he needed to stand firm. 'Hush! Hush, Abbu…don't cry…please…hush, Ashraf.' Iqbal whispered softly as he tightened his grip around both of them. But then the reality of his mother's death impacted his body like the steel edge of a knife and he felt the fact of her death like a visceral wound. Like the life blood seeping out of a gut-shot man. *How could she have left us alone? Had she not known that she was the anchor that had held us all together?* He struggled to understand that his beloved mother was no longer among the living. *I wonder how Navaz is taking this? She is closest to Ammi.* Iqbal shuddered as he thought of how distraught and lonely his little sister would be. *The poor kid, she must be totally devastated.*

Suddenly he realized that she had not come running when she had heard the doorbell and knew he had returned. He fought back the panic in his voice. 'Where is Navaz?' he asked already dreading the answer. *'Where is she?'*

The sobs intensified. Iqbal was about to ask again when Abbu spoke: 'They killed her too…the bastards... so horribly…. so brutally…'

Iqbal's mind froze. Everyone and everything else fell away from him, forgotten for the moment. He pulled back from them. His brain refused to accept the unacceptable things his father and brother kept telling him. He didn't believe them. It wasn't possible. *Who kills innocents? Who kills defenceless little girls?*

That is when Iqbal learnt about the savage end his beloved mother and sister had met; the two people who had meant everything in the world to him. Iqbal felt the world inside him give way, he felt his very being crumble and implode. The anguish and pain he felt at the loss of his mother and sister slowly transformed into a revulsion for himself. *I am responsible for their deaths.*

In his mind's eye Iqbal saw the look on the Maulana's face as he had stood proudly in front of the television and told them all of the great deed his brave trainees had done. Just behind him was the shadowy face of the other man who had been there at that time. Salim. The famous Brigadier Murad Salim of the Pakistani ISI. 'Today a great blow has been struck for the jihad,' the Maulana had said in triumph.

How could the killing of innocent women and children be called jihad? What God would ever condone such senseless violence?

The snow-flecked images on the television that evening flickered through Iqbal's tortured mind. But now two of the dead bodies on the ground wore faces he knew and loved. The self-revulsion inside him exploded and he felt the darkness of despair and guilt flood through him.

'O Allah, I have oppressed my soul and undoubtedly there is no forgiver of sins but You alone. O Allah, forgive me

and have mercy on me. Undoubtedly You are the most forgiving and most merciful...'

From somewhere deep within him the words of the *Salaat* ran through Iqbal's head in relentless circles.

He wanted to lie down and die.

Part Two

THE COUNTER-ATTACK

FORCE 22

1150 hours, 30 October 2005, Kasauli Hills, Himachal Pradesh.

The most critical set of orders sent out at the behest of the Prime Minister were going to be the hardest to implement. It was Colonel Rajan Anbu, the Commanding Officer of Force 22 who received this set of orders. The orders of the Joint Chiefs of Staff were absolutely clear and concise. It took him barely two minutes to go through them. Absorbing the import, and the twenty files that accompanied the order, took longer. He sat in the solitude of his command post and gave the matter serious thought.

Many people knew about the existence of Force 22, but not more than a handful knew what it was capable of doing. Born in the bloody crucible of the decades-long low-intensity conflict that had been thrust upon India by Pakistani military and intelligence establishments, Force 22 was created to provide a rapid, highly professional and covert response to certain situations that could not, due to tactical, strategic, diplomatic or political reasons, follow standard procedures.

Force 22 comprised officers drawn from the Indian Army, Navy, Air Force and the RAW (Research and Analysis Wing – the Indian Intelligence Agency). All of them were carefully handpicked volunteers every detail of whose personal and professional life had been thoroughly scrutinized before they were allowed to join Force 22.

Each of these officers had some basics in common: they were all commissioned officers not below the rank of Captain, all in superb physical condition, all high achievers amongst their peers, all trained to fight over land, sea and air, all skilled in most known methods of killing and destruction and all highly motivated. In thought, word and deed they all manifested and depicted the credo of Force 22 – *speed, stealth* and *surprise*.

To keep the existence of Force 22 as quiet as possible it was located in a small secluded barracks a few miles away from the picturesque hill town of Kasauli. In this sparsely habited area there were not many people around to take any notice of these tough looking men in camouflage uniforms as they punished themselves with a variety of arduous physical exercises at all hours of the day and night. Yes, the sound of gunfire and sporadic explosions did echo through the hills, but these are normal activities associated with any military unit and did not attract undue attention.

However had someone walked into the barracks that housed Force 22 and taken a close look around, he or she would have been in for a surprise. On the surface it was a typical army set-up, but at its core it was a state-of-the-art, ultra-sophisticated facility equipped with highly secure, multi-mode communications and could latch on to any database in the country and, if the need arose, overseas.

Colonel Rajan Anbu, the first Force 22 Commanding Officer, had been specifically picked by the PM in consultation with the army, navy and air force chiefs when the force was set up about a year ago. An innovative and resourceful mind coupled with a rugged physique, a lead-from-the-front attitude, and a decade of experience in counter-terror operations made the forty-one-year-old Colonel the ideal choice for the job. In the past year, Anbu had interrogated hundreds of potential candidates and put them through a battery of physical, mental and psychological tests. He had finally put together a small but lethal team. He had also used his generous budget to shop for a variety of state-of-the-art weapons, communications and support systems to enhance the potency of the force.

Finally he had set about blending his chosen warriors to fight as a team. Anbu was a firm believer of the more-you-sweat-in-peace-the-less-you-bleed-in-war school of thought. The result of this belief was a training regimen that made Force 22 a hell-hole for those who had been chosen. Despite the rigid selection criteria, six of the twenty-six handpicked officers did not cut the ice and were duly reverted to their parent battalions. Of the remaining twenty, one chose to opt out for personal reasons.

Now the time had come for him to set his team in action. Anbu picked up the intercom. 'Get me Tiwathia and Sami,' he told his staff officer.

When they walked in two minutes later, Anbu pushed the bundle of files at them: 'Each of these files is about a specific individual. The data on these individuals has been systematically collated over the years and kept up-to-date by our intelligence agencies. Each of these individuals is a proclaimed offender who has played a major part in the various heinous terrorist activities that have plagued India all these years. For each one of them a Red Corner alert has already been issued by Interpol. As you know, all twenty of them are living a life of comfort in Pakistan.'

'We've been following the intelligence summaries,' Tiwathia cut in as Sami and he flicked through the names on the file covers. 'All these guys are being sheltered and supported by the bloody ISI.'

'The whole world is aware of who and where they are but this is the age of plausible deniability. Even though their weddings and funerals are front-page news, nobody is ready to acknowledge their whereabouts,' Sami added.

'Our government has released extensive proof about all of them a dozen times but the damn Pakis deny it blatantly.'

'I want you both to study all twenty files.' Anbu explained what the PM wanted: 'Look for patterns and avoid those for whom there are no confirmed sightings. Give me your independent views...four each...okay?'

For the next forty-five minutes only the rustle of pages being turned broke the silence as the three men scrutinized the files. Sami was the last to finish. Anbu looked at him. 'You go first.' Sami plucked out four files from the bundle and handed them over. Anbu placed the files face down and turned to Tiwathia. 'What about you? Which ones do you recommend, Vikram?'

Tiwathia took four names without missing a beat.

Anbu gave a small smile as he heard the names then he flipped over the files Sami had handed him. 'I thought as much,' he said quietly. 'You guys have also picked out the same three people that I had identified. We only differ on the fourth. That's okay...this time we take down only three.'

Colonel Anbu outlined the operational plan in a calm measured tone. Tiwathia and Sami were the two most experienced officers in Force 22. In fact, Sami was the official second-in-command. They both listened carefully as Anbu spoke and gave their input when he finished. An hour later when they finally got up, each knew exactly what had to be done; they had played out many such scenarios in various war games. It did not take Anbu long to fine-tune the plan and hammer out the operational details. Activating his laptop he checked out the availability of men and materials. Then he called in his staff officer and issued precise orders.

Anbu requisitioned a series of satellite and aerial photographs. While these were being uploaded to his machine he put together the Op Orders. Thirty minutes later, twelve of the nineteen Force 22 officers were assembled in the briefing room. Anbu put them through the paces. 'That's it, folks. Any doubts so far?' he asked when he had finished.

There were. Several. Anbu took another fifteen minutes to clear these and then in accordance with the commonsense rule that nothing goes as planned he spent another thirty minutes carrying out some detailed contingency planning. Finally he handed over a Compact Flash Card and some photos to each one of them. 'Everything you need is here. Study it en route and erase the files when you are done.' The men were filing out of the room when Anbu called out: 'And folks, keep your GPS locators on at all times once you leave the base.'

'Don't worry about us, boss.'

'I'm not. I just need to be able to find you in case you get lost.'

The laughter that rang out was a welcome change from the sombre mood that had prevailed during the briefing.

IQBAL

Iqbal spent the whole day on a settee in the far corner of the room. He could not bring himself to speak to anyone. It was as if he had battened down the windows of his mind. Finally, a distraught Nawab sought Omar's help: 'Beta, please talk to him. He is not talking to any one of us. He is very disturbed...he loved them very much...specially his sister...I am very afraid he will try to do something to himself...please...I will die if something happens to him also.' Nawab's voice quavered.

Omar stood up and held the old man's folded hands between his own. 'Please calm down, Uncle. Everything will be all right, I promise. You just need to stay calm.'

Embarrassed that a stranger was giving him solace Nawab choked back his tears and abruptly left the room. Ashraf looked uncertainly at his brother sitting silent and unreachable on the settee and then followed his father out.

Omar sat next to Iqbal and tried to speak to him. His voice was like a drone in Iqbal's ears. He felt its vibrations but heard nothing of its content. Omar was trying very hard to intrude on Iqbal's thoughts but everything he said was deflected by the one thought playing on and on in Iqbal's mind: *You are responsible for the death of the two people who meant the most to you. You killed them almost as certainly as if you'd planted the bombs yourself.* The echo inside Iqbal's head grew louder with every passing minute. *'Murderer!'* the voice within him mocked.

Omar put his hand on Iqbal's shoulder. 'I know how proud you must be feeling at their martyrdom.' It was the word 'martyrdom' that caught his attention and wrenched Iqbal back to reality. It suddenly became imperative for him to know what Omar was saying. He made an effort to clear his mind.

'Remember what Rehman Sahib used to tell us?' Omar was speaking in the calm, reassuring tone an adult uses when talking to a sick child. 'There are always casualties in every war. You must remember that the sacrifice made by your Ammi and your sister will not be in vain...They were martyrs for the jihad...'

Martyrs? *How can you be a martyr for someone else's cause*? Iqbal suppressed the urge to reach out, shake Omar hard and scream at him. He turned and looked at him incredulously. How could Omar even think that it was all right to sacrifice innocent people for a cause that had no meaning to them? He was just a deluded, misinformed, juvenile idiot with no sense of the value of another's life. A mindless monster. And then he thought: *I am one too.*

Suddenly Iqbal knew with blinding clarity what he had to do. He knew his new mission as surely as he knew that no God or religion could ever teach or expect anyone to kill innocents. *We have been misguided. Misguided and used. The Prophet (Peace be upon Him) would never condone the slaughter of women and children in Allah's name.*

Iqbal would have to kill Omar. He knew this as surely as he knew he was going to kill each and everyone who had led him on to this path. The Maulavi who had recruited him; Maulana Fazlur Rehman; Brigadier Murad Salim who was the brain behind the entire operation; and all those other merchants of death who had trained with him – they would all die. He had to kill them not because any of the wrongs they had done would be rectified by this. He had to kill them as part of his penance. *This is going to be my way of saying sorry to all those countless innocents whom we have brought grief to. To Ammi and Nawaz whose lives were cut short by their own flesh and blood...It is going to be my way of ensuring such things do not happen again.*

'Thanks for talking to me, Omar.' Iqbal sat up straight and looked him in the eye. 'I feel better now.'

Omar's eyes searched his face deeply. Finally he nodded, relief flooding his face as he reached across and held his friend's hand.

Iqbal stood up. 'Now, if you don't mind, I need to be alone with my father.'

When Iqbal entered his father's room Nawab was lying on the bed staring up at the ceiling. He must have heard his son enter but he did not acknowledge his presence. Iqbal did not disturb him. He sat through the long night by his father's bed massaging his father's feet in a silent plea for forgiveness. When dawn broke and his father had fallen into a fitful slumber, Iqbal stood up. His body was stiff from sitting for so long, but his mind was crystal clear. The time had come for him to get moving. Back in his room, Iqbal left a message for his father:

'Please forgive me for leaving you at a time like this. I need to be alone. The wound in my head is too fresh and everything in the house reminds me of Ammi and Navaz. I do not know how to tell you how much I love Ashraf and you.'

As he wrote the note his eyes grew moist. The first tears he had shed after learning of his mother and sister's deaths were not for them. They were for his father; for the old, grieving, broken man alone in his room. He realized that this was the first time as an adult that he had told his father he loved him. He had always been sure of his love for his mother but Abbu had always been...Abbu...a remote and somewhat scary person; love was not a word he had readily associated with him.

Having finished the note Iqbal went and quietly woke up Omar: 'Get ready. We are leaving.'

Omar gave him a long look. 'You haven't told your folks that you are leaving?'

Iqbal turned away without answering him.

'Where are we going? At least tell me that,' Omar asked as he got up and started hurriedly pulling on his clothes.

Iqbal ignored him as he quietly transferred the two grenades he had carried back from Chakoti into his rucksack. He had already packed in some tools from Nawab's toolbox knowing he would need them soon. The events that lay ahead were so clear in his head that he could pin them down with military precision.

The night had not yet fully receded into the light of the new day when Omar and Iqbal began to walk down the road that led towards town. They had gone about a hundred metres from the house when Iqbal stopped. He turned back and for a very long moment just stared at the house they were leaving behind. 'Where are we going?' Omar asked again when they had gone some distance.

'Delhi.' Iqbal answered without breakin his stride, 'I need to meet Maulavi Sahib.'

Omar came to a dead halt. 'He is going to be pissed as hell. We had been told very clearly to return to our homes and await further orders. Especially after these blasts and all...do you think it is wise to try and meet him?'

Iqbal stopped and gave Omar a long cold look before he answered: 'I am going to see him. You come if you want to.'

Omar felt a twinge of fear run through him, but he didn't know what else to do. He hefted his bag and started to walk alongside Iqbal.

SPEED

1440 hours, 30 October 2005, Force 22 Base, Kasauli Hills.

A MI-8 helicopter belonging to the Indian Air Force landed at the Force 22 base near Kasauli. It was a machine that the Indian Air Force commonly used and it attracted no untoward attention. The brainchild of Mikhail Leontyevich Mil, who was involved with Soviet gyroplanes and helicopters until his death on 31 January 1970, the Mil helicopter is an unparalleled success story. Today every fourth helicopter in the world is either of Mil construction or origin.

When the chopper lifted off again, nine of Force 22's superbly trained killing machines were on board carrying an odd assortment of gear with them.

Anbu was at the helipad to see them off. None of the stress and tension that he was feeling showed on his face. 'Remember, gentlemen, this is our first major mission. There will be hundreds of eyes on us so we need to do this right. Remember our motto – speed...'

'...stealth and surprise!' The assembled team chorused in unison. Then they laughed: 'Don't worry, Chief...just keep the beer chilled.'

Anbu shook hands with each of his men as they boarded the craft. The clatter of the engines ramped up to a crescendo as the chopper lifted off. Anbu stood on the edge of the helipad for a very long time watching with unseeing eyes as the helicopter disappeared into the blue skies. It is never easy to send your people off into battle; no matter how many times you do it. A cold coil of stress began to knot itself in the pit of his stomach.

A short haul later the helicopter landed in Chandigarh and the men transferred their gear from the chopper to the Air Force jet waiting with its engines already thrumming a few metres away. The strike force was soon winging its way towards the western coast. Barely an hour later the jet touched down at Bikaner Air Force station in Rajasthan. Six of the Force 22 commandos offloaded with their gear and moved to another nondescript MI-8 chopper waiting for them. This chopper was headed towards Khajewala, the small desert town on the Indo–Pakistan border, which had the dubious distinction of counting Afzal the smuggler as one of its own.

The remaining three Force 22 officers continued towards the Indian coastal town of Bhuj, located on the western coast. Except for the crew of the choppers, the jet and the few people who helped them move their gear no one had seen them come and go.

Meanwhile, elsewhere, four more seemingly unrelated events had begun to unfold. These had started within a few minutes of the helicopter taking off from the Force 22 base and did not appear to be even remotely linked with it.

An Indian Navy warship on routine patrol along the western coast received orders to divert. It immediately altered course and set sail towards Bhuj. Around mid-afternoon, just off the coastline, it transferred a container to the fishing dhow that linked up with it. The sorry-looking dhow then continued its leisurely journey seawards on a north-western course. Nothing about its appearance hinted at the real power of its superbly maintained engines, the sophistication of the surveillance and communication equipment it carried on board or of the highly trained and specialist Indian Navy crew manning it.

Having delivered its cargo the warship turned around and headed out for the open sea. An hour later two Indian Navy missile boats linked up with it. Maintaining visual distance from each other the trio continued seawards with a slight north-western tilt in their bearing. By evening they would take up position in international waters and start a random patrol. As and when they were noticed, which they would definitely be, no one would be unduly perturbed; the Indian Navy routinely kept an eye on Karachi port.

Though not much activity was visible on the decks the watch on all three crafts had been doubled, all weapon systems had been readied and the crew primed to take up battle stations instantly. The warship and its accompanying missile boats were ready and loaded for bear. So was the flight of fighter-interceptors at the Indian Air Force base at Bhuj. The pilots had been briefed, the jets readied and moved to the highest operationally ready platform (ORP One). They were ready to touch the skies at almost negligible notice. At all times the three crafts made sure they were within comfortable striking distance of the fishing dhow – just in case the need arose for them to move in and protect it.

The warship had been transferring the container to the dhow when a convoy of three very ordinary looking vehicles left the Force 22 base and headed towards Amritsar. Moving with the convoy were two Force 22 officers – Ankita Bhatnagar was busy with her laptop in the leading vehicle while Manoj Khare played Spider Solitaire on his Ipaq in the third vehicle.

The demure Ankita was a flight lieutenant in the Indian Air Force. She was just over five-feet-two with a build that could best be described as spare. She made an odd pair with the tall dark and burly Captain Manoj Khare. Though on the face of it the two appeared to have little in common both were capable of doing things with computers that would have made Bill Gates sit up and take note. Had they walked into a computer company anywhere in the world they would have been instantly employed. Both were also physical fitness freaks, adept in a variety of martial arts and unarmed combat. Anbu had pulled them out of the humdrum of a regular Army life just as it was beginning to pall. The duo had been humorously nicknamed 'Beauty and the Beast' by their comrades in Force 22. 'Bloody hell, Ankita. They're calling you a beast!' Khare had roared across the room when he heard the appellation the first time.

The convoy moved at a steady clip as it chewed up the miles across Punjab. They had just crossed Chandigarh when Khare's mobile phone beeped. It was a text message from Bhatnagar: 'Stop playing mind games and check your mail.'

'It takes a mind to play mind games,' Khare texted back before putting away the mobile phone and hauling out his laptop. The Net-Connect Data and Voice Card plugged into it allowed him to connect to the Internet whenever and wherever he pleased. He watched as his emails downloaded into Outlook. There were forty-five mails waiting for him. Forty-two of them peddled Viagra, various weight loss drugs, online gambling, stock alerts, pornography and home loan offerings. Of the three that remained, one was from his mother reminding him to be regular with his prayers and his meals, the second was from the Force 22 Accounts Officer informing him that his last batch of expense vouchers were not being processed for reimbursement since the signature was supposed to be *on* the revenue stamp and not beside it and the last was from Ankita. It had a huge attachment that took its own sweet time to open.

It was a map of the Indo–Pakistan border with the focal point being the area ahead of Amritsar. Overlaid on the map were the details of all Pakistani radar sites that covered this border. An arc defined the coverage areas of every radar. There were two such overlays; the first one marked the horizontal coverage and the second marked the vertical coverage. Meandering through these overlapping arcs was a thin red line. It seemed to probe through the radar coverage and find gaps in the vertical or horizontal planes as it went along. Khare whistled in admiration. The detailing Bhatnagar had done was impressive. Khare began a detailed study of the file as the convoy steadily wound its way along the highway towards Amritsar.

They would reach their destination – a cluster of trees flanking a little village just short of Amritsar, a few miles from the Indo–Pakistan border – by midnight. The site had been carefully selected after a detailed study of photographs downloaded from the Indian spy satellite that had passed overhead a few hours ago. No road or track led up to that cluster of trees, but the terrain seemed easily fordable by a 4 x 4 vehicle. All three vehicles in the convoy were four-wheeled drive and would face no difficulty navigating the terrain.

Right near the cluster of trees was a narrow piece of flat uncultivated land about 200 metres long. With no rain in that area for almost a month now the ground was firm and hard. For almost two kilometres on all sides there was no habitation barring the sporadic farmer's hut. The nearest airfield, in Amritsar, was well over sixty kilometres away. All said and done it was an ideal spot for what the Force 22 officers had in mind.

A few minutes after Khare and Bhatnagar left Kasauli for Amritsar, two jeeps started out from the Military Intelligence detachment located in Bikaner. Both jeeps were the typical beat-up variety found in abundance on both sides of the border. In fact they were almost carbon copies of the one that Afzal and his ilk used. What the casual eye would miss was the souped-up engine and the fancy noise suppressors fitted on one of the jeeps. Everything possible had been done to reduce the audio and infrared profile of this vehicle and radar absorbing material had been extensively used to minimize radar detection. The same had also been done for the motorcycle which lay covered by a tarpaulin in the rear of the jeep. It sported desert tyres. A jerry can of fuel was lashed alongside it, and also concealed under the tarpaulin. The other four jerry cans of fuel that would be required by the jeep were lashed onto the small metallic brackets fitted on either side. This was more the norm than the exception in almost all such areas where fuel stations were few and far between. The speedometer and odometer of the jeep and motorcycle had been artfully replaced by state-of-the-art GPS systems. The jeeps headed out at a steady pace for Khajewala. All at once life in and around this small sleepy town in the Rajasthan desert was becoming a hotbed of activity.

The jeeps had barely left the city limits of Bikaner when six trucks moved out from the small town of Pugal, midway between Bikaner and Khajewala. All six were loaded with contract engineers, labourers and an assortment of engineering and electrical equipment required for the fencing that had been installed by India along the Indo–Pakistan border. Comprising two fences approximately three metres high and erected a few metres apart, the border fence is a formidable deterrent to cross-border movement of the illegal kind. Normally the gap between the two fences is covered with concertina coil. In addition floodlights, electrification, radars, thermal imagers, night-vision devices and sensors stand sentinel at all likely infiltration points.

The Indian Government had started the border fencing sometime in 1980 when it became clear that Pakistan would not desist from smuggling drugs, counterfeit currency and terrorists into India. It was decided that every inch of the 1800-mile-long border with Pakistan would be secured with this kind of a fence. With a total projected cost of about 2 billion US dollars it was a very expensive and tedious job, but then sometimes, when neighbouring nations lack responsibility, fences are required.

On that particular day most of the Indo–Pak border in Rajasthan and Punjab had already been fenced and work was on in deadly earnest to achieve the same in Jammu & Kashmir. In fact, as far as Rajasthan was concerned precisely 1066 kilometres of fencing had already been erected and 1061 kilometres of this had been augmented with flood lighting.

Pakistan, of course, foresaw the huge negative economic effect such a fence would have on its drugs and terror export policy and was objecting to it strenuously. 'How can you guys not object to it?' An affronted Pakistan Foreign Minister had asked his American counterpart during the former's visit to Washington. 'After all, it is almost the same as the fence that Israel has put up along the West Bank. You guys were definitely vocal about that one.'

'I don't think that is inherently correct...the two fences cannot be equated. The Indian fence is well within its boundaries, unlike the Israeli one that crosses into and eats up parts of the West Bank.'

Ironically, this was the same Pakistani Minister who, a few months later, announced that Pakistan was going to be putting up a border fence along the Pakistan–Afghanistan border. He had been considerably put out when he was asked by a Western journalist, 'What exactly is this fence supposed to do, Minister, other than limit the number of terrorists entering into Afghanistan?' The look on the Minister's face made it more than clear to the journalist that a visit to Pakistan any time in his life might well put an early end to it.

As the six trucks from Pugal wound their way to the border fence, four more trucks moved out from Anupgarh, another border town to the north-east of Khajewala. Like the trucks from Pugal these were also filled with men and equipment, however not all the supplies had to do with border fencing. Tucked safely out of sight of prying eyes was an odd assortment of arms and ammunition. Enough, in fact, to fight a small war. Had a careful watcher been observing this particular convoy he would have also noticed that the labourers in these trucks were considerably more physically fit.

Both convoys moved out at short intervals from each other, joined up on the solitary road that lead to the International Border between India and Pakistan, and headed straight for the border fencing.

The six trucks from Pugal split up into two smaller convoys with each one heading for different sections of the border. The four trucks from Anupgarh headed for yet another section of the fence.

If one were to stand in the Indian desert town of Khajewala and draw a straight line to the Pakistani town of Fort Abbas, that lies towards the north, the Pakistani BOP of Ranabhana would lie almost bang on that line about two kilometres ahead of the Indian border fence. Two platoons and the headquarters of a company of Pakistan Rangers man this BOP. The third platoon of this company mans the Majnuwala BOP, which lies about seven kilometres to the west of this BOP.

Likewise, on the opposite side, six kilometres to the east of Ranabhana is the Lambawala Toba BOP, also manned by another Rangers platoon. Both the platoon commanders, at Majnuwala and Lambawala, report to and are under the command of the Rangers'

Company Commander located at Ranabhana BOP.

On the Indian side, the area right up to the border was green, well-developed and almost completely cultivated. The well-laid-out Indira Gandhi Canal network provided the water required for irrigation, and sunflower was the favoured produce of the area.

In direct contrast, the area on the Pakistani side was totally undeveloped and barren right up to Fort Abbas, about thirty kilometres north of the border.

The trucks carrying the labourers arrived at the border fencing and the men started repair work on the fence at several different places, right from the section of the fence facing Majnuwala to the section ahead of the Lambawala Toba BOP. Two kilometres away, the Pakistan Rangers took note of this activity.

'Majnu for Rana. We have movement on the IB. There are trucks with people who have come up to the fence.'

'Rana for Majnu. The jokers must be carrying out repairs and maintenance of their precious fence.' There was a sardonic laugh. 'Some contractor must be in need of money. Keep watching and inform us if you see anything out of the ordinary.'

'Roger that Rana.'

'Lamba for Rana. We have the same thing happening here also. There are three trucks in our area also.'

'Roger Lamba. I guess the contractor must be in need of a lot of money. Keep watching.'

'Yeah, right, Rana. With contractors like that who needs enemies?'

The radio operators at all three BOPs sniggered. It was the same old story no matter what side of the border you stood on. None of the Pakistani BOPs did anything beyond recording this activity in their daily log. None of the BOPs even bothered to send out a cursory patrol to take a closer look at what was happening on the fence or inform their force headquarters.

Even if they had sent out their patrols they would not have noticed anything amiss. Although if someone had been observing the work closely they might have noticed that the gang working at one of the sites seemed to be doing more dismantling than repairing. This was the gang working on the section of the fence almost exactly in the centre of the six-kilometre gap between Ranabhana and Lambawala BOPs.

At this particular site, just a little away from where the men were working was a small, sand-coloured tent pitched in the lee of a dune. The tent blended in perfectly with the surrounding sand and would have been hard to pick out even in an aerial photograph.

Even if the tent had been spotted no one could have seen the pile of automatic weapons neatly stacked on a wooden rack in a corner of the tent. Nor could they have seen the radio set installed on a small table in the other corner.

The radio set looked exactly like the ones used by most Indian Army units. It operated on VHF frequency and was the standard frequency hopper used to degrade enemy Electronic Warfare attacks. The difference was that this radio set was far more sophisticated than the ones it resembled. A team of top-notch Indian scientists, who had once figured on the payrolls of communication giants like Motorola and were now more gainfully employed by the Indian government, had assembled this particular model. The radio set was virtually impossible to hack into within any reasonable time frame. Barely a hundred sets of this model had been pressed into service so far and most of these were with the Indian Special Forces.

Today this particular set had been activated just once since the tent had been set up. 'Chengiz for Tiger.' The Team Leader had reported to Anbu as soon as the tent had been pitched, 'We are in position. Over.'

'Roger Chengiz. This is Tiger. Remain on listening watch and maintain radio silence. Out.' Sitting in his well-equipped command post in the Kasauli hills Anbu kept close track of each development. So far things were moving per plan. 'I wonder how long that will last,' Anbu mused; he was a seasoned veteran and knew it was only a matter of time before Murphy's Law came into play.

1640 hours, 30 October 2005, Khajewala Sector, Rajasthan.

The innocuous-looking helicopter that had taken off from Bikaner carrying the six Force 22 officers and their gear landed near a small hut outside Khajewala. The spot was barely three miles as the crow flies from the house of Afzal the smuggler. Afzal was of course nowhere near his house when the chopper landed. On the way from Bikaner to Khajewala along with his two terrorist charges, he had suffered a couple of punctures that set him back an hour.

The Indian Army and other not-so-overt agencies used this particular hut once in a while. It had a dilapidated exterior but the interior was more than adequate and a small generator ensured power at all times. It boasted the basic amenities required for a short stay, including a well-equipped medical kit and some seriously unpalatable ready-to-eat Army meals. Legend has it that once a senior Army General was questioned about the awful quality of these meals and the unfortunate effect they had on human tastebuds. 'Why doesn't the Army do something about it, General?'

'It is because we eat such stuff that we are always ready to fight,' the General is reported to have replied.

A Military Intelligence man who had driven down from Bikaner was standing by. He stepped forward as the men began to get off the chopper. 'The vehicles we have to hand over to you are here. They are in very good shape. We have also placed some critical spares and extra fuel in the jeep. Here, let me help you with that.'

'Thanks.'

As the MI officer helped to unload the chopper, one of the Force 22 officers left to check the vehicles.

Despite the cordiality, no introductions were made; it was nothing personal, just the way things happen in such operations.

It was almost sunset when four of the Force 22 officers who got off the chopper, Captains Tony Ahlawat, Mohammed Sami, Vikram Tiwathia and Pradeep Katoch of Force 22, had re-checked and loaded their gear on the jeep with the motorcycle strapped in at the back. They were ready to move.

While they were busy the other two Force 22 officers, Squadron Leaders Gautam Vashisht and Rajesh Tiwari, quickly unpacked their gear and started setting it up in the hut. By the time the four officers were ready to leave, the small hut in the middle of the desert had been transformed into a mini *StarWars*-style command centre. Tiwari activated the first piece of machinery as soon as the command centre was operational. It was a radio set that was identical to the one deployed in Chengiz Khan. He too reported in to Anbu. 'Tango for Tiger. Foxtrot Bravo is up and running. Over.'

'Tiger for Tango. Good. Keep me posted. Out.'

It took Vashisht and Tiwari another twenty minutes to open the two long wooden containers that had also been part of their cargo and to start setting up the two Unmanned Aerial Vehicles (UAV) packed inside.

As darkness fell upon the desert the four Force 22 Captains climbed into the jeep and headed for the border. All four men were natives of the desert. In fact, like Afzal, two of them, Mohammed Sami and Tony Ahlawat, were from this very area of Rajasthan. They could well have taken a short detour and dropped in to say hello to their families, but home was the last thing on their minds just then.

'Fox One for Tango.' Ahlawat made the call when the jeep was a couple of miles away. 'Report my signal.'

'Tango for Fox One. You are strength five,' Tiwari replied confirming that communication with Foxtrot Base was working well.

'Fox for Tiger. That's it then. We are off.'

Tiwathia gunned the engine and they headed straight for the section of the border fence between Ranabhana and Lambawala Toba BOPs that had been codenamed Chengiz Khan. 'Happy hunting Fox. See you tomorrow.'

Then Fox was off; moving fast and silent through the rapidly gathering desert night.

The first prong of the Indian counter-strike had been unleashed.

Based on a platform akin to the American Predator UAV, though several technological steps ahead of it, the Krishna UAV was the latest and most covert addition to the Indian arsenal. It had not been revealed to the Indian public. Nor, if the Army had a say in the matter, was it likely to. The Indian Army had no desire to let the world in on their real capabilities in this field.

After all, what the enemy didn't know about it couldn't counter.

The Krishna did full justice to the ingenuity and hard work that had been put in to it by a dedicated team of scientists working for over two years. Made from a mixture of carbon and quartz blended in a composite with Kevlar, the UAV's airframe is supported by Nomex, foam and wood laminate pressed together in layers. A sturdy fabric sandwiched between these layers provides the required insulation to the sensitive equipment carried on board the UAV.

The ten-metre-long Krishna has a 21 metre wingspan and is powered by a highly fuel-efficient 4-cylinder, 4-stroke, 120 horsepower engine. It has a minimal RCS (Radar Cross Section) and a reduced infrared footprint thus making the Krishna almost impossible to detect. With a flight endurance of about forty hours and the ability to operate up to an altitude of 14000 metres, it is capable of carrying a payload of about 250 kilograms in addition to the fuel load that it carries in its twin tanks.

The payload carried by a Krishna could include an ultra-sophisticated surveillance package comprising a full colour nose camera, a Variable Aperture camera, a Variable Aperture Infrared camera for low light or night viewing and a Synthetic Aperture Radar for seeing through clouds, haze and smoke. The data can be transmitted in real-time through a Ku-band satellite communication system fitted onboard the Krishna. The complete package is a formidable force multiplier and presents a bird's-eye view of the complete battlefield to a commander sitting hundreds of miles away.

In its other, deadlier avatar, the Krishna can also carry a weapons-load of up to four highly lethal, precision-guided weapons. The weapon system is an electro-optical infrared one with a laser designator and a laser illuminator. As and when required the Krishna can also carry a mix of both, an abbreviated surveillance system and a reduced missile load. It is an ideal weapon for a precise, selective strike against a small target without exposing expensive aircrafts or even more valuable manpower to risk.

Tonight the two Krishnas operating ahead of the Force 22 team were equipped with the most sophisticated surveillance package possible. They silently clawed their way into the cold night air and gained height rapidly. A few seconds later they had vanished into the darkening night sky.

'Isn't this beautiful?' Vashisht said admiringly to Tiwari, pointing at the real-time data streaming in on the array of monitors before them. The data feed was also being simultaneously piped across to the main command post at the Force 22 headquarters at Kasauli, to enable Anbu to keep an eye on things. This was always a dangerous and double-edged proposition since a lot of commanders tend to get into the thick of an operation and try to fight ground action from hundreds of miles away without realizing that things are never as simple and clearly defined as they appear on the screens in front of them. Anbu was mature enough not to get too closely involved and start micro-managing the operation, but human enough to want to know every last detail of what was happening.

'Technology! A real bitch!' Tiwari grinned as he looked at the monitors. Sitting at the command post they had a fabulous panoramic view of the desert ahead. 'Just look at that!' He pointed at one of the monitors as the Rangers' sentry at the Lambawala BOP stepped out to take a leak in the desert. The imagery was so sharp that the urine hissing away from the man glowed red through the thermal imagers. 'Tango for Tiger. Are you getting the feed?'

'Roger that Tango. I'm getting it loud and clear.' There was a smile in Anbu's voice. 'Stop pissing away the tech, guys and show me something worthwhile.'

Sitting in the improvised control room near Khajewala both Force 22 officers grinned as they put their heads down to the task at hand. High up in the air, the two Krishna UAVs moved into a carefully calculated pattern a little ahead and over the four Force 22 officers as they raced through the desert night in the jeep.

Travelling a couple of kilometres towards the east, but following a path very similar to the one that Afzal was taking the two terrorists out on, the jeep with the Force 22 officers headed straight for Chengiz Khan where the slightly implausible labour gang had carefully created a gap in the fencing.

'Tango for Fox.' Tiwari's voice crackled into the headset Tony Ahlawat was wearing. 'You are six hundred now. Chengiz get ready to rock.'

'Roger Tango. We are ready. Come on in, Fox.'

The Chengiz team leader turned away from the radio set and signalled to his second-in-command. Immediately the work on the fence speeded up. The eight-foot-wide section of fence covering the gaps in both the fences was removed just as the jeep drove up to it. It barely had to check its speed as the fence section was swiftly moved out of the way. The minute the jeep went through the gap the workers replaced the section of the fence. However they did not fix it back in a particularly permanent manner.

It was going to be removed again tomorrow. If all went as planned.

The jeep was crossing through the cut in the border fence when, a couple of hundred miles to the west, another MIL-8 chopper with Indian Coastguard markings, pulled into a hover over an Indian Navy warship on the high sea around which two missile boats were busy frolicking. The chopper alighted lightly on the deck and Lieutenant Commanders Chandan Deopa, Ranjit Dhankar and Sunil Jaggi of the Indian Navy, all presently seconded to Force 22, jumped out. It took them a moment to retrieve their gear from the chopper, which then took off immediately and returned to the Air Force Base at Bhuj.

A few minutes later, the warship launched a small speedboat that sped away from it at high speed. The tiny speedboat did not reflect on any radar or raise any alarms as it skimmed over the choppy waters and headed for the fishing dhow, which was still moving at a steady pace and by now was barely forty miles out of Karachi.

Deopa and Dhankar were on board the speedboat along with two other sailors from the warship. It closed in on the dhow and tied up with it. Both Force 22 officers got on to the dhow while the two sailors returned to the Naval warship on the speedboat. Deopa activated his radio set and called in almost as soon as they were onboard the dhow. 'Dolphin for Golf. We are on now. Confirm strength.'

'You are strength five Dolphin,' Jaggi replied from the warship.

'Roger Golf. See you tomorrow.'

Both Deopa and Dhankar had cut their teeth in the Navy SEALS and were just beginning to feel frustrated with their careers when Anbu proposed Force 22. Both snapped up the offer since they no longer found anything special about the Special Forces.

From a small village in Haryana that boasted one son from every household in the Defence Services, Dhankar could have walked onto a movie set anywhere in the world and signed on as the archetypal villain; there was something hard and brutal about his eyes that sent an involuntary shiver up one's spine. He was definitely not the kind of person you would like to bump into in a dark alley. Or anywhere.

His buddy Deopa, on the other hand, was amiability personified. He had an infectious smile and talked as much as he grinned. Deopa was so short and stocky that his course mates used to say that he qualified the minimum height stipulation in the medical selection test for the National Defence Academy because they had measured his girth instead of his height.

Appearances notwithstanding, the two men gave each other close competition when it came to the speed and skill with which they handled all kinds of weapons. Dhankar could hit a bird in the eye with almost any gun as efficiently as Deopa's knife could slit a throat. The two men were as much at ease in water as they were on ground and equally adept at fighting in both elements.

Arriving on board the dhow they checked their gear and then, with the help of two crewmen, unpacked the Chariot mini-submarine that had been delivered to the dhow by the warship earlier that day. With a length of around seven metres and a diameter of about one, the Chariot mini-sub can accommodate two men and their complete weapon-load and stay submerged for over twelve hours covering ten knots per hour; it is the perfect vehicle for a covert insertion into enemy territory.

Just before midnight, about eight miles out of Karachi, the fishing dhow changed tack and released the Chariot into the sea. The Chariot took a minute or so to right itself and settle down on an even keel. Then it slid silently through the water as Dhankar guided it towards the Karachi coastline.

'Why can't they make these things a little more roomy?' Deopa said and smiled when this elicited a string of curses, as Dhankar roundly abused the mothers and sisters of the Chariot designers for the mingy dimensions of the craft.

IQBAL

Omar was right. Maulavi Sahib was not pleased to see them. In fact it was clear from his expression that had he known they were coming he would have refused to meet them. 'Hadn't you been told to wait for orders? Didn't they clearly tell you that I was not to be contacted?' he said curtly when he saw them waiting outside his room.

Omar was mumbling a reply when Iqbal cut in: 'Something important came up. It was imperative that I meet you.' His tone was mild but there was nothing remotely apologetic in it.

Maulavi Sahib unlocked the flimsy looking lock on the door and irritably ushered them inside the same small room that they had met in everyday soon after he had recruited them. Despite his obvious ill humour, which he made no effort to hide, the Maulavi was a man of fixed habits. He motioned for them to sit down as he went straight to the small metal box in the corner of the room. He opened the box and emptied the contents of his pockets into it. It only took a brief glance for Iqbal to confirm that there were still several bundles of cash in the box. Iqbal watched the Maulavi replace the key in his pocket.

Iqbal heard Omar recount the story of their adventures in Pakistan. He saw the Maulavi listen to everything keenly yet with a pretence of impatience. He was clearly torn between his curiosity to know everything about the terrorist camp and the troubled restlessness of being burdened with a situation he did not wish to have to deal with.

When Omar finished with his narrative the Maulavi took up his usual refrain: 'Allah's will...the jihad...a blow to the kafir...martyrdom...'

Iqbal was not really listening. He felt detached and removed. The Maulavi's words no longer swayed him. He sat in stony silence, his fingers caressing the knife that was stuck in his waistband and concealed by the shawl he was draped in. He longed to pull out the knife and drive it deep into the withered body of the man talking at him but he restrained himself.

Somewhere during the one-sided conversation the Maulavi sensed that he did not have Iqbal's attention. He looked up. What he read on Iqbal's face unnerved him. He stopped talking abruptly and stood up. 'I would like both of you to leave now.'

The Maulavi scribbled something on a piece of paper and handed it to Omar. 'This is my phone number in case you need to talk to me. Let me talk to the others and find out what you should do next.' He gave Iqbal a long searching look, as though seeking concurrence. 'Okay? But don't call me unless it is imperative. And don't come to see me again... no matter what happens...'

Iqbal nodded briefly as he felt Omar take his arm and tug him towards the door. 'Let us go to my home now. You can stay with me for the time being, okay?' He looked at Iqbal questioningly, but did not wait for a reply. 'Let's go.'

The two men walked out onto the road and up to a waiting autorickshaw. Iqbal and Omar climbed in and Omar gave directions to the driver. 'Mohammedpur.' The autorickshaw pulled out into the chaotic traffic that flowed all around them as Omar began to save the Maulavi's mobile number on his own phone.

STEALTH

As the Chariot sped its underwater course to Karachi, the four jeep-borne Force 22 officers used the gap between the Rangers' BOPs at Ranabhana and Lambawala Toba to cross into Pakistan. Due to three halts forced on them by the movement of the Rangers patrols they took a little over four hours to cover the next seventy kilometres. The patrols of course did not pose any significant threat to them since they were being guided by the Krishna UAVs circling overhead and unseen in the sky.

The terrain they traversed was rough and undeveloped. 'I guess they are too busy setting up madrassas, training terrorists and growing opium to develop their economy,' Tiwathia muttered. The others laughed, softly: 'Why the hell would you want to grow sunflower and wheat when you can grow opium instead?'

They were deep in enemy territory now. Danger lurked behind every sand dune; anyone and everyone they might run into was the enemy. The slightest mistake or error in judgment could result in death. And, if they had the misfortune of being taken alive, death would be exceedingly painful. Anyone who had seen the mutilated bodies of the soldiers of the Indian patrol whom the Pakistanis had captured during their Kargil intrusion could bear testimony to that.

It was almost 2300 hours when they skirted the Pakistani military garrison at Fort Abbas and hit the road to Bahawalpur a little ahead of the town. Just before getting onto the road they stopped for a minute. 'You take the rear plates,' Tony told Sami as they both jumped out.

A tall lanky man with an unruly head of hair, Captain Kuldeep Ahlawat was an an expert with explosives. For some strange reason his mother had nicknamed him Tony. In direct contrast to Tony, Captain Mohammed Sami, his operational buddy pair, distrusted explosives. Although he was quite adept at using them he much rather preferred the scoped sniper rifle that he carried today.

Working swiftly together it took them barely two minutes to change the plates on the jeep. When the jeep hit the road to Bahawalpur it bore a Pakistani number plate.

'There is no way the number plates or the vehicle will stand up to a close scrutiny, but it should get you past the casual glance of other passing vehicles. In the worst case it may create doubt and give you those few critical seconds that you need to act,' the Force 22 Intelligence Officer had said. 'In any case, the road is not very heavily used. There is not likely to be much traffic on it at that time of the night. I have personally reviewed the satellite logs of the past few weeks and barring the odd military vehicle the road is mostly deserted.'

The four men rode in silence as the jeep kicked the gravel through the chilly October night, burning the 117-odd kilometres to Bahawalpur.

'Tango for Fox.' The radio set in Tony's hand squawked to life. Tony double-clicked the transmit button. He did not want to transmit unless it was absolutely imperative. 'Get off the road now. You have three inbounds. They're about fourteen hundred. Sorry for the delayed warning but they seem to have come out of nowhere.'

Tiwathia, who was at the wheel, swerved off the road immediately. He hit the lights and killed the engine as the jeep came to a halt behind a small sand dune about forty feet from the road. The four men waited in silence as an Army jeep and two three-tonners thundered past in the night. Their grip on their weapons relaxed as the vehicles vanished in the distance. Tiwathia waited for another few minutes before he gunned the engine and hit the road again.

Set amidst sand dunes and poorly cultivated cotton fields stretching on all sides, the remote rocky outcrop two miles outside Bahawalpur town was not only sans houses or population it was also at easy striking distance from the target.

Bahawalpur town was notorious for the rabid religious fundamentalists and the hardcore criminal types who gave the cops a perennial run for their money. Surrounded though it was by fields of cotton and corn, the sleepy little town had a reputation for Sunni extremism. Consequently, the town police was up and about at all times and more than quick to pull the trigger when they saw something out of the ordinary. 'Buying a gun there is as easy as ordering a pizza from Dominos,' the Force 22 Intelligence Officer had said wryly, adding, 'and not half as expensive.'

Tony and Sami got off the jeep, quickly offloaded the motorcycle and wheeled it out of sight into the rocky outcrop. The jerry can of fuel required for the motorcycle was buried next to it. Sami retrieved three almost identical rocks and placed them in a neat triangle exactly ten feet to the right of the spot where the bike and fuel were buried. The rocks would mark the spot. Katoch took two jerry cans from the four strapped onto the sides of the jeep and emptied them into the jeep's fuel tank. The empty jerry cans were carefully strapped back onto the jeep.

Then the four men shook hands with each other.

Courtesy the Krishna's miracle eyes, sitting far away in the Khajewala and Kasauli command centres, Tiwari, Vashisht and Anbu saw the one green dot split into two on their electronic battle boards. Fox One stayed static on the outskirts of Bahawalpur while Fox Two began to move away silently.

Katoch and Tiwathia climbed back into the jeep and drove off into the night. They headed back towards the road that ran from Bahawalpur to Multan. Just short of Lodhran was the bridge they had to use to cross the Sutlej.

'Tango for Fox Two. The bridge is clear. Also, we are now at the end of our tether. Another few minutes and then we have to close shop for the night. Stay loose guys and God speed.'

The safety blanket of the night was retreating fast and they still had another ninety kilometres to go. Tiwathia double-checked their location on the GPS as they moved off.

Katoch and Tiwathia had the advantage of having trained together at the National Defence Academy. They had taken well to being back together again, though it did take some time for both of them to adjust their ideas of each other, from the RAW recruits they had known each other as, to the men they had grown into. They drew up the jeep and killed the engine. Working quickly they dug a small pit in the side of one of the sand dunes and concealed the tarpaulin-wrapped motorcycle in it. The tarpaulin would keep the bike safe from damage by the sand. It took them twenty minutes. Then they both sat down to wait. 'We have a couple of hours at least.' Tony checked the luminous dial of his wristwatch. 'Might as well get some rest.'

'You go ahead and take a nap. I'll take the first watch.'

Before Tony hit the sack, both men took a little time to memorize the spot where the motorcycle was buried and fix down its relative location from the town. They knew there would not be much time for scouring the desert on their way out after the mission.

Two hours later, hefting their small packs, they moved off at a brisk pace towards the town. Reaching the outskirts they stopped again for a closer, more careful look at the town of Bahawalpur. Somewhere in the labyrinth of lanes and houses clustered ahead of them slept the man they had come this far for.

At about the time Tony and Sami set out for Bahawalpur, Katoch brought the jeep to a halt in a remote stretch of the desert about two miles south-west of Multan. Even though the chance of it being discovered was remote, they covered it with a camouflage net. Then Tiwathia and Katoch grabbed their gear and set off for the town at a brisk pace.

Tony and Sami were starting their approach to Bahawalpur and Tiwathia and Katoch were throwing the camouflage netting on the jeep outside Multan when Deopa and Dhankar emerged silently from under the ocean and slipped onto the beach.

Deopa and Dhankar had sunk the Chariot at a spot deep enough in the water to ensure it was not found in a hurry. They'd covered the remaining distance with powerful, silent strokes till they'd reached the shore. Running on light feet till they hit a grove of trees some distance from Gotismailkarachi, a fishing village about four kilometres outside Karachi, they'd slid out of their wetsuits and buried them deep in the soft ground.

Up ahead they could see the sparkle of Karachi city lighting up the horizon. Changing into more appropriate clothing for what lay ahead they hoisted their packs and started on the last leg of their journey.

Fox One comprising Mohammed Sami and Tony Ahlawat was entering Bahawalpur; Fox Two comprising Pradeep Katoch and Vikram Tiwathia was on the outskirts of Multan; and Deopa and Dhankar had entered the suburbs of Karachi. Three prongs of the Indian counter-strike had moved into place.

As he paced the floor of the control room in Kasauli, Colonel Anbu watched the tiny green dots converge on their destinations on his glowing battle board. The stress of impending combat coiled tighter in the pit of his stomach. As promised by the Indian Prime Minister, justice was about to be delivered.

IQBAL

The autorickshaw had a little problem getting to the house as it was located at the end of the narrow, twisting alley that broke off from the main road just after the bus stop opposite Safdarjung Enclave. Despite the late hour the door was answered almost as soon as they rang the bell. The pretty young girl who answered the door looked at Omar in surprise and delight. 'Bhaijaan!' she squealed as she hurled herself at Omar. They hugged hard as she shouted – 'Ammi, Abbu! Look who is here!' Breaking free from her brother's embrace she caught hold of his hand and whooping with delight began to drag him inside. Omar was laughing as he allowed himself to be pulled inside. 'Come, Iqbal,' he waved at him with a wide grin.

Within minutes the room was full of people as Omar's parents and siblings materialized from the rooms within. Iqbal watched the family reunion awkwardly and felt his head begin to throb. The agony of his own loss was stark as he watched Omar's mother and sisters cluster around him. 'This is Iqbal,' Omar introduced him to his relatives. 'We were together at the training institute...he is a good friend.'

'Salaam Waleikum,' Iqbal smiled politely. He noticed the wide-eyed look that Omar's teenage sister was giving him. It unsettled him further. As soon as he could Iqbal pleaded a headache and tiredness. He could not wait to be alone.

Omar took him to a room as soon as dinner was over. 'I know what you must be going through. You get some sleep.' He paused apologetically. 'I would like to spend some time with my family. I'm meeting them after very long.' He gave a small smile. 'I hope you don't mind.'

Iqbal gave him a brief tight smile and watched him leave the room with relief. Then he placed the rucksack on the bed beside him and began to construct the device he needed for his next move.

When Omar came into the room next morning to wake up his friend he found the room empty.

Iqbal knew the man he sought would not be in his room when he reached there; he would be at the mosque attending the Fajr prayers. He was right. It took Iqbal only a few seconds to pick the small lock on the door. Bolting the door from inside, he went to work swiftly. The lock on the metal box took a little longer. Iqbal quickly went through the contents. He removed the bundles of cash, the small address book and the mobile telephone that was inside and transferred them to his rucksack. The cash was in bundles of thousand-rupee notes. There were eight of them.

Then Iqbal took out the device he had constructed the previous night and placed it gently inside the box.

He looped the end of the string to the inner side of the latch on the lid of the box and carefully tested the length – it had to be exact – before attaching the string to the small metallic ring. Finally he locked the box again and left the room after replacing the lock on the door.

Iqbal was standing at the bus stop at Malviya Nagar when the morning prayers finished and the Maulavi returned to his room. The old Maulavi let himself in and going straight to the metal box, opened it. As he lifted the lid, the taut string tied to it pulled the small metallic ring that was tied to the other end. The metal ring had a pin-like spike attached to it. It had been oiled. Both prongs of the pin slid soundlessly out of the two tiny holes they had been nestled in. The metallic lever holding the plunger shot free. The plunger lunged forward and hit the detonator with a tiny metallic thump. The sound of the detonator triggering off was lost in the creak of the opening lid. Precisely four seconds later the hand grenade that had been taped by Iqbal to the base of the metallic box detonated with an ear-shattering roar.

Getting off the bus, Iqbal set off for the inner circle of Connaught Place. At this hour the traffic was light and the brisk walk helped him keep the chill of the winter morning at bay. The city had started coming to life by now, but most of the shops were still closed. Iqbal came up to a congestion of eating joints along the road just outside the Super Bazar. He vaguely remembered coming here with his friends from engineering college.

The food at Kapoor's Kitchen located just ahead of the Super Bazar was piping hot and delicious. Iqbal sat and ate slowly as he watched the traffic flow along the outer circle of Connaught Place. He enjoyed every morsel as he waited for the bank across the street to open. It was the same bank where Iqbal's father had opened an account for him to pay his college fees. He had come here often to withdraw money during his college days. Iqbal was one of the first people who walked into the bank when it opened for business that morning. He deposited most of the cash into his account.

Leaving the bank Iqbal hailed the first passing cab and told the driver to head for the Delhi Cantt Railway Station.

'What is your name?' Iqbal asked the cabbie as he pulled away from the kerb. Something inside him wanted to reach out and connect with another human being, even if it was as casual and meaningless as this. Or maybe, it was because it was casual and meaningless that Iqbal felt safe talking to him.

'Satnam Singh,' the cab driver replied more than happy at the chance to make conversation. After a short pause he volunteered some more information about himself: 'I am from Firozepur, but I have been in Delhi for almost twenty years now. This is my own taxi, you know.' The pride in the cabbie's tone was evident.

The traffic was heavy since the office rush hour was in full flow by now. They crawled along in companionable silence. It was almost noon when Satnam halted the cab outside the station. When Iqbal finally dismissed him, Satnam Singh was more than happy at the obscenely large tip that Iqbal gave him.

I have taken the life of one human being today. I have made another human being happy. Now I am about to take a life again.

Iqbal reached into his pocket and pulled out the mobile phone he had taken from the Maulavi's metal box. Powering the phone he waited impatiently as it glowed to life and then he dialled the number he had memorized earlier that morning.

THE FOURTH PRONG

The fourth prong was awaiting a signal from Ahmed, the MQM activist who had been recruited by the Indian RAW some years back, and who was now a vital and trusted part of their intelligence gathering apparatus.

Ahmed had returned home from a dinner party the night before when his phone rang. 'It's been a long time, Ahmed. How have you been?'

He recognized the voice immediately. 'Oh, hello, khalajaan, how are you?'

'I am well, Ahmed, but there is a problem I need you to help with immediately. Two of my son's friends came over to Pakistan yesterday. I want you to go and meet them and see if they need help. I have sent you an email with all the details. Please check on them and call me immediately...what?...yes, I am still in London... ' There was some more idle chitchat before the lady rang off; both of them knew that the ISI was in the habit of monitoring overseas calls and they were too experienced to forget such basic precautions.

Getting off the phone, Ahmed logged on to the Net to find the details of the two terrorists who had travelled in by the Attari Express. There were no photographs, just the names, descriptions, dates and times of arrival and the fact that they were most certainly being helped by the ISI. But then Ahmed was a bright guy. It did take him almost the whole day but not only did he track them down he even managed to confirm that they were still present in the ISI safe house in Mari on the outskirts of Lahore.

He left his assistant armed with a mobile phone to keep watch on the safe house and returned to his hotel room in downtown Lahore to call his aunt with the details.

His assistant rang at about 0430 hours on 31 October 2005. 'Ahmed Sahib,' the man keeping watch on the ISI safe house at Mari said, 'this is to confirm that both items are still safely stored in the same place.'

'Good. Stay there for another twenty minutes. Just in case there is any change in status. After that go back home. You have done a good job today, my friend.'

Ahmed immediately called his aunt again. 'Khalajaan, I am sorry for calling so early but I was about to leave for the Fajr prayer.'

'That's okay, Ahmed. Tell me, were you able to meet them?'

'Yes, I was. They are both fine...both are still staying at the address I emailed you.'

'Thank you, son, and do let me know if there is anything I can send you from London.'

The lady who had taken the call from Lahore did not even bother to put down the handset; she immediately dialled again and was soon speaking to Captain Khare who had been waiting for her call in the shadows of a small grove outside Amritsar. This call was short and to the point: 'Both the men are present in the house,' she said and then called out a series of numbers. The numbers were the grid reference coordinates of the ISI safe house at Mari. Khare carefully checked the digits and read them back to her slowly.

Replacing the mobile phone in his pocket Khare walked towards the waiting vehicles parked a few metres away and called out to Ankita. Within a couple of minutes the two of them were busy programming another Krishna UAV. They used the data on the location of the Pakistani radar sites that Ankita had forwarded to Khare and which he had vetted out during the drive. Since most low RCS radars exploit Doppler filters to increase the signal-to-noise ratio, knowing their precise locations and areas of coverage allowed the Force 22 officers to plot a route with zero radial speed. This would render the Krishna virtually invisible in the short time that it would overfly Pakistani airspace.

Khare dialled again. Miles away to the north, the Nokia mobile phone lying on the table before Anbu began to ring.

Anbu had been awake the whole night. In fact, barring short snatches of sleep, he had been awake ever since the choppers carrying his strike teams had taken off from base. Picking up the phone Anbu heard the caller out in silence. Then he glanced at his watch. 0501 hours. Anbu took a deep breath. It was the first major operation for Force 22.

'A lot of eyes are going to be watching your people, Colonel.' Anbu remembered his conversation with the Prime Minister. He had been unusually sombre when they had spoken just a few hours back. 'India has a lot at stake here. You pull this off well and every damn terrorist in the world will think twice before they decide to meddle with us.'

'Don't worry, sir. Force 22 will not let the country down.'

Anbu had full faith in his men, but he knew that in battle a million things could go wrong. He took one long look at the huge electronic battle board that took up an entire wall of the Force 22 command post. He could see the six tiny green dots glowing over the huge area the map presently displayed. The GPS locators carried by his teams fed back their positions in real-time to him. Anbu could tell where his men were whenever he wanted to, but he could not know how they were. He could not tell if they were captured and dead, or alive and racing towards their objectives. Eight of the dots represented the men and women who would actually be carrying out the strikes and delivering India's message to her enemies. Only two of the eight were located on the safety of Indian soil. The other six were deep in Pakistan and squarely in harm's way. As he spoke into the phone, his tone was cold and crisp, betraying none of the tension that coursed through him, 'Let's go for it, Khare.'

At 0506 hours the solitary Krishna UAV was airborne soaring silently into the air as it gained height and closed in on its target. However, unlike the pair that had guided the four Force 22 officers through the Rajasthan desert the previous night, this Krishna carried four precision-guided missiles. The missiles were third-generation laser-guided ones that needed to be shown the target and then guided to it.

The Krishna UAV streaked unseen through the still, early morning air as it headed for Mari. It was flying the course painstakingly plotted out for it by Ankita Bhatnagar and was not noticed by the host of Pakistani radar operators who keep a relentless eye on Indian airspace all along the borders. Even if they had detected the Krishna it is doubtful that the Pakistanis would have anything readily available in their arsenal that was fast enough or accurate enough to take it out in mid-air in the short time that it was in flight.

SURPRISE

0519 hours, 31 October 2005, Mari, Pakistan.
The solitary Krishna UAV reached its target area and came into a holding pattern on the outskirts of Mari town. Like a falcon getting ready to swoop it took one complete circle of the small town as it located, identified and aligned itself with the target. There was a very brief pause as a series of relays and circuits clicked into place on board the Krishna. An unseen laser shot out from the Krishna and lit up the target. The target designator showed the awaiting missiles their target. The missiles acknowledged the signal and confirmed that they had the target in their capture fields.

With a silent click the Krishna released the first set of missiles, one from each wing. A few seconds later it released the second set of missiles. Having done that the Krishna hung around for a few more seconds to ensure the missiles were heading out properly in the right direction and going to do their jobs properly. Its full-colour nose camera whirred as it captured the missiles streaking towards the target. It saw the missiles strike home before it turned around and raced back towards its handlers at optimal speed, weaving its way back along the skilfully plotted path.

Another twenty-seven minutes later the Krishna was safely back in its cradle. An hour later it was back on board the small truck that followed the jeep as the three vehicles sped back towards the Force 22 base in the Kasauli hills.

'The bird is back, sir,' Khare told Anbu as Ankita completed the data transfer from her laptop. 'The BDAR (Bomb Damage Assessment Report) is being uploaded to you right now.'

'Give me a second.' Anbu cradled the mobile phone against his shoulder and punched a few keys on the command centre computer.

All three watched as the feed from the nose camera began to play back on the screens in front of them.

Falling away from the Krishna the four precision-guided missiles swooped down on the target like a pack of eagles. They hammered into the safe house in rapid succession and disappeared inside. With their advent the safe house ceased to be safe and became a death trap instead. The two terrorists of Team Three of the Lashkar, their ISI handler and the three ISI support personnel present in the safe house at that time were fast asleep when the first two missiles struck the house a few seconds after 0520 hours. The sharp, precisely focused explosion brought the house down like a pack of cards. They died instantaneously.

The second set of missiles simply demolished the house and ensured they were all given a thorough if not decent burial. Fifteen minutes later, when the dust and debris began to settle, the house had ceased to exist. Barring the odd cracked window here and there, none of the neighbouring houses had been damaged.

The killers had been delivered to their maker for final justice. There was no loss of any innocent lives at Mari. Unfortunately the same did not hold true for Karachi; substantial collateral damage took place there.

0505 hours, 31 October 2005, Clifton Area, Karachi, Pakistan.

The plush Clifton Area in Karachi town belied the actual state of Pakistan's teetering economy. The streets were wide, well laid-out and in an excellent state of repair. The houses that bordered both sides of the streets were palatial, mostly double-storeyed structures built on acre-sized plots. Most of them belonged to top-level industrialists, senior civil service and military officers, serving and retired. Anybody who was anybody in Karachi owned a bungalow in the Clifton Area. Sprinkled amongst the wealthy elite of Karachi were an assortment of drug-lords, weapon-traffickers and so-called religious leaders. However they were not your average criminals. All of them, without exception, were major players in the narco-nuclear-terror networks that the ISI had fielded over the years.

'Let me tell you, guys,' the Force 22 Intelligence Officer had told them, 'in that area there are more guys who have had Red Corner alerts issued for them by Interpol than there are labour unions in Kerala.' He may have overstated it a bit, but there was substantial truth in what he had said.

Deopa and Dhankar reached the Clifton Area just a few minutes after five in the morning. At this time of the morning the streets were almost completely deserted, save for the security guards in some of the houses. The milkmen and newspaper boys had yet to begin their morning rounds. It took them ten minutes to complete their reconnaissance and mesh ground reality with the satellite pictures they had used to study the target on. The house selected by Force 22 as the operational base after studying the satellite pictures, was ideally located. Although it had a security cabin right next to the main gate there was no security guard on duty that morning. 'Good! That is one less problem we have to deal with,' Dhankar thought to himself as he silently opened the main gate and the two commandos let themselves in.

A small driveway ran up from the main gate to the front door of the house thirty feet away. There were two cars parked in the drive. They provided valuable cover since they partially screened the front door from the street beyond the gate. Dhankar positioned himself roughly halfway between the main gate and the front door while Deopa, moving rapidly on silent feet, completed a circuit around the house. He nodded briefly to Dhankar as he came around and then approached the front door, the commando knife in his hand gleaming dully in the early morning light. The chimes of the bell ringing inside the house echoed out faintly through the door as he raised his hand and rang the doorbell.

The middle-aged man who answered the door was shaking off sleep as he opened the door, cursing whoever it was disturbing him at this unearthly hour. The sharp edge of the knife cut open his jugular with surgical precision. He was already dying as Deopa caught his falling body and moved him away from the doorway quickly, just in case someone was watching from the street. Dhankar moved swiftly out of the shadows. Skirting the car parked right outside he raced up the stairs as Deopa swept through the ground floor. The knife was put away and now silenced pistols in their hands were poised ready to cough out their lethal cargo. The magazine of each weapon housed nine death-dealing rounds. The tenth was already in the chambers of both pistols.

There were two other people in the house. Both asleep at the time. They were dispatched with due diligence. Dhankar did not hesitate as he fired. They died without even knowing it.

Elsewhere, the Krishna UAV had already unleashed its missiles and was on its way home, when Dhankar and Deopa began to set up their equipment in the bedroom on the top floor of the house. The room had two very large windows. One of these windows faced west. It overlooked the palatial bungalow across the street.

The large bungalow was set in the middle of a sprawling garden. The only entrance was through a massive gate made of sheets of solid metal. The gate was painted an ominous black and, as always, it was shut. Through his binoculars, Deopa could clearly see two men in the guard-room next to it.

'There are two at the gate and three patrolling the garden,' Dhankar whispered to Deopa.

'Got them. You get some rest now. My watch.'

It took Deopa a little longer to spot the two men positioned on the terrace garden atop the house. They were standing in the lee of the water tanks and, like the guards in the garden and guard-house near the gate, were carrying automatic rifles. Deopa could read the Chinese markings on some of the weapons as he scanned each one of them through the small, but powerful binoculars he was using.

Though it appeared formidable Deopa knew that the security set-up was cosmetic at best. The man in the house and the government hiding him did not really think the security men would be ever called into action. Or maybe the guards were meant to contain the threat of other rival gangsters; a task for which they appeared adequate. Of course, taking on a trained military force was a totally different ball game.

'According to Indian Intelligence, the security is there more to ensure the man does not get away from the country,' the Force 22 Intelligence Officer had told them. 'That is the most likely scenario,' Anbu had agreed. 'The man knows too many secrets about the Pakistani terror factory to be allowed to get away alive. His criminal network is also a vital part of the covert nuclear proliferation network set up by the Pakis. A chunk of the drug profits are used to fund the global jihadi terror factory. There is no way in hell the Pakis will ever allow him to walk out of their country alive...he knows too much and they have too much at stake riding on him.'

All this ran through his mind as Deopa settled himself down into a comfortable crouch behind the window and watched with unwavering attention. He did not speak to or disturb Dhankar who was lying on the bed in the centre of the room; rest was their ultimate weapon and they would both need it.

'We know for a fact that the man is in Karachi. He has been regularly sighted in his home and was last seen there just a few hours back,' the Intelligence Officer had told them during the briefing. 'It is also an established fact that he follows a pretty fixed routine.' Despite all this, Deopa and Dhankar had no way of knowing if the target would emerge at all that morning or how long they would need to hold fort in the house; a million unforeseen factors could come into play.

'If he does not emerge from the house before nightfall you are to implement Plan B just before first light and then get the hell out of the area,' Anbu had said. 'You will ensure that you pull out latest by the next morning, no matter what happens. Otherwise the extrication is going to get really tough.'

'Plan B is way too uncertain,' Dhankar had voiced the concern that had been in Deopa's mind too. 'It is too loud and messy and there is simply no guarantee that the target will be taken out.'

'I understand,' Anbu's voice had been very firm. 'But if there is no choice then that is what we will have to live with. In the worst case, it will at least deliver a loud and clear message to the Pakistanis and the terror groups hiding there that we can get at them anytime, when and wherever we wish. Anyway, let's not discuss this further. Those are the orders and that is precisely what you will do.'

Even if either man had been the worrying kind they had no time or reason for worry up until then since fortune rode squarely with them. God was with the good guys that morning in Karachi.

Dawn was breaking over the posh Clifton Area of Karachi when the target emerged. Even at that early hour he was wearing his trademark dark glasses with a white tracksuit as he stepped out onto the terrace and started to jog, stopping after every round and taking deep breaths.

Deopa scanned the face carefully and compared it with the photo lying beside him. The photograph was from the same file that had been handed over to Interpol, yet again, the day after the Delhi blasts. It was the same one that had been handed to the Pakistan government, along with the pictures of the nineteen others wanted for terrorist and criminal activities in India. As always, Pakistan had denied any knowledge of their whereabouts.

Despite the uncertain early morning light, there was no doubt in Deopa's mind that the person jogging on the terrace in front of him was the man behind the March 1993 bombings that had caused horrific death and destruction in Mumbai.

Deopa tracked him through his binoculars as he took his first round, just to ensure he had made no error. When he was sure he nudged Dhankar awake. 'Up, buddy boy,' he hissed. 'The target is out. The hunting season is open.'

Dhankar rose instantly and scooped up the scoped sniper rifle that had already been assembled and kept ready beside him.

The American manufactured 7.62 mm bolt-action M600 sniping rifle is a weapon that any gunsmith would be proud to wield. In the hands of an expert it is a superb killing tool. Dhankar was beyond all doubts an expert. Although he personally favoured the Russian Dragunov rifles he was more than adept with the weapon in his hand. Moving to the window he took up position. There was no glint off the sniper scope since the rising sun was coming up behind them. Dhankar ranged in on the target with minimal motion.

Through the sniper scope the soon-to-be-dead man's head loomed large and clear. Dhankar could even make out the small twisted birthmark on his right temple. It offered an irresistible and automatic aiming mark.

Dhankar steadied his hand. His breath stilled for a fraction of a second as he gently took up the slack and squeezed the trigger. He felt the recoil of the spring as the weapon discharged. The M600 uses a subsonic cartridge to reduce the noise. There was a muted bark as the weapon fired. It was not very loud, but in the quiet of the morning it rang out with unmistakable clarity. The rifle's muzzle brake hider reduced the muzzle flash and recoil. There was no giveaway flash as the tiny lead projectile shot out from the chamber of the weapon and spun its way through the long barrel. The rifling in the barrel gave the bullet the spin required by it to maintain the desired trajectory as it cut its way cleanly towards the target.

No second shot was required. The bullet whistled through the air and entered the head of the man just above the birthmark. It drilled effortlessly through the skull and ploughed through the soft brain tissues before it exited at the other end with explosive force, spraying flecks of bone and gore into the air. Life left the terror merchant as his body jerked back sharply and crumpled to the floor.

The instant that Dhankar saw the bullet strike he abandoned the rifle and slid away from the window. 'Let's go.'

They were already out of the room when one of the terrace guards in the bungalow across the road raced up to the fallen man and began to shout.

'What's happening up there?' The other guards near the gate abandoned positions and ran to the terrace as the echoes of the rifle shot lingered hauntingly and then died out in the early morning air. Immediately weapons were drawn and the cold metallic snicks of them being cocked filled the air. Blood was starting to stain the collars of the white tracksuit when Dhankar and Deopa exited from the rear door of the house across the street and strode away, casually peeling off the thin latex gloves they had been wearing. Moving at a steady pace it took them barely five minutes to cross through the rear by lanes and exit the area.

The two commandos had just cleared the Clifton Area when luck ran out.

Deopa was leading the way when they took the turn out of the small alley between the rows of mansions. He almost banged into a policeman who had stopped at the street corner to light a cigarette. The man was facing the wall of the building overlooking the road and using it to shelter the matchstick from the wind. There were two more policemen a few feet behind him. Neither Deopa nor Dhankar knew that they were the beat constables of that area on a routine patrol.

'Shit!' Seeing cop uniforms Deopa's highly conditioned reflexes automatically swung into battle drill. He reacted on instinct, without any conscious thought or plan. His hand swept out the commando knife and drove it hard in a straight, forward thrust into the policeman's heart. The policeman was dead even before he realized what had happened.

The two policemen to the rear watched open-mouthed as their comrade fell with a harsh yell. The speed of the assault numbed their senses and stunned them for a moment. Despite the shock they recovered creditably fast and reacted with the speed that had become a basic survival criterion in Karachi, a major hub on the narco-terror trail where guns ruled the day. Luckily only one of them carried a firearm. He pulled it out and began firing as Deopa withdrew the knife from the dead cop's chest and Dhankar, coming up a few feet behind, went for his pistol.

The first shot fired by the cop spewed chunks of brick and cement out of the building. The second took Deopa plumb in the chest. Deopa threw the knife at almost the same instant as the cop fired the second time. Luckily the knife had left his hand a split second before the bullet hit Deopa. That is why the knife still flew true. It covered the short distance between the two men and buried itself into the base of the cop's throat. Deopa and the cop hit the ground simultaneously as Dhankar cut down the third cop with a clean shot to the head.

The immediate threat was over but the flurry of shots had attracted unwanted attention. Luckily there were not too many people about at this early hour. Also, luckily for them, the gun-hardened people of Karachi knew that gunfire in the street meant they needed to be inside their own homes minding their own business.

Dhankar was not sure how much time he had, but he knew there would be a only small respite before the shit hit the fan. Even as he moved swiftly to take a look at Deopa he knew that their original escape plan had to be shelved. There was no way in hell that Deopa would make it out that way...not with a bullet lodged in his chest.

He was plotting the next move when a battered Honda car swept around the corner. Dhankar knew that this was not the time to wait for anything fancy. He ran onto the road and pulled over the Honda at gunpoint. Hauling out the terrorized man from the driver's seat he clubbed him hard on the head. The man crumpled to the road, unconscious. Dhankar raced back and helped the semi-conscious Deopa to his feet. He half pulled, half pushed him onto the rear seat of the car. The bleeding had already thickened and Dhankar knew he would have to do something about it soon, but right now it was imperative to get away from this place. It would be crawling with cops very soon.

About ten minutes and almost as many kilometres away, Dhankar slowed the car and began to plan his next move. He knew the wound was bad and Deopa would not make it if it wasn't tended to soon. Dead or alive, Dhankar knew he had to get him home; the Indian Army did not leave its dead or wounded behind. And seeing as they had been together a long time now, he would much rather be taking his friend home alive. *I am sure Deopa would subscribe to the same school of thought.* Despite the circumstances he grinned grimly at the thought.

Dhankar was still weighing his options when providence stepped in and made the decision for him. He had been slowing down to take the turn ahead when he saw a familiar little red cross painted on the nameplate of the house across the street. He drove straight for the house and brought the car to a halt at the gate. Leaving the engine running he jumped out, opened the gate and drove the Honda into the driveway before he jumped out and closed the gate again. There was already another car parked inside so it was a really tight fit, but he managed. Turning off the car engine he turned to Deopa who was semi-conscious and moaning in pain. 'I'm going to get hold of a doctor.'

Getting out he crossed over to the door marked CLINIC and rang the bell. The sleepy man in his late thirties who answered the door looked wealthy and successful.

'Are you the doctor?'

The man nodded. He was about to say something when Dhankar, pushed for time as he was, pulled out the automatic from his waistband and jabbed it into his soft stomach. 'I need your help. You will come quietly and do what I say or I will kill you...I do not wish to do so, so don't compel me...' Dhankar's tone was all the more menacing because he kept it low and matter-of-fact.

The blood fled from the doctor's face and he swayed slightly. For a moment Dhankar thought he would faint. He steeled himself to reach out and steady him but the wide-eyed doctor managed to keep his balance. He nodded at Dhankar who immediately nudged him towards the Honda. 'Come with me. Your patient is in the backseat.'

The doctor took one look at Deopa lying on the rear seat and whispered, 'That's a gunshot wound! He's hurt bad...too much blood loss. I don't know if I can help him.'

Dhankar gave him a cold, hard look. 'Get this straight, doc, if he dies, you die. Get him inside and dress the wound.'

The doctor had a small examination room next to the consultation chamber of his private clinic. They had put Deopa on the table when Dhankar asked him, 'Who else is at home?'

'Only my wife and two small children.' The doctor gave him a panic-stricken look. 'Please don't harm them. Please.' He was literally begging. 'They never come down to this part of the house when I have patients. Please don't do anything to them.'

Dhankar pointed to Deopa, 'Take good care of him, doc...' He left the rest unsaid.

The doctor worked like a madman for almost an hour while Dhankar stood in the half open doorway and kept an eye on him and the passage outside. No one passed that way and no other patient came to the clinic at that early hour.

However, every so often Dhankar heard a police siren sweeping past. The worry of this threat nagged him constantly. He knew they were not far enough away from either the Clifton Area or the spot where he had seized the Honda. By now the police would be scouring the streets for the Honda with two men in it. Even so there was nothing much he could do to hurry the doctor along. The stress in his head escalated with every passing moment.

Precisely what the doctor did he had no clue, but Dhankar was happy to see Deopa's breathing become less ragged and a bit of colour return to his face after his administrations. The doctor stood back and gave him an anxious look. 'I have done all that I could. The bullet is still inside. You need to get him to a hospital soon or he will not...' The doctor stopped abruptly, shocked by what he had been about to say.

'I hope not, doc...for your sake.' There was no pity on Dhankar's face; he could afford neither the emotion nor the time. 'You're coming with me, doctor. Get your bag.' He motioned roughly with the pistol as the doctor opened his mouth to protest. 'Is that the intercom?' Dhankar pointed at the instrument on the doctor's table.

'Yes.'

'Call your wife and tell her that you have been called out for an emergency. Tell her you will be back soon, but she should not worry if you get late.'

'But...'

'Do it, doc...' Dhankar's tone was harsh. 'For their sake.'

That shut up the doctor immediately. He picked up the intercom and spoke to his wife. Dhankar watched him carefully. 'What? No! You don't need to come down. No!' He threw a panicked look at Dhankar who was watching him closely. 'Don't worry I have to rush off now. I will eat something there. Bye.' He slammed the phone down hurriedly and picked up his bag. All at once he was in a hurry to get out of the house. He was worried his wife would come down; the doctor did not even wish to think about that possibility. 'Let's go.'

'We will take your car,' Dhankar said as they carried the barely conscious Deopa out again and put him on the rear seat of the doctor's car. They used a couple of cushions to prop him up. A large shawl covered the bandages, but there was no way they could stand up to a close scrutiny if the cops stopped the car.

There were some tense moments as Dhankar got the doctor to manoeuvre the Honda to one side and then drive his car out on to the road.

'Don't try anything clever, pal. Just remember your family is still inside the house. Even if you run for help I will ensure they die before anyone gets here.'

The doctor nodded grimly. 'I won't.'

Dhankar waited impatiently as the doctor backed the Honda onto the road. Luckily no police car drove past and he swiftly closed the gate and got into the doctor's car. 'Use side lanes only and get us out of the town. Head for the coast. Take us to Gulamullah or Thatta.' Dhankar named two fishing villages on the coast about ninety kilometres south-east of Karachi.

Both of them were in the direction of the closest Indo–Pakistan border. It was for exactly such an eventuality that Deopa and he had studied the villages and terrain along the coastline on the flight down from Chandigarh the previous day. *Thank God for contingency planning.*

'Look, doc, I don't need to keep reminding you, okay? I can get to the coast on my own also...so don't pull any numbers on me. I would hate to kill you, but I will do it without a thought if you try anything.'

'Don't worry, please. I will not do anything,' the man pleaded. 'I'm just a doctor.'

Sure you are, boy. That's the only reason you are here. I need you to keep Deopa alive. Dhankar didn't reply. They rode in silence as the doctor navigated the car towards the suburbs. Dhankar could feel the stress coiled inside the man.

'Who are you?' the doctor asked finally. 'Are you going to release me?' He paused to catch his breath. 'Please don't kill me. I have nothing to do with this. I promise you I will keep my mouth shut.'

'You get us where we have to go and I will release you,' Dhankar hardened his voice and motioned to him to keep driving. 'But I promise you that if you try anything you will die. Just stay off the main roads and get me to either one of the two villages.'

It was late afternoon by the time they managed to cross the town and head out for Gulamullah. The track they were driving on was barely discernible and badly cratered. It ran through patches of cultivation; the doctor had a tough time navigating the car through it.

By now the stress and fatigue was getting to Dhankar. His sleep and food deprived body was on edge, his mind on the verge of playing tricks on him. He could see the doctor starting to get increasingly restless and edgy. *The bugger is going to try something sooner or later,* his gut told him. He forced himself to stay alert.

'What is that?' Dhankar pointed to a cluster of rooftops that suddenly emerged in the distance as they turned a corner.

'That should be Gullamullah…in fact I am quite sure it is.'

'Good going, doc.'

'You are going to let me go?' the doctor asked with a sideways glance. 'Aren't you?'

'You need to have faith, doc.'

They were barely a kilometre from the village. Hardly four hundred metres away was the narrow but metalled road that led to the village. They could even hear the occasional vehicle go past although the road was not clearly visible through the cultivation all around. Just then the car engine began to sputter. 'Shit!' Dhankar muttered under his breath as the engine missed and then just died out.

There was a shocked silence as the two men watched the cloud of dust settle down around them. Deopa's harsh breathing and an intermittent clicking and hissing from the engine were the only sounds that punctuated the silence.

Dhankar shook his head and collected himself. 'Come on, doc, out of the car,' he gestured with the pistol.

The minute the car doors opened, they heard the familiar and, at this point, dreaded sound of human voices in the distance. Dhankar steeled himself and studied the landscape carefully. The doctor had his head cocked to one side in an oddly canine fashion. 'Isn't that the sea?' he pointed in the distance. 'Can you hear it?'

Dhankar listened harder. Sure enough it was. He could hear the muted roar of ocean water breaking against the shore. He felt a sudden lightening of his senses and a wave of relief. The sea beckoned to him like a long lost lover. Water was his element. Now he knew that he would be able to get both of them home.

'What is that, doc?' As he spoke Dhankar transferred his pistol to his right hand and turned towards the doctor who was peering around anxiously. The doctor was turning to see what Dhankar was pointing at when Dhankar's hand rose and then with a rapid downward arc he slammed the butt of his pistol on the doctor's head. The hit was nicely placed and professionally executed. The doctor slumped neatly to the ground. He was out cold. *Sorry, doc, but I'm sure you'd rather wake up with a headache than not wake up at all with a hole in the head.*

Dhankar hoisted the unconscious doctor on to his shoulders and jogged about two hundred metres into the fields that bordered both sides of the dirt track.

He stopped when he came to a bushy outgrowth in an uncultivated patch. Putting the doctor down he tied him securely with his own belt and strips of cloth cut from the doctor's pants. He was pretty sure the doctor would be out for at least an hour. Even when he came around he would not be able to free himself easily. That would give them enough time to get clear.

Being the professional that he was Dhankar had no desire to kill any more than strictly necessary. Not that he would have hesitated to do so had the situation demanded it.

Having taken care of the doctor Dhankar jogged back to the stranded car. Throwing a quick look around to check if there was anything on the horizon he leaned into the car and pulled Deopa out carefully. Deopa groaned; more asleep than awake. 'Easy, pal, easy does it,' Dhankar whispered. Carefully taking him on to his shoulders in a fireman's hoist he began to skirt round the village as he headed for the ocean at a slow but steady pace.

The sun was on its way down when he finally managed to reach the shore. Putting down the semi-conscious Deopa in a clump of bushes he made him as comfortable as he could. Then he shook him awake. The wounded man stirred with a groan. 'Open your eyes. I need you to stay alert for a while.' Dhankar took out Deopa's pistol and removing the safety catch put it in his hands. 'Stay awake for a while, buddy, and keep this handy...just in case. I'm going to go and requisition a boat for us.'

His words registered. 'Prop me up a bit,' Deopa whispered as he firmed his grip on the pistol. 'Where are you going to get the boat from?'

'A fishing village back there,' Dhankar pointed. 'I'll be back ASAP.'

'Do that. And listen…'

'Yes?' Dhankar turned back.

'Don't forget to give the owner a receipt when you requisition his boat.' The joke was lame, but it cheered Dhankar no end to find his buddy in good spirits.

Dhankar found a boat almost as soon as he hit the beach. In fact he found a whole lot of them. There was a cluster of boats pulled on to the beach and lined in an uneven row. Several fishermen hung around the boats, talking and laughing as they wound their nets after returning from the sea. Despite the sense of urgency, Dhankar found the sight oddly comforting.

Forcing himself to be patient he lay hidden and waited as the small knot of men standing around and talking on the beach slowly started to drift towards the village. Dhankar's patience was severely tried as they took their own sweet time about it. Finally, the sun went down and with it all signs of humanity vanished from the beach. Darkness engulfed the area.

Dhankar watched for a few more minutes to make sure there was no one around then he moved back swiftly to the spot where he had left Deopa.

Deopa's breathing was ragged and his face pale with exhaustion. Nonetheless he was awake and fighting gamely to keep the pistol steady in his hand.

'Come on, pal. Time to get going.' Dhankar again hoisted Deopa on his shoulders and made his way back to the boats. He could feel the heat of the fever that had started raging through Deopa.

Reaching the beach Dhankar went to the group of boats and checked them out. 'Crap! None of them are powered.' With that option gone Dhankar settled for the nearest, lightest and sturdiest looking boat he could spot. Gently laying Deopa down into it he cut the boat loose and pushed it into the water.

As the shoreline receded Dhankar felt the familiar rhythm of the water calm his nerves. The sailor in him took comfort at being back in the element he was most comfortable with.

For almost an hour the man rowed steadily and evenly. By now even his sturdy SEAL's body had started to give up on him. He had to fight to keep the waves of tiredness at bay. He wanted to rest his aching muscles but his mind called up reserves from deep within and drove his body on relentlessly. Dhankar knew he was in the final stretch. Safety was within reach. He just had to keep going for a little more time now.

'What is it that dude used to tell us?' Dhankar forced his mind back to the commando instructor who had trained them during his induction into the SEALS. *Your body can do what your mind wills it to*. 'Deopa! Do you think we are far enough from the coast? How long do you think I have been rowing?'

There was no answer. Deopa had passed out. Reaching out, Dhankar felt his pulse. 'Shit! It's definitely weaker than before.'

That decided him. Shelving the oars he retrieved his radio set. 'Dolphin this is Golf Nine One One. I have major trouble with the starboard engine and require assistance on priority.'

On board the Indian Navy warship cruising just outside Pakistan's maritime limit Sunil Jaggi picked up the signal. So did Anbu sitting in the Kasauli Command Centre.

Both were already aware that something had gone majorly wrong to make Deopa and Dhankar abort the overland escape route and return via sea. The 911 suffixed to the call sign used by Dhankar confirmed this. It let them know that the situation was critical and hostile pursuit was imminent or already underway.

This was serious enough without the added complication that Dhankar had brought up. The reference to the starboard engine told him that Deopa had been injured. He knew Dhankar well enough to know that the situation must be really serious for him to invoke emergency procedures.

'Thank God the old man had told me to stay put in this part,' Jaggi thought as he blessed Anbu's extensive contingency planning.

'I read you Dolphin. Stand by,' Jaggi responded more calmly than he felt. 'Golf for Tiger. Do you read? Over.'

'Tiger for Golf. Go and get Dolphin. Required tech support is on the way.'

'Roger Tiger. Stand by Dolphin I am on my way.' Jaggi waved at the two Naval personnel who had been detailed to assist him. 'Let's go!' The three men raced for the speedboat.

Jaggi was getting into the speedboat when the fisherman's wife came out of her house to throw out the garbage. She saw a half naked man staggering towards her and screamed.

'No...no...it's all right. I am a doctor.' The semi-nude apparition ran towards her speaking in what he thought was a calming manner. The fisherman's wife was anything but reassured and in no mood to wait around and get medically examined. She screamed louder and ran for her life. A few minutes later the semi-nude scion of the medical sciences found himself on the ground surrounded by a mob of very irate people brandishing an assortment of wicked-looking weapons.

The poor doctor had made a superhuman effort to free himself when consciousness returned and he found himself freezing in the cold damp field with most of his clothes gone. At this last onslaught on his senses he snapped and began gibbering. That did not go well with the mob.

'Do you think he is the maniac who has been killing all those women in Karachi?'

'Let's read out the kalma for him.' One of the more aggressive types leaned forward brandishing a huge fish-cleaning knife. Luckily for the doctor one of the saner village elders was also present.

'Wait...let us at least hear him out.' He waved back the others and turned to the doctor. 'Who are you? What are you doing here like this?'

The tone was kindly and the doctor responded to it. It took him ten minutes to spill out the whole sordid tale, beginning from the time he had opened the door to a pistol-wielding villain that morning.

'I think he is telling the truth.' One of the villagers piped up. 'I saw a car blocking the old road. In fact it is still there.'

'Let's get him to the police station.'

'Better still, why don't we take him to the phone and let him talk to Karachi?'

That is how another ten minutes later the freaked-out doctor was talking to a sleepy inspector of the Karachi police department.

'There were two of them. One was badly wounded. He had been shot in the chest,' the doctor told him on the phone. 'They seemed to be soldiers, or something like that. Very fit looking guys.'

'What time did you say this happened?'

'Pretty early in the morning. Around six thirty or seven...I'm not sure.'

'And where do you live?'

The doctor told him.

'Hmm...that is like seven or eight kilometres from the Clifton area...isn't it?'

The doctor was about to hang up when one of the fishermen shouted, 'Tell him that one of our boats is also missing. It was there till just before sunset.'

The doctor dutifully complied.

'Really? Boat is also missing? What kind of boat?' The inspector's sleep vanished within seconds of the story sinking in. Even though he was not noted for his intellectual prowess it did not take him and his superiors long to link the two men and the missing boat with the multiple deaths at Clifton and the three dead cops that morning.

The minute Jaggi was off the air, Anbu made a series of urgent calls as he activated the operational back-ups and support that could be required to extricate his team. The PM had literally given him carte blanche on this one. He intended to use it to the fullest and do whatever it took to get his men back.

'I need to speak to the Base Commander...right now,' he told the Duty Officer of Air Force Station Bhuj after introducing himself. As luck would have it the Base Commander was an NDA batch-mate.

'Dhillon, I have a problem.' He rapidly explained the situation to him. 'This is what I want you to do.'

'The first part is no problem, Anbu, but for the fighters you need to get me clearance from on high.'

'Just go ahead and activate both things,' Anbu replied quietly. 'The clearance is on the way. You will get a call within the next few minutes. Thanks, buddy.'

A few minutes later a helicopter took off from the Bhuj Air Force Base. With two medics and extensive medical equipment and supplies on board.

'Golf for Dolphin. I have you on my scope now. Stay put we're almost there.' Pause. 'I also have three other crafts heading your way. They are almost as close as we are. Keep your eyes peeled.'

The Indian Navy warship heard the radio exchange and altered course slightly. The two missile boats floating around the warship also moved cautiously forward, but ensured they stayed out of Pakistani waters.

'Don't worry Golf,' the warship chipped in. 'We have the scenario mapped out. We're watching your back.'

Miles away in Kasauli Anbu felt the coil of stress get tighter. He was about to get up and start pacing again when the phone rang.

'Anbu? Dhillon here. I have the sanction. The chopper should be landing on the warship anytime now. The fighters also are on the go. They can be over your target within minutes.'

'Great!' Anbu felt his muscles relax. 'Just hold them over the horizon unless they are required. We don't want to spook the Pakis needlessly.'

Seconds later a flight of Indian Air Force fighter-interceptors hit their afterburners and thundered away towards the designated area.

All at once a very lethal arsenal was moving into play. Each one of the players involved knew that if either the fighters or the warships came into action the fight would escalate and it would escalate fast.

So be it. This time there was deadly resolve in Indian minds. They would definitely not be the ones to blink first if push came to shove.

The rowboat carrying Deopa and Dhankar and the speedboat rushing towards them were too small to register, but the Pakistanis had had all three Indian Naval ships on their radars since the afternoon. However at that point in time this was just one meaningless bit of information for them. Though all the relevant information relating to the killings in Karachi was already with them, the bits and pieces were with different people in different departments and organizations. That is why no one in authority had been able to put the larger picture together.

The Pakistan Navy Monitoring Station in Karachi also picked up the signal transmitted by Dhankar. The signal was scrambled and they did not know what it signified, but they knew that it was something out of the ordinary and so needed to be investigated. The message was recorded by the Signalman on watch and passed on to the Duty Officer.

'What the hell is this?' the Duty Officer asked irritably.

'I have no clue, but there seems to be a lot of chatter out there tonight.'

'Isn't there always? The bloody ocean is full of old women these days,' the Duty Officer grumbled. He was not one of those high-initiative types.

'Not this kind, sir...that's the Indian Navy frequency and they are chattering like crazy. I have a feeling something is up, sir.'

'Feeling? You have *feelings,* sonny?' The Duty Officer gave him a contemptuous look; he turned away and putting his feet back up on the table returned to *The Rubaiyat of Omar Khayyam.* The Duty Officer was convinced that he was a poet who had missed his true calling when he had joined the Pakistan Navy.

'I feel we should call up the Commanding Officer and brief him, sir,' the Signalman persisted.

'At this time of the night? Are you crazy?'

It's not my ass on the line. Turning away with a shrug the signalman filed the report. That simple action of his made sure it delayed the start of the Pakistani search by almost forty critical minutes.

Two miles away, the Duty Officer at the Karachi Police Headquarters wore a perplexed look. 'What do you mean a boat is also missing? What the hell does the rowboat have to do with those guys?'

'I think those two guys stole the boat to make a getaway. My gut tells me they are the Clifton killers,' said the Inspector who had spoken to the doctor from Gullamullah.

The Duty Officer mulled over this; the whole thing was a bit bizarre. 'Where the fuck do you think they're going to go in a rowboat?'

'Maybe there is someone waiting for them out there?'

'Well, let me run this by the navy, the coastguard, port security and sigint. Let's see what they have to say.'

A few minutes later the big picture began to fall into place.

Cops the world over have the same pathological hatred for cop-killers. The Karachi police were no different. A flurry of phone calls disturbed the sleep of many other people in the police, the Navy, the coastguard and a host of other departments. Even so, it took almost half an hour for someone to connect the whole thing to the signal that had been caught just off the shore.

'You did *what*?' The Sigint Commanding Officer asked.

'I filed it, sir,' the poetry-loving Duty Officer sheepishly replied. 'I didn't think it was that critical, sir.'

'You didn't think it was critical?' The Commanding Officer's tone was cold and caustic. 'You have Indian Navy ships chattering around in your frontyard and you don't think it is critical?' Pause. 'Just wait for me to come in tomorrow morning. Make sure you meet me before you go off duty. And tell the coastguard, the Fleet Duty Officer and Post security to move their butts *now!*'

A little while later the first naval and coastguard boats left the harbour or were diverted from their patrol routes and began to scour the sea ahead of the fishing village for the missing boat and the two men. One of the smaller coastguard boats got lucky and actually spotted the rowboat. Immediately three of the search vessels altered course and started bearing down on it.

The Pakistani coastguard boat was barely minutes away when the speedboat with Jaggi on it rendezvoused with the fishing boat stolen by Dhankar, who was by now absolutely at the end of his tether. The GPS locators had helped Jaggi to swiftly home in on Dhankar.

Dhankar helped the medic shift Deopa into the speedboat as Jaggi held the boats together. Then they were off. Jaggi handled the small craft as the medic went to work on Deopa. The speedboat raced away into the night.

'Golf for Tiger. We have Dolphin. Two is in urgent need of evacuation.'

'Cas evac is standing by Golf. Get back to Golf Base now.'

The Pakistani Navy now took serious note of the Indian warship and missile boats that were patrolling sedately just outside their maritime limit. They were still trying to figure out what they could or should do when their coastguard took possession of the stolen rowboat and reported in.

'It's empty now but there is some blood in it.'

'So they've moved out in another boat?'

'I guess.'

'Shit!' There was long pause. 'Do you think that's why those Indian Naval ships are hanging around?'

'How would I know?'

'There is whole load of chatter out there. Any idea what's up?'

'Negative PortSec. They are out of our waters.'

'What do you want us to do?'

'Stand by till I check back from HQ. Nobody get trigger-happy.'

'Roger Control. We are standing by.'

A few minutes later he was back on the line:

'This is control. No one is to do anything as long as they are outside our waters. HQ does not want an incident in international waters. Is that clear?'

The Pakistani crafts moved into a holding pattern as they kept watch on the three Indian Naval crafts hanging around just outside Pakistani maritime limits.

The helicopter was landing on the Indian warship as the speedboat zoomed in out of the darkness and pulled up alongside. Eager hands helped to get the men on board. Soon the helicopter took off again. Deopa was on board. The naval medic positioned on the warship accompanied the wounded man. So did Dhankar. The minute the chopper landed near the Air Force hospital at Bhuj they rushed him straight into the operation theatre. The operation lasted four-and-a-half hours.

'Another hour or so and you could have taken him straight to the morgue,' the stocky Air Force surgeon told Dhankar when he came out.

Dhankar gave him a relieved smile. 'He is a hard man to kill, doc.'

IQBAL

Omar started when the cell-phone jangled to life. He was huddled in an armchair watching the news-anchor taking viewers through the death of the Maulavi once again. The television camera took in the large crowd gathered in front of the Savita Nagar mosque. The crowd was angry and chanting slogans. Omar jerked up and stared at the phone. Then he noticed the number the call was originating from and his mind went numb.

Omar had been sitting in the living room sipping his tea when he first switched on the television. By this time the news teams had reached the scene of the Savita Nagar blast and details of the horror were being telecast on every channel. Omar watched in horror as the cameras focused on the headless corpse of the Maulavi again and again. His mind whirled. He knew beyond doubt that Iqbal had killed the Maulavi. Somehow he knew this as clearly as he knew that he was going to be the next to die. He picked up the phone which was still ringing persistently.

'Omar?

A frisson of fear tingled his spine. 'Iqbal? *Why?*' he asked in a whisper throwing a quick look around the room to ensure he was still alone. 'He was a man of God. How could you...?'

'No one who preaches death can ever be a man of God. He was a plain and simple terrorist. In fact he was the shaitan himself.'

'What the hell is wrong with you, Iqbal? I understand how you feel about the loss of your mother and sister, but it was not intended like that. No one targetted them...'

'That is the point, Omar,' Iqbal broke in harshly. 'Can't you see that, you stupid bastard? It could have been anybody. No one knew who would be maimed and who would die when the bombs went off. Or what, if anything at all, any of them had to do with the jihad. That is why it is wrong.'

He paused briefly; his anger making him unable to speak. Then he continued: 'I believe, Omar. I believe. I believe in our God. I am ready to go to battle for him. Kill for him. But not women and definitely not children. If we are the true God's Lashkar then we should meet the enemy head on. We should fight them to death. Kill them, but not like this. Not women and children...'

'You...it is because of wimps like you that that the jihad will fail.'

'Jihad!' The vehemence in Iqbal's voice shocked Omar. 'Do you even know what jihad means? You are always busy spouting the Koran, do you even understand the meaning of the word?'

'Of course I do!' Omar recited authoritatively: '"It is the right and duty of every true believer to defend ourselves, our religion and our community from those who seek to destroy us."'

Iqbal gave a harsh, disdainful laugh. 'I am sure that even a fool like you knows that jihad means to strive...to strive for purity within oneself and goodness in society.' His tone hardened suddenly. 'But stupid shits like you...'

'You are mad!' By now Omar was literally shaking with anger. 'Don't you try to teach me religion, you crazy fool...'

'It is stupid bastards like you who ensure that the real beauty of Islam is never seen by the others! The antics of fanatics like you give Muslims the world over a bad name. We are the true believers, but because of lunatics like you where ever we go today all we arouse is suspicion, hatred and violence...' Iqbal's voice trailed off. As though the fight had gone out of him. Or as though he did not care to explain himself any more.

'Tell me, Iqbal, what makes you any different? You have killed also. What makes you think what you have done is right?'

'The man I killed was responsible for many deaths. He deserved to die.'

'Really? Our brethren are being killed in the thousands in Palestine, Chechnya, Kashmir, Afghanistan, Iraq and all these other places. What of them and the people who are killing them? Who has to decide who will live and who will die? What gives you the right to decide who deserves to die? At least we are fighting for a cause. You have just killed in cold blood for totally personal reasons.'

'Omar, you bloody fool, are you blind? Can't you see that you are fighting only because you have been conned into it? Those scheming Pakistani bastards, whose only aim is to destroy our country and the fabric of our society because their own has failed, are taking you for a ride. In the end, that is all there is to it.'

There was a very long pause. Omar could hear Iqbal breathing heavily into the phone. Then he heard the sound of a train hooting in the distance. Omar's mind registered the sound. *He is at the railway station. I wonder which...?*

'I am going to kill you, you know that, don't you, Omar?' Iqbal spoke again breaking his chain of thought. 'Just as I am going to kill all the others who had anything to do with these blasts. I want you to know, Omar. I am going back to the training camp...to where it all began. I am going to find the man who started it all and I am going to kill him.'

For a long time after Iqbal had hung up Omar sat holding the phone. He had to find a way to get word to Maulana Fazlur Rehman. He had to warn them and get them to stop Iqbal before he did any more damage. Omar knew that Iqbal was heading straight for the training camp at Muzaffarabad. And that he couldn't go there without going to Hari first. Omar got up and headed for his room. It took just ten minutes for him to throw some things together in a rucksack. Talking to his parents and getting them to understand that he had to leave immediately took much longer. Despite all this, at 1605 hours when the Jammu Tawi Shalimar Express pulled out from the Delhi railway station Omar was on it.

The flight from Delhi was almost an hour late, but it got Iqbal to Srinagar just twenty minutes after Omar's train left Delhi for Jammu. Omar did not know this of course. Just as Omar did not know that Iqbal had wanted him to hear the train in the background when he had spoken to him on the phone earlier that day.

Bluff and counter-bluff. The deadly endgame had begun.

0435 hours, 31 October 2005, Bahawalpur, Pakistan.

Except for the occasional stray, the streets of Bahawalpur were deserted when Mohammed Sami and Tony Ahlawat entered the town. An early winter fog shrouded them in semi-darkness as the two commandos swiftly made their way towards the target area. Despite the poor light it did not take much time for the two men to correlate the layout of the town with the satellite pictures and the map they had used to prepare for the mission. Moving at a steady pace it took them about twenty minutes to reach the target. Casing out the area and confirming the suitability of the operational base took another ten. 'That looks like a decent spot.' Sami pointed to a flat-roofed house with an old, uninhabited look.

'You check out the left flank,' Tony said moving swiftly to the right part of the building. The two men met back at the same spot a few minutes later. 'Let's do it.'

Sami pointed at a pile of debris and rusted junk lying on the roof. 'Couldn't be better for us.' The two men moved to the side of the roof and peered out. The target was perfectly laid out in front of them.

'Field of fire is good. Let's set up.'

By the time the call of the muezzin rang out for the Fajr prayer the two commandos were comfortably ensconced in suitable fire positions.

'Get ready. The prayers are over,' Sami hissed as people started emerging from the mosque. Most of them came out and started to leave. However a few diehard fanatics still hung about listening to the man who stood outside the entrance waving his hands and talking non-stop. 'That guy haranguing the crowd, isn't that him?'

The man Sami was referring to was one of the three terrorists released by the Indian Government after the hijacking of the Indian Airlines flight from Kathmandu to Delhi. He had been handed over to the hijackers at Kandahar.

'Definitely him,' Tony Ahlawat agreed looking at him through his binoculars.

'I think so too.' Sami followed the target through the sniper scope of his rifle. The man was standing in the midst of a crowd as he gestured and postured grandly. The Maulana needed only the slightest opportunity and a one-man audience to start dispensing his pearls of wisdom. 'The guy really loves the sound of his own voice, doesn't he?'

The Maulana's penchant for discourse was a well-known habit. It had been duly noted by a host of intelligence agencies the world over, who made it their job to monitor such personalities. Accordingly, this fact had found due mention in the RAW file maintained on him. The file was always kept up to date. The RAW had been more than happy to pass it on to the Crisis Management Committee when they got the orders from the PM's office. Today they were banking on this particular personality trait of the Maulana to cut short his stay on earth.

Neither man wished to kill any more than was essentially required, but that morning they had a mixed bag of luck. The target was present and out in the open. That was the good part. But as their weapons zeroed in on the target there were almost fourteen people around the Maulana. It was unrealistic to hope for a clear shot with all those people clustered about him in such close proximity. That was the bad part. The good part was that one of the fourteen men present in the crowd around the Maulana was Maqbool Zargar. He was among the terrorists who had been released along with the Maulana by the Indian Government after the hijacking. Of course, that morning when the two Force 22 officers pulled the triggers of their weapons almost simultaneously they did not know they were going to get two for the price of one.

Sami used the same model of sniper rifle used in Karachi by Dhankar. It was a standard American make, found in abundance in this neck of the woods; a legacy of the American support extended to the mujahideen in the fight against the Russians and of the ISI support for the jihadis in their fights in numerous battlefields the world over.

Sami sighted carefully as he pulled the trigger of the rifle. He was hoping he would get lucky despite the crowd. Tony, the back-up, just in case his luck did not hold true that morning, held the GP-25 Grenade Launcher.

The 40 mm GP-25 is a self-cocking, under-barrel grenade launcher that can be fitted on all types of full-sized Assault Kalashnikov rifles. It is a versatile weapon that always found huge favour with the Russian Spetsnaz. There was a fair sprinkling of them present in this region, most of them war booty captured from the Russians during their Afghan misadventure. They were capable of firing a grenade up to a range of 400 metres. They could fire two types of grenades, the VOG-25 fragmentation grenade and the VOG-25 fragmentation 'frog' grenade that would airburst at a height of 50 to 150 centimetres above the target and spray the target area below with metal shrapnel. Both types had a 14 second fuse. A trained soldier could fire a grenade every 4 to 6 seconds.

Captain Tony Ahlawat was a lot more than just a trained soldier. Firing rapidly he got three grenades to fly through the early morning air in quick succession as Sami sent off a well-aimed bullet towards the target. The first grenade hit the target just a fraction of a second after the bullet.

Overall, for the Force 22 officers, luck was just middling that morning. Though the sniper rifle did manage to strike the Maulana, because he was busy mingling with the crowd and constantly moving about, it hit him high in the upper right arm. It was nowhere near fatal. The Maulana felt the shock of the bullet strike home and stared at it in horror and disbelief. His hand moved instinctively towards the wound as the excruciating pain followed a microsecond later. His hand had just about managed to reach the wound, when the grenades came into play.

The first grenade overshot the small knot of men and hit the wall of the madrassa behind them just as its 14-second fuse ran out. It was a simple fragmentation one. As it exploded some fragments sprayed into the small crowd, but did not account for anything much beyond some cuts and bruises.

The second grenade landed bang on the head of the man closest to the Maulana. He literally lost his head as the grenade exploded. A satisfyingly large number of fragments also cut into the Maulana. Most of the fragments were quantitatively and qualitatively large enough to dispatch him to his maker although the one that won that honour was the fragment that lacerated his left eye.

The third grenade fired by Tony was a 'Frog' or the aerial airburst variety. It detonated approximately sixty-five centimetres above the small cluster of men surrounding the Maulana. It accounted for three more dead and wounded almost everyone present. One of the three who died was the ill-fated Maqbool Zargar. The other two were misguided youth who had just arrived from a peaceful London suburb to further their education in the Maulana's terror academy.

The two Force 22 men dropped their weapons and raced down from the roof of the building they had chosen to launch the strike. Moving swiftly, but without showing any undue haste, they quickly escaped into the winding, narrow lanes. Their luck held good. Somewhere in a less-populated alley the thin latex gloves came off and found their way into their pockets. They had almost reached the outskirts of the town by the time the police arrived on the scene.

'Shit! What a bloody mess.' The Inspector commented when he saw the pile of bodies being sorted out by the ambulance people. 'Who the hell could be behind this?'

'Just about anybody, sir. Times are bad.'

'True. Hmmm...' The Inspector surveyed the scene with a critical eye. He was an old hand. Even so, by the time they managed to re-construct the crime scene and find the sniper rifle and the grenade launcher Sami and Tony were well clear of the town and heading back for the dune where their wheels awaited them.

Given the number of terror groups that had a free run in Pakistan, it took a while before the police managed to get information of the other killings at Mari, Karachi and Multan and pieced together the fact that this was more than just a gangland killing by some rival group. The state police responded with the usual profusion of checkposts that broke out like a rash along the roads leading in and out of these towns.

Sadly, the search operations lacked a discernible sense of direction.

By the time the local police managed to lock down Bahawalpur, Sami and Tony were already well on their way out. 'That is the one.' Tony pointed to a cluster of dunes about 200 metres away. The two men altered course slightly to jog towards it. It took them about ten minutes to recover the motorcycle from the sand. Tony jumped on to the pillion seat as Sami gunned the engine.

'Go easy, man. It shouldn't take us more than two hours to get to Akbar.' Akbar was the designated link-up point. It lay almost plumb south of Fort Abbas.

'That should be about it,' Sami said pointing in the direction they had to travel. 'Hope Akbar is clear.'

Two hours later the two men came to a halt at Akbar. Once there, they went to ground again as they waited for the safety of the night. It would have been madness to try and get across the border in daylight.

'Wonder how long it will be before those two get here,' Tony said as they settled down to wait.

'They should be here soon. Either way we pull out at sunset.'

'Yup...Wonder how the buggers are doing though...'

Sami opened a packet of food. 'Knowing them the poor fucker they went after will be six feet under by now.'

Tony smiled gazing in the direction of faraway Multan.

'Here...' Sami tossed an absolutely unpalatable ready-to-eat at Tony. 'Poison yourself.' The two men munched the rations in silence, washing them down with a swig of water.

'I'll take the first watch,' Sami said after they had eaten. 'You get some sleep.'

Tony nodded, 'Sure, we'll need to be on the ball tonight,' he replied as he made himself comfortable in the sand.

It was during Tony's second sentry duty shift that the Pakistan Rangers patrol found them.

0605 hours, 31 October 2005, Multan.

Ibrahim Azhar, the man who had masterminded the hijacking of the Indian Airlines flight from Kathmandu to Delhi to get the leader of his terrorist cell freed from an Indian prison was a zealot of the highest order. He knew beyond doubt that Allah had blessed him when he had set him on the path of jihad.

He was a smart, if brutal and shortsighted leader. Though lacking strategic vision he was a sound tactical man and a firm believer in planning things meticulously. That is why the hijacking operation had gone like clockwork. That, and the fact that Salim's hidden hand had been guiding him at all times. The hijacking had established him as a hero for dozens of misguided youth who flocked to join the jihad.

'His one fault is that he follows an unvaried routine when he is home.' During their briefing the Force 22 Intelligence Officer had read aloud from the file maintained on him by RAW. 'These days he is home. We have a confirmed sighting of the man as of 2240 hours last night.'

'In fact, that is the reason why we have picked him out from amongst the twenty of India's Most Wanted,' Anbu had added. 'Immediately after the Fajr prayer the man heads to the park for a morning walk. He has been doing so all these months. No reason why he shouldn't do it tomorrow.'

Clearly Allah was not watching over Ibrahim Azhar that morning when he stepped out of the mosque and headed to the park behind the house for his morning constitutional. As usual, he was surrounded by four bodyguards who accompanied him as he proceeded at a leisurely pace.

Pradeep Katoch and Vikram Tiwathia had reached the park well before sunrise. They now watched the small entourage coming up to the park and compared the face of the man in the centre of the group with the picture that they carried. 'It's him.' Pradeep gave the thumbs up to Tiwathia – the designated commander for this mission.

The two commandos turned their attention back to the group of men who had now entered the park and were walking briskly down the jogging track that ran along the sides of the park. They had concealed the souped-up Claymore mine in a cluster of rose bushes just ahead of the third tree along the jogging track where it waited patiently to put a fiery end to its target.

*

Named in all probability after the large two-handed Scottish sword invented by Norman A. Macleod, the M18 Claymore antipersonnel mine was first developed and deployed by the Americans. The improved, deadlier M18A1 was developed well in time for use during the Vietnam War. The mine has a plastic casing that is 21 centimetres long, 8 centimetres high and 3 centimetres deep. It stands on two adjustable legs that can be used to balance it in all kinds of terrain and make basic height adjustments. The plastic casing has a steel sheet at the back, 680 grams of plastic explosives and 700 steel balls in the front. When triggered the device fires these steel balls in a 60 degree horizontal arc inflicting deadly damage within 50 metres and is capable of causing injury as far away as 250 metres.

The Claymore is an excellent anti-infiltration device and is very effective in ambushes. During 1969 to 1992 the United States exported over 1.36 million Claymore mines to 28 countries. Cambodia, Iran, Saudi Arabia, and Somalia were amongst those that benefitted from this largesse. So, in the aftermath of the US support to the Afghani mujahideen it was Pakistan where these mines were readily available. That is why Force 22 had chosen it for this mission.

Today the word Claymore mine is a generic term for any round or rectangular directional fragmentation munitions that can function either in a command-detonated mode or the victim-activated mode. The 1997 Mine Ban Treaty clearly prohibits the use of such mines in the victim-activated mode, since one never knows who or what will trigger it off. However its use in the command-assisted mode is considered acceptable.

Vikram Tiwathia was a God-fearing and law-abiding man. He had a deep respect for the law, even for some of the ones he had never heard about. That possibly is one of the reasons why the beefed-up Claymore deployed by the Force 22 officers was command-activated and not the banned victim-assisted mode type. Another even more appropriate reason was that they needed to ensure it took out the right man and not just the first poor sod who happened to trip over it.

The bodyguards were scanning the faces of the few other early morning walkers in the park with the casual manner of semi-trained people, not mentally involved with their work. Even so they were careful to go through the motions since the man they protected could be bad-tempered and abusive when things did not go his way.

Watching through his binoculars from about three hundred metres away, Tiwathia kept a close eye on the small but prominent white mark he had notched on the trunk of the third tree. The tiny aiming mark was at a height of about seven feet and clearly visible to Tiwathia. It would not be obscured from sight by anyone walking under it. The aiming mark had been placed so as to give enough lead time for the target to be in optimum position when the mine exploded.

Tiwathia involuntarily held his breath as the target closed in on the aiming mark. 'Now!' He whispered to himself the minute the target's body came in line with the white mark and pressed the tiny remote he was holding. An unseen signal leapt out from the remote and raced across the park to the tiny radio receiver attached to the detonator in the beefed-up Claymore mine.

There was a barely audible hiss and a click as the detonator triggered. The mine detonated almost immediately unleashing a hail of shrapnel and pellets along the arc in which the target was located. Almost one thousand pieces of deadly steel bearings saturated the area in front of the Claymore.

From across the park, Katoch and Tiwathia watched the explosion keenly. Katoch swept the fallen target with the sniper scope of his rifle. He was the back-up to take out the target in case he survived the blast. Tiwathia used his binoculars. He raked through the mass of bodies lying across the park.

'We got him.'

'Let's make sure.'

They both scanned the fallen men carefully for another moment. 'I can see one of the men moving but the mark is definitely down.'

The two men swiftly crept out of the bushes. After a careful look around they rose to their feet and casually merged with the crowd that had started to gather around. The sniper rifle had been abandoned in the bushes, the latex gloves peeled off and returned to their pockets. They stood in the crowd for a few moments. As the crowd increased the two men broke away from it unobtrusively and casually walked out down the bylanes crisscrossing the colony around the park.

As they were about to turn a corner and get out of the line of sight of the park, they stopped. 'Fire in the hole,' Tiwathia half whispered to himself as he triggered the tiny remote in his hand once again. The second bomb was placed high in the tree, about fifty feet away from where the Claymore mine had been. It went off with a loud bang and sent everyone scurrying for the outskirts of the park.

'That should keep the buggers busy for some time,' Tiwathia grinned at Katoch as they turned and moved off, this time at a much faster pace.

1550 hours, 31 October 2005, Link–Up Point Akbar, Somewhere South of Fort Abbas, Pakistan.

Tony checked his watch again to see if it was time to wake up Sami. He was looking forward to his second share of shut-eye. Like every good soldier he knew that one could never get enough sleep. 'Tiwathia and Katoch should be here soon. Then we will all get some rest,' he muttered to himself as his eyes relentlessly scanned the area around. Not that there was anything casual in the manner in which he kept watch. He was a hardcore professional and knew that careless sentries got people killed.

The late afternoon sun had started to throw its redness across the desert sands and the silence around them was almost complete. That is why Tony picked up the sharp metallic sound almost instantly. 'Get up. There is something out there,' he hissed as he shook Sami awake. 'Check out the other side,' he added as he crawled a little higher up the sand dune to enhance his field of vision.

Sami awoke instantly in the catlike way that Special Forces men the world over do. He picked up his weapon and headed for the opposite dune silently and swiftly. Climbing to the top of the dune Sami immediately spotted the Pakistan Rangers five hundred metres away. Instinctively, he pulled himself back to ensure he was not spotted. Not that there was any real danger of that happening, seeing the manner in which the patrol was advancing.

The patrol was blundering along in the casual fashion of bored men on a routine patrol.

Naik (Corporal) Hameed, the NCO leading the Pakistan Rangers patrol, was one of those stalwarts who rose through the ranks by the sheer weight of the number of years of service that he'd put in and not by the slightest hint of merit. Paramilitary forces the world over have an abundance of his type thronging the ranks. In times of peace they are the last ones to retire from service simply because, despite all their cribs and gripes, they know the outside world will be hard for them to survive in. During times of war and conflict they are generally the first to die, simply because they have never bothered to cultivate the skills required to survive. This in itself is not much of a problem, but for the fact that more often than not their stupidity causes many others to die with them. Hameed, the NCO in question today, had only a vague idea about reading maps and a vaguer idea still of what patrolling entailed.

'This way,' Sami mouthed as he gestured in the direction of the patrol coming towards them. He held up five fingers to let Tony know that there were five men. Tony rapidly checked the other direction to ensure that the coast was clear on his side before he slid down the dune and stealthily made his way towards Sami. Both men watched the patrol carefully, cocking their weapons as they did.

'The buggers are lost,' Tony observed. 'See the way they are all clustering around the map.'

'Stupid jerks. If these fuckers had been moving around like this in the Valley or even on the island they would have been dead meat by now.'

'Who gives a shit? I just hope they stay away from us.'

But that was not to be.

'Crap!' Sami swore as the Rangers patrol started moving. 'They are heading straight for us.'

'We'll have to take them down.'

Both men contemplated the situation for a moment.

'Okay. Here is what we will do.' Tony and Sami had trained together as a team long enough; it took them only a moment to decide on a plan of action. 'You stay here. I'll take that dune. Keep the bike between us. If they wander up to us you take the lead guy out. I'll handle the rear.'

'Let's just hope no one else is around to hear the gunfire.'

The two men swiftly moved into position on the two dunes shouldering the track that led up to the motorbike lying in the sand. The motorcycle was to be the bait that would draw the patrol's attention. The path between the dunes leading up to it was the killing ground of the ambush. The two men tightened their grip on their weapons as the Rangers patrol drew inexorably closer.

The lackadaisical attitude of the Rangers was clear from the way their weapons were slung across their shoulders and the fact that they were busy talking to each other rather than paying attention to their surroundings. 'I guess one can't really blame them,' thought Tony as he watched the Rangers ambling into target. 'Most of these guys are posted to bleak borders like this one for far too many years; nothing ever breaks the monotony.'

That was a fact. The only people the Rangers ever saw traversing this godforsaken stretch of desert border were the occasional smugglers, like Afzal, young terror recruits being sent into Pakistan for training and trained terrorists being sent back into India, whom they provided launch pads for. All three categories were a good source of income and provided a much-required break in the tedium. They always looked forward to bumping into them.

'Holy shit!' The man leading the patrol exclaimed loudly as the five men came through the path between the dunes and saw the motorcycle lying in the sand. There was a moment's stunned silence before a verbal storm erupted:

'What the hell...' began the patrol leader.

'It's a motorcycle!'

'We can see that, you idiot...'

'Where the hell did it come from?'

The man leading the patrol began to unsling his weapon from his shoulder as they all started towards the bike. He was the one Sami shot first. This was the signal for Tony to start firing. He fired a short two-round burst cutting down the last man in the patrol a split second after the first man dropped. The sudden volley of shots galvanized the remaining three men. They ran helter-skelter, grabbing for their weapons as they scrambled to get off the track and run for cover. The second last man tripped over the body of the last man as he turned. He did not get up; Tony's next burst opened two gaping holes in his chest. The last two Rangers managed to get almost to the edge of the killing zone before Sami cut them down.

The action was over in a matter of seconds and the crash of gunfire settled into the silence of the desert once again. After the ear-shattering hail of gunfire the silence that descended seemed even more ominous.

*

About 500 metres away from Akbar, Katoch and Tiwathia heard the crash of gunfire. They exchanged worried glances. 'That's from the direction of the link-up point.'

Tiwathia, who was driving, quickly veered towards the nearest dune and brought the jeep to a screeching halt in the lee of the dune. Seconds later, they were racing towards Akbar with their weapons at the ready. They split up as they got closer and began to move alternately in short hops, each covering the other man as he moved forward. Moving swiftly but cautiously it took them almost ten minutes to close in on the link-up point.

Yet again it was Tony with his animal instincts who sensed rather than heard them first. He nudged Sami and hissed, 'Someone else is coming up.' He cocked his head slightly and pointed, 'That way.'

Immediately, they both took cover again as Katoch and Tiwathia converged on the link-up point from different directions. Tiwathia covered Katoch as he closed in on the cluster of dunes. Sami spotted Katoch first. 'Tony...cool it,' he called out urgently. 'It's Vicky and Katoch.'

Tony emerged from behind the dunes. 'Next time just honk, okay?' He had a wide grin on his face. 'What's happened to your field craft, guys? We heard you coming a mile away.'

Suddenly there was an eruption of sound and static from the cluster of bodies lying beside the motorcycle. Someone seemed to be trying to raise the Rangers patrol on the radio set. For a second all four of them froze.

'That's torn it!' Sami reacted first. 'We can expect a search party real soon. You guys get ready to pull out. I'll just take a minute to leave a welcome mat for the next lot that comes along.' He began to rummage through his rucksack and pull out what he needed.

By the time the other three men had grabbed their gear Sami had set the explosives and wired the booby trap to the motorcycle. Then the four men raced off into the desert, back towards the jeep. Like all military plans this one too had a back-up.

'Do you think we should tell Tiwari that we are heading for Birbal, the alternate link-up point?' Tony asked as they climbed into the jeep.

'I'd rather not transmit anything right now. It would really put the wind up the Pakis and they would know for sure where we are.'

'I agree,' Katoch concurred. 'Let's watch and see how things unfold.'

A silence descended on them as the jeep raced away into the desert. They all knew that the operation was not going to be simple any longer. Sooner or later the patrol would be missed and people would come looking for them. It would not take a genius to link the death of the patrolmen with the killings in Multan and Bahawalpur.

1630 hours, 31 October 2005, Ranabhana BOP on the Indo–Pakistan Border.

The officer commanding the Pakistani BOP who had sent out the patrol under Naik Hameed was very irritated when his radio operator told him the patrol was overdue and not responding. 'Why? Why the heck aren't they responding?' he demanded to be told.

'I don't know, sir.' The man shrugged helplessly at the senseless question.

'The bloody fool!' This was not the first time that Hameed had returned late from a patrol. However this was the first time that he had failed to respond on the radio set. 'I'm going to kill him when he gets back. The stupid...' he muttered under his breath. To the radio operator he said, 'What the hell are you hanging around here for? Go and keep trying to raise those morons. Let me know as soon as you get those idiots on air. That motherfucker Hameed! He is going to be on everybody's shit list tonight. I swear I will kill him...'

The Company Commander would have been a lot more perturbed if he had known that the hapless Hameed was already dead, as were the four others in his charge.

Ten minutes elapsed. The Company Commander could not control his impatience. He walked up to the radio hut.

'Anything from them?'

'No, sir,' the radio operator replied. 'Not a peep.'

By the time the Company Commander finally decided to send out the second patrol, darkness was barely an hour away. 'I just hope he does nothing to jeopardize my retirement,' he thought to himself as he cursed Hameed for the enth time and went out to brief the second patrol.

The second Pakistan Rangers patrol was just starting out from Ranabhana BOP when the four Force 22 officers reached Birbal, the alternate link-up point about four kilometres south-west of Akbar. The four commandos were now almost directly north of Chengiz Khan, in the gap between the Pakistani BOPs of Ranabhana and Lambawala Toba. This is from where they had entered Pakistan and this is from where they were to exit tonight.

The commandos had no way of knowing that they were now almost directly in the path of the second Rangers patrol that had just left the border outpost seven kilometres to their north-west and was going to retrace the original route of the first patrol.

Nor had they anyway of knowing that the point on the map known to them as 'Birbal' was known as 'Bound Three' to the Pakistanis. It was one of the selected bounds that all Pakistani patrols moving between Ranabhana and Lambawala halted at. But then it is these small coincidences that acquire critical mass in battle and result in people getting killed.

IQBAL

1540 hours, 07 November 2005, Terrorist Camp in Jungle above Hari, Kashmir.

Iqbal deliberately avoided the route that Omar and he had taken when they had left the camp five days ago. *It's the most logical way in and out of the camp. I am sure there will be a sentry keeping an eye on it.* He skirted the base of the mountain for almost an hour till he saw a ravine that seemed to run all the way up to the top. Surveying the climb carefully he then started his ascent to the camp.

Half an hour later, he realized that it was a very bad climb. The gradient was steep and the loose shale was treacherous. More than once his foot lost its grip and he went tumbling down a few feet. The cold and the rapidly descending darkness of a long winter night added to his misery. Still, the rigorous training he had undergone in the camp in Muzaffarabad and his determination to get there were to his advantage. Eventually, the rhythm of the mountains began to return to him. His grip steadied. The craggy terrain felt familiar once again. His mind and feet stopped playing tricks on him. With every passing moment his movements became more surefooted as his body acclimatized to the incredible cold and darkness of the night.

Cresting the last fold of the ravine, Iqbal was confronted by a small, flattish ledge. There was something familiar about it. He looked around it as he stopped to catch his breath. It took a few moments before realization dawned. *This is where we buried the instructor.* Iqbal squinted in the dark. Yes. Definitely the same spot. In his mind's eye Iqbal once again saw the sentry leaning against the shovel as they took a break from the digging. 'Motherfucking Pakis…the only good ones are the dead ones,' he had said. The harsh laugh that had followed the sentry's words rang so clearly in his head that for a moment Iqbal almost thought there was someone with him. He thought about what the sentry had said:

Don't you see? It is all about money. Only about money. Twenty dead mujahideen like us cost them less than one dead soldier. Plus they have the comfort of denying that they are the ones who train us and task us to fight their war. They get to fight a cheap war at almost no cost to them. Even the few bucks they throw at us we earn for them by bringing out their drugs. Do you have any idea how many millions of dollars those shit-eaters earn from drugs?

Shaking his head to clear the ghosts from his past Iqbal slowly turned a full circle. His eyes fell on a raised spot further ahead. It was the cluster of rocks where the sentry had made Omar and him bury their weapons. Iqbal automatically began to plot the route to the rock cluster. It would be easier to get to the camp from there. He was about to start around the ravine and head for the rocks when something within made him pause. *Would they have posted a sentry?* After all, this was where they kept their weapons...some of them at least. There was bound to be a sentry.

Standing stock-still in the lee of a tree Iqbal focused his attention in the direction in which he knew the camp huts lay. *If there is a man on guard then, logically, he should be in that general area.* Iqbal focused his eyes in that direction, straining in the dark for any tell-tale signs but could not spot a thing. Twenty minutes later, just when he was about to give up the vigil and start moving a tiny flicker of light shone briefly about a hundred and fifty metres away. An unseen hand cupped a matchstick as a cigarette was lit. In the mind-numbing darkness that tiny transient flame of light was more than enough. *Smoking is injurious to health.* Iqbal smiled mirthlessly in the darkness. *Don't you guys read the warning on the packet?*

Lowering his rucksack to the ground Iqbal drew his knife from his belt and started forward on light feet. A chilling calm descended on him. The field craft that had been grilled into him at the training camp surfaced effortlessly as Iqbal inched forward soundlessly in the dark. In his mind the man he was going to kill had ceased to be human. His death was simply one more formality to be completed in the interest of his mission. A job to be done; a roadblock to be eliminated. Swiftly. Efficiently. The transformation of the decent young boy from a small-town, middle-class home into a heartless killing machine had been rendered complete. And Iqbal had no idea when and how it had happened.

Hoping to break the monotony of the watch, the man who was supposed to be standing guard was leaning against a tree trunk toying with a pack of cigarettes when Iqbal's hand clamped down on his mouth. As it opened into a startled, instinctive 'O' of surprise the cold steel of Iqbal's knife pierced his skin and slit his throat.

Iqbal silently lowered the dead man to the ground, careful not to make any noise. He checked the blood-streaked face of the man he had killed as he wiped his hands and the blade of his knife clean on the corpse's clothing. It was not the sentry Omar and he had stayed with earlier. That meant the rest of the group operating from this camp had returned. *I hope there are not too many of them.* Iqbal had no illusions about his ability to take on a band of hardened jihadis.

Iqbal dragged the body of the sentry to a clump of bushes a little away from the designated sentry post. If the present inmates of the camp had been trained at camps similar to the one he had been trained at Iqbal knew that sentry duty would not last more than two hours. Normally most people started duty on the hour, if not for any other reason than that it was easy to remember and keep track of shift-change timings. That meant Iqbal had about forty minutes before the dead sentry's replacement came to relieve him.

Iqbal made his way towards the cluster of rocks where the weapons were buried. He knew exactly where they were buried, but he had no tools to dig them out. Working with his knife it took him almost half an hour to recover a rifle, as much ammunition as he could carry and a few grenades. Then Iqbal crept back to the sentry post. He had barely settled in when he heard a rustle a little distance behind him. A swift backward glance confirmed that someone was approaching. *The guy has just come out of the hut; his eyes have obviously still not adjusted to the darkness.*

Iqbal watched as the man blundered through the undergrowth. He was making a lot more noise than he should have been. Iqbal held the knife close to his belly as he waited.

'Anwar!' The man called out softly, just a little louder than a whisper. 'Anwar!' Again that muted whisper. This time there was a clear note of irritation in his voice. 'Oh…' he saw Iqbal. 'There you are.' The man changed direction and headed for Iqbal who was slumped forward pretending to be asleep at the post. He placed a hand on Iqbal's shoulder to shake him awake, cursing him all the while.

The minute the man's hand touched his shoulder Iqbal grabbed it and lunged forward with the knife thrust out. In the circumstances, there was no way Iqbal could have aimed it any better. The knife broke through the skin. It hit the man's breastplate and skidded to the side, tearing through more skin and flesh. The man screamed as he fell forward almost on top of Iqbal. Actually it was more like a howl. The primeval death howl of a dying animal. It rang out loud and fearful and reverberated in the mountains around.

Iqbal froze. The others in the camp would definitely have heard it. The scream subsided into a whimpering moan. Iqbal raised his knife hand and slammed the hilt down on the man's temple, silencing the whimpers.

Iqbal was moving away from the unconscious sentry when he heard the sound of breaking undergrowth. Several people were on the move. Iqbal tensed as he reached for his rifle and prepared to meet the imminent assault.

Then he stopped. He listened more attentively. The sounds were moving away from him. For a minute he was perplexed. He listened even harder. Yes, they were definitely moving away from him.

Suddenly understanding and comprehension dawned.

You must never get into committed battle with the security forces. They are better equipped, armed and trained. They also have a far higher capacity to absorb losses. So, when you are attacked you must run for it. Get away. Then come back and hit them when and where they least expect it. Always remember, the attacker has the latitude of selecting the time, place and method of attack. Come back and fight them on your terms, at the time and place of your own choosing.

The words of the instructor conducting the tactics class at the training camp echoed in his memory. Iqbal knew for a fact that his erstwhile terror mates must have assumed it was a raid by the Indian security forces and were making a run for it. Of course, they would return. Once they realized there was no pursuit.

This suited Iqbal just fine. It gave him enough time to do what he had to do. For Iqbal this was the most critical part of the mission.

Iqbal used the bootlaces of the unconscious sentry to lash his hands behind him. Then snatching up the rifle he cocked it. The blood lust in him was now in full fury. Holding the weapon at half port so that he could bring it into action instantly Iqbal moved forward hoping he wouldn't have to actually fire. Noise carried far in this terrain. It could actually get the security forces here.

Moving rapidly, Iqbal circled silently along the ledge, pausing every now and then to recheck his surroundings before he moved again. He paused for slightly longer as he scoped out the huts. The door of the main hut was ajar and a faint glow came from within. He resisted the illogical temptation to go inside. There was nothing in there that he sought. Somewhere in the recesses of his mind Iqbal could hear the faint hiss of the radio set he had heard that morning when they had reached here after the ambush. The sound reverberated in his memory guiding him to the spot he thought he had heard the sounds from. It took him only a few minutes to find the radio. He used the rifle butt to smash it before he resumed his circuitous patrol. The camp was completely deserted.

Iqbal returned to the spot where the sentry lay. He was beginning to recover consciousness and starting to moan. Iqbal knelt beside the man and shook him till he saw the man's eyes open.

It did not take very long for Iqbal to get the information he needed from the traumatized and terrified man. Having learnt what he needed Iqbal stepped away from the wounded man; looking at him made him nauseous. The dying man beseeched Iqbal to spare his life with eyes full of fear; eyes that pleaded with him to show some compassion. A part of Iqbal wondered at himself, at the level of evil to which he had fallen, even as the other part plunged the knife expertly into the man's heart, ending the agony of the night.

Shouldering his rifle Iqbal went back to the top of the ravine and retrieved his rucksack. Then he started the descent.

An hour later Iqbal had reached the base of the mountain. By now his body was a screaming mass of pain and fatigue. He forced himself to push on, knowing that if he sat down to rest even for a moment he would not be able to get up and get moving again.

By the time he found the small cave in the side of the mountain that the sentry had told him about his his numb and exhausted body had lost all sensation. Dropping the load he was toting he fell to the hard, cold floor as though he had been pole-axed.

Sleep had just engulfed him when, on the other side of the mountain, Omar hopped off a ramshackle jeep two miles away from Hari.

1800 hours, 31 October 2005, Birbal/Bound Three, Somewhere in the Desert, South of Fort Abbas, Pakistan.

Sami checked his watch yet again. The hands of the watch seemed to have frozen. He must have looked at it more than twenty times before the small luminous dial glinting in the dark confirmed that it was finally time. He nodded to Tiwathia.

Tiwathia checked his watch and returned the nod. Turning on his radio set Sami sent a brief signal into the ether. 'Fox One Four for Tango. We are leaving Birbal now.'

The tiny burst of disturbance in the electro-magnetic spectrum was picked up and heard by many people. After all, this happened to be one of the hottest and most active international borders in the world. There were more guns deployed on this border and more people keeping eyes and ears on it than there were hookers on Sunset Boulevard.

Sitting in the ad hoc control room near Khajewala, Tiwari and Vashisht heard the transmission. Their radio set was on the same frequency hopping sequence as Sami's so they received the transmission in the clear.

'Birbal?' Tiwari who was standing near the door asked Vashisht. 'Did he say Birbal?'

'He did.'

'They must have run into trouble at Akbar...Damn! Hope they are okay.'

'But he did add One Four to his call sign. That means all four of them are still together and okay.'

'Great! Let us get the birds up.'

'Roger that Fox. Stand by for five. Big brothers are on the way.'

The two men raced out to launch the waiting Krishnas.

The various Indian monitoring stations keeping an ear on that border heard the signal too. None of them got it in the clear since the transmission had been automatically coded by the radio set and they were not on the same frequency hopping sequence. Most of them duly logged it since it originated in Pakistani territory. A few of the sharper operators observed that it was a typical Indian Army frequency transmission.

Almost a dozen Pakistani monitoring stations also picked up the signal. Once again they got the scrambled version of the transmission so they had no clue what it meant.

'What the heck was that?' The Sigint man asked his Controller.

'No clue, but it is definitely on the Indian Army frequency. Much like the new frequency hoppers they have inducted recently.'

'Should I pass it on to the cipher guys to decode?'

'Do that...not that it will be any good to us. By the time they make any sense of the signal it will cease to be relevant.' The Operator shook his head in disgust. 'Well, I do have a fix on their location, sir.'

'Good!' The Controller called up the others. 'Charlie One to Charlie Seven. Do you guys have a fix on that transmission?'

'Charlie Five I have a fix.' The Operator passed on the coordinates.

'Copy that Charlie Five. Who else picked it up?'

'Charlie this is Two. I also picked it up. Here's the reference.'

'Roger that Charlie Two.'

The Controller triangulated the location and had a fix on the precise location of the transmission a couple of minutes later.

Within minutes telephone wires burned all along the front.

'I am positive, sir. It was one of those newfangled Indian Army frequency hoppers. Though what the hell they are doing in our neck of the woods beats me.'

'You don't beat your brains about that.' The Garrison Commander at Fort Abbas was in on the information loop. It did not take him long to put two and two together. 'Just keep your ears open and keep me posted about everything happening there.'

He was pretty sure it was connected to the incidents at Bahawalpur and Multan.

*

The officer commanding the BOP Rangers company who had sent out the second patrol was horrified when he was ordered to step out of the safety of his BOP and investigate it personally.

'I want another patrol out. Also send one section out from each of the BOPs on the sides...fully loaded and properly briefed. And listen–' The Garrison Commander was fully conversant with the abilities and capabilities of the Company Commander– 'let's try not to make a mess of it this time.'

The stricken officer moved his ample bottom as fast as he was able to. 'Get another section ready,' he told his Platoon Commander. 'I will go with them myself. You jokers are useless.'

He then got on to the radio and briefed the second patrol about the radio that was transmitting from that area. 'Keep your eyes peeled. Check out area Black Rocks and Twin Dunes thoroughly. And maintain radio contact at all times.'

He also ordered the BOPs at Lambawala Toba and Majnuwala to launch patrols into the area. 'One section strength both of you. Lamba, you cover the area between your BOP and Black Rocks. Majnu, patrol the IB (International Border). Warn your people to be careful. Really bloody careful. And get everyone on the BOP on high alert. I want everyone on the ball. Okay?' He repeated his instructions twice more, revealing his nervousness more than reinforcing the orders. 'And, remember, we have two more patrols out. No friendly fire, okay? I'll personally annihilate anyone who shoots at each other.'

All three Rangers patrols moved out within minutes of each other. At about the same time two helicopters took off from the Pakistan military garrison at Fort Abbas.

Although six American AH-64D Long Bow Apache attack helicopters had been inducted into service by Pakistan in early 2002, the Pakistan Army detachment at Fort Abbas was considered a low priority area and had only two ageing AH-1 Cobra helicopter gun ships available to it.

Inducted into service during the Vietnam offensive the AH-1 Cobra had definitely seen better days. However, geriatrics though the two birds were, the 20 mm cannon capable of unleashing 750 rounds in a matter of seconds, the four TOW missiles and the 19-tube M261 2.75" rocket launchers fitted on to them made them more than capable of dealing with the situation on the ground that particular day. The choppers moved towards the area triangulated by the monitoring posts, onto which the three Pakistan Rangers patrols were also rapidly converging.

Unknown to the four commandos, all at once the desert around them was coming alive. Of course, they were clearly aware of the dangers of staying put in the same location once they had used the radio set. They knew how deadly and effective technology was; they may as well have placed a 'We are here' marker on the Pakistan battle board the minute they used the radio.

Sitting in the Force 22 control room Colonel Anbu heard the transmission. His eyes were automatically drawn to the tiny green dots pulsing brightly on the electronic battle board. *One, two, three, four…yes…all there.* His mind mulled the possibilities of what could have gone wrong at Akbar even as he tried to visualize what was happening on ground. Then the imagery on the screen before him changed. The Krishnas had come into their holding pattern over the target area. Live feed from them began streaming in.

'Tango for Fox. We are up and about now. Screens are lighting up. Give us a moment to get a fix on things.'

Sami double-clicked the transmit button in acknowledgement.

Both the Krishna UAVs slashed their way unseen through the night sky. The ever-vigilant shepherds were going out to guide their flock home again. They spotted the four commandos almost immediately. The small IFF (Identification Friend of Foe) system fitted into the GPS locators carried by the Force 22 officers shone like welcome beacons.

The Krishnas also spotted the second Rangers patrol from Ranabhana BOP and the two Cobra helicopters that had taken off from Fort Abbas, heading straight for the Force 22 officers.

'Fox, this is Tango. You've got mail.' Vashisht's voice came through crisply on Sami's headset. 'Ten inbounds, dead ahead. Eighteen hundred and closing.

You also have a couple of Snakes coming at you...ETA approximately fifteen minutes.'

'Snakes? Shit!' The last thing they needed right now was a pair of attack helicopters looking for them. Things were beginning to get hot and hairy.

'Roger Tango. We're going to need assist with the Snakes.'

'Stand by Fox. Let's work on that.'

Sami hated to transmit again. He knew that the more often they transmitted the faster and more accurately the Pakistanis would be able to pin them down. *On the battlefield that we operate, we are safe only as long as we are not detected,* he remembered Anbu telling them more than once during training. *Problem is, modern technology makes it almost impossible for anyone or anything to remain undetected for very long. That is why the key is to move fast and move smart.*

'We're hot now...' Sami alerted the others as he repeated the message transmitted by Vashisht to the other three. They assimilated the information with grim nods. Instinctively their grips tightened on their weapons and they altered course to ensure they would not run head-on into the incoming Rangers patrol.

'Those damn choppers are not good news at all,' Tony remarked as they raced through the desert, putting the maximum possible distance between themselves and the place they had transmitted from last. 'I wish we had a couple of MANPADS (Man Portable Air Defence Systems) with us. I would have shown those buggers a thing or two.'

IQBAL

0700 hours, 08 November 2005, Terrorist Camp in Jungle above Hari, Kashmir.

Omar's stomach heaved as he looked at the mutilated body of the sentry lying before him. The rank odour of death hung heavily about. Omar did not want to look at the body, but was unable to drag his eyes away from it. He was trying to shake the horror from his mind and figure out what to do next when he heard a faint rustling sound. Nervously he imagined Iqbal creeping up on him with a blood-soaked knife in his hand. He was turning to run when he heard a man say: 'Hold your fire! Don't shoot! I know this man.'

Omar's mind screamed in relief as he recognized the sentry who had been guarding the camp when Iqbal and he had gone there last week.

'You?' The sentry was accompanied by two other men, one of whom looked about the same age as Omar. 'What are you doing here? Why did you kill...?'

'I-I didn't.' Omar tried but couldn't overcome the quaver in his voice.

'And where is the other chap who was with you?'

'He is the one who did this.' Omar pulled himself together with a huge effort and began to talk, the words tumbling out of his mouth. The shattered radio set and missing weapons convinced them of Iqbal's grim purpose more than Omar's breathless narrative did. He noticed the glance that the sentry exchanged with the older man. 'You have to help me,' Omar pleaded.

'Of course we will. We will come with you,' Hasibul, the younger chap, assured him.

The older men exchanged glances again. 'I have a better idea,' the sentry said. 'You and Hasibul go ahead to Chakoti. Meanwhile, we two shall go across to Camp Shamsher which is two valleys away. We will use the radio set there to warn the Maulana.'

Before Omar could object the two had turned around and trudged off. Omar watched them go. He turned to Hasibul, wanting to share his misgivings about whether the other two would even head for the next camp at all, then he stopped, unsure if it was the right thing to do. 'Don't you think we should also get a move on?' he asked instead.

'No. We will wait for sunset before we move out. The Pakistan Army post at Chakoti is barely three hours away. It would be suicidal to move around near the LOC in daylight. We wouldn't last a minute,' Hasibul replied.

No matter what route you take to Chakoti, that point has to be crossed; you cannot avoid it. Iqbal remembered the words of the dying guard. Iqbal forced his mind away from the man whom he had tortured and killed the previous night. He scanned the track lying ahead of him. It stood still and silent. Almost five hours had passed since the darkness of the night had silenced the sun when Iqbal heard a faint scraping sound. Iqbal was about to pass it off as a figment of his overwrought imagination when the first man hove into view, silhouetted against the skyline. He was barely forty metres away. The second man appeared a little behind him. They were moving slowly and cautiously, picking their way up an almost non-existent mountain track.

Iqbal knew he would not be seen as long as he stood still. *At night it is generally motion that gives us away,* the field craft instructor had told them at least a hundred times during their training.

As he continued to watch Iqbal realized that the man leading the way seemed to know the route well. The second man was a few feet behind him. Iqbal only recognized Omar when he came over the ledge and for a few seconds was clearly outlined against the skyline. The presence of the other man bothered Iqbal. He had visualized a special encounter with Omar with no room for another person in it. Iqbal's mind shifted gears furiously as he tried to improvise and figure out a way to handle this new development.

Omar and the other man were now even closer. At one point they were so close to Iqbal that he could have reached out and touched them. He could hear Omar's breath wheeze in and out of him as he walked. *How can he not pick up my presence?* Iqbal's hands tightened on the rifle butt and he got the weapon ready to cut them down the minute that happened.

The man accompanying Omar stopped suddenly. As though he had heard the working of Iqbal's mind. He cocked his head as he listened harder. Behind him Omar also froze. Then they moved on.

According to the sentry he had interrogated last night, the Indian patrols were the most active from this point onward. Iqbal waited for them to get a reasonable distance ahead before he got up and started to follow them.

Omar and the other man silently skirted the Indian post. Iqbal, maintaining a constant hundred to hundred and fifty metres distance behind them, followed suit. Given the ruggedness of the terrain that little distance seemed a lifetime away.

The light of a new day was beginning to creep through the darkness of the night when the muted sounds of Chakoti Post fell upon Iqbal's ears.

'Hoy! Who goes there?' The voice of the Chakoti Post sentry pierced the early morning fog. He seemed to be using some kind of a hailer since his words echoed hollowly.

Iqbal hit the ground immediately and lay very still. The two men walking ahead also stopped. Iqbal heard one of them shout something back. The wind was blowing away from him so he was unable to make out what was said. Whatever they said did not convince the post sentry. 'Wait there!' The sentry's amplified voice boomed again.

Iqbal saw the Chakoti Post sentry turn towards the inner part of the post and gesticulate repeatedly towards the minefield, in the direction where Omar and the other man were standing. He seemed to be calling out to someone.

A minute later Iqbal saw another man emerge from the depths of the post and join the sentry. The two men spoke for a moment before the sentry turned and called out something to Omar and the second man. Iqbal heard Omar shout back. This time it was clearly Omar who was doing the talking. Finally the sentry stepped forward and began to weave his way through the minefield that lay along the entire front of the post. *He must be following the same kind of markings that they had used for us when we had crossed the minefield. The marking must not be so obvious…that is why he is stopping to check every now and then.*

Seeing that everyone's attention was diverted Iqbal quickly moved to a more advantageous position. It took the sentry almost fifteen minutes to get across to where the two men waited on the outer fringe of the minefield. By now Iqbal had taken position behind a rock about a hundred metres away. Through the sights of his rifle he watched the sentry come up to the two men. The three of them stood together and conversed for a moment then the sentry turned and started walking back towards the post. Omar and the second man followed his lead. They were following him closely, like a line of geese.

The best time to hit an enemy patrol is when it is about to enter its camp or post. The familiar camp right in front of their eyes makes them feel safe psychologically and their guard is down. The words of the tactics instructor at the training camp echoed in Iqbal's mind. *They think they are safe because they can see their post clearly. Troops seldom realize that they are still as exposed as when they were a kilometre away from camp.*

The three men had covered another twenty metres when Iqbal crawled to the flank and took up position behind a larger rock just off the trail. He settled himself in as comfortably as he could against the cold damp earth and sighted carefully on the sentry leading the way. The three men were now almost midway into the minefield. Iqbal could feel them slowing down for yet another route check. Iqbal's breath stilled for a fraction of a second as the rifle steadied in his hands. Steeling himself, Iqbal fired.

The sound of the rifle shot echoed in the stillness of the morning. Iqbal was sure it would give away his position. Instinct urged him to cut and run. Training and logic held him back. *Nobody would be expecting it. Why would anyone be watching this area? The next shot will be dicier. The third will definitely locate me and the minute they find me I am dead meat.*

Iqbal held his position as he saw the shot strike home. It gave him a strange sense of satisfaction as he saw the clearly visible puff of dust and debris that spurted in the air as the bullet slammed into the sentry leading the way. The man was flung forward. Rapidly switching targets Iqbal fired another two shots in quick succession at Omar and the man with him. Both shots were a waste of ammunition.

As the first shot rang out and the sentry leading the way fell, the two men following closely behind him froze for a long second. Then some half-remembered battle drill must have erupted in the mind of the man accompanying Omar.

Run-Drop-Crawl-Sight-Fire. That is what they teach you to do when you are confronted by enemy fire. *Run*...It is imperative to get away from the spot where the enemy has already ranged in his weapon. *Drop*...to ensure he cannot hit you easily. *Crawl*...It is equally imperative to move away from the spot where you dropped because the enemy has seen you drop there and will be sighting on it very soon. *Sight*...Having evaded the enemy thus you must now try to see where he is firing at you from. And then...*Fire*...to make sure you kill the enemy before he kills you.

Hasibul followed the drill instinctively. He had gone about three steps when there was a sharp thunderclap and a loud, hideous scream. This was followed a second later by another thunderclap as a black cloud arose from the spot where he had been. The poor sod had run smack into the minefield. He must have stepped on a mine and then landed on another one when he fell. Unfortunately both the mines were simple anti-personnel mines. Had they been the fancier, jumping fragmentation ones that leap out of the ground and detonate at waist height spraying the area around with deadly metal shrapnel, Omar would have died with him.

The early morning light was still not good enough and the situation too confusing for anyone to determine exactly where the fire was coming from. Iqbal raised the sights of his weapon and fired two more rounds at the men rushing towards the Chakoti sentry post.

Iqbal had not bothered to aim the last two shots properly because whether he hit anything or not was irrelevant. The fact was that the return fire was going to be immediate and plentiful.

Iqbal had not been wrong to bank on the inherent instinctive trigger-happy response of sentries on active border posts the world over. On this particular line of control nerves were always on edge and sentries almost obsessively keyed up. The roar of several guns broke out as Iqbal pulled back. The Pakistanis let go with everything they had on hand. They aimed for Omar and the area around. This was logical since he was the only stranger on the scene and his arrival had coincided with mayhem breaking loose on their post. It was easy to assume that he was responsible for it.

In any case, Iqbal had no intention of hanging around any longer. Moving rapidly he left his position and started crawling back to the dip in the ground about thirty metres down the trail.

He knew the Chakoti Post would launch a patrol soon. So would the Indian post on the other side of the mines and fences, not too far away. He had no desire to be anywhere in the area when that happened. He chuckled as he fled deeper into Pakistan Occupied Kashmir. *Friendly fire is such a bitch.*

1815 hours, 31 October, 2005. Somewhere in the Desert, South of Fort Abbas.

The Pakistani monitoring stations once again picked up the signal transmitted by Sami. Brief though the message was, it was enough for them to home in on the Force 22 commandos. By now the Pakistanis were fully aware that something seriously untoward was brewing on their western borders.

The Fort Abbas Garrison Commander's phone rang again. 'No matter what happens, no matter how many they are, they must not be allowed to get away across the border.'

'Don't worry, sir. I'm pulling out all stops.'

'Yeah, do that, but nothing goes across the IB.'

Putting down the phone the Garrison Commander got on to the radio set and started getting on everyone's case.

This second set of transmissions allowed the Pakistan monitoring stations to triangulate the location of the radio set on the ground and get a precise fix. 'Control for Mike One and Two. This is your new bearing.'

Immediately the two Cobra choppers altered course as they got a more specific area in which to concentrate their search.

Back at the command post, Vashisht saw the whole picture developing. He had a bird's eye view of both of the Pakistani patrols, the two attack helicopters converging on them and the Force 22 officers. He also had the advantage of knowing exactly what was going on whereas the Pakistanis were still struggling to put together the larger picture. 'Tango for Fox. Head south-west, approximately twelve hundred.'

He gave them a bearing that sent them straight in the direction of the Pakistani patrol from Ranabhana BOP heading their way. When they were about six hundred metres short of the patrol Vashisht transmitted again. 'You're now heading straight for the bandits from Romeo Bravo.'

Click. Click.

'Tango for Fox, halt now and acknowledge my transmission, but keep it short. The Snakes are close now. Coming up on your port side. ETA five minutes at max.'

'Reading you loud and clear Tango,' Sami acknowledged crisply. 'Port? Don't you bloody go Navy on me at this time...what the fuck is port side?'

Vashisht laughed as he told him.

'Roger Tango. I'm getting the drift.' By now Sami had understood what Vashisht was planning. 'We are standing by.'

Sami's subsequent transmissions had given the Pakistanis ample opportunity to home in on him. He knew they would only be able to pick up the transmissions, but not read them since the transmissions were coded.

The coding process was not very simple, but given the modern code cracking technology that was available these days it would not take much time for the messages to be read in the clear. However, the Force 22 officers knew that by the time the message became readable it would also become redundant. That was the problem with most real-time battle intelligence; it was only worth something if it was available immediately. Otherwise it was only good for operational post-mortems and military history books.

'Tango for Fox. Get ready to rock. Ground bandits at three hundred and Snakes coming up overhead now.'

Click. Click.

The Pakistanis were tracking the transmissions continuously.

'Mike One and Two the target is now in area...'

It took another minute for the Pakistani controller to guide the Rangers patrol to the new location. He had to do both separately since the choppers and the Rangers were operating on different channels primarily due to the different types of sets the two were using. In fact, in the heat of the moment no one had remembered to even tell the Rangers that the choppers were also on the way.

Vashisht saw the change in course of both helicopters and also the men on ground. He watched carefully for a few moments, confirming that they had taken the bait.

'Fox this is Tango. Move now as advised. Guns hot. Radio silence till Chengiz Khan. Chengiz stand by to cover Fox. Over.'

'Chengiz for Tango and Fox. Roger that.'

Sami did not reply. He just double-clicked the transmit button in confirmation.

Then the four commandos were off.

The Pakistani helicopters took another two minutes to reach the precise area they had been given. During this time the Force 22 officers had withdrawn from the location. Moving rapidly in a short arc they circled the Pakistani patrol that was by now almost at the same spot from where Sami had transmitted the last two signals.

Vikram reconfirmed the bearing and location with his GPS locator. 'This way, guys!' he pointed. 'Tony, all yours...and catch up fast.'

The three men raced away as Tony Ahlawat, who was bringing up the rear, stopped and took up position. He waited till one of the helicopters was almost directly over the Pakistani patrol. It was circling slowly and noisily, scanning the desert with a huge searchlight. He knew that most of the Pakistani patrolmen would be busy following the light with their eyes. The glare would render them totally night blind for a while.

Using the rifle he had retrieved from the jeep he fired two deliberate shots into the helicopter. 'Got you!' he hissed triumphantly when he saw the chopper lurch momentarily before steadying itself. That was good enough for him. Shouldering his weapon, he ran after the other three commandos towards the Indian border.

The sound of the two shots was almost completely lost in the roar of the helicopters' rotors. Most of the Pakistani patrol party was not even aware of the firing. But there was no way the Pakistani pilots could have missed it. The co-pilot took one of the two bullets in the tender-most part of his anatomy. His startled yelp and sudden start as he soiled himself almost caused a total loss of control and sent the helicopter plunging wildly towards the ground. 'What the hell are you doing?' the pilot screamed in panic as he wrested back the controls and managed to correct it just in time.

'I've been shot,' the co-pilot moaned.

'Shot?' The pilot instinctively pulled away from the sudden threat that had emerged from the desert. He banked the helicopter away and aligning it towards the general area, from where he assumed they had been fired upon, cut loose with his machine-guns. With honour duly satisfied, he gave an urgent call to his base.

'Control, I have taken fire. My co-pilot is hit. I also have possible damage to the bird. Returning to base now.'

'Mike one where is the fire coming from?' The agitated Controller asked trying to get a clear picture of what was happening out there.

'Who the hell knows Control! There are lots of people down there. I need to go now. We're hit. I don't have time for this shit.' He wrinkled his nose as he spoke. The smell of crap was getting stronger. He just couldn't wait to get out the chopper.

The pilots of the second helicopter heard the entire conversation. They duly noted the threat that had suddenly emerged from the desert sands and arrived on the scene with guns blazing. The desert sands churned madly as hundreds of machine-gun shells blazed out from the twin guns mounted on either side of the chopper.

'What in God's name are those idiots doing?'

The Pakistan patrol on the ground was amazed at the sudden hostility and fire that it was drawing from up above. Frantic calls on the radio set to their Company Commander, since they had no means of communicating directly with the helicopters, resulted in more panic and confusion all around.

It took almost twenty minutes before temperatures cooled sufficiently and some semblance of order returned to the area. In those twenty minutes the Rangers fired off enough ammunition to win a small war. Most of it fell harmlessly on to the empty desert. Some whistled past the four commandos racing towards the border. One of the bullets got lucky and nicked Sami's right ear, taking off the lower lobe.

'Shit!' he cursed as he instinctively turned to return the fire, but then he restrained himself. There was no sense giving away their positions by opening fire. That chopper could cause serious problems if it managed to locate them again. Clasping a handkerchief to his ear to stanch the bleeding he resumed running with the others.

The second bullet was a little luckier. It slammed into Tony's upper thigh felling him to the ground. Katoch was running almost abreast with Tony when he saw him stumble and fall.

'Man down,' Katoch hissed urgently bringing the others to a halt. Swiftly he knelt down and checked the wound. The bullet seemed to have missed the bone. Even so the flesh was ripped apart. 'There is no way in hell he can move with this leg. Here...' Katoch tossed his weapon to Tiwathia and hoisted Tony onto his back. 'Man! What the hell have you been eating?' he said as Tony's weight settled on him. Then they were off again. Sami led the way as Katoch followed and Tiwathia brought up the rear.

Those twenty minutes of confusion between the Pakistan Rangers and the choppers clattering noisily overhead gave the four Force 22 officers enough time to put over a kilometre between themselves and the Pakistani patrols. The Pakistanis did not know who, how many, or where exactly they were.

'Whoever it is, has to be heading for the bloody border, you idiots,' the frantic Company Commander screamed in frustration. 'Where else do they think they will be going? Stop them! Just head for the border and stop them.'

By now the four commandos had given up all pretence at stealth and were heading hell for leather for Chengiz Khan. They were in superb physical condition, but there was just so much speed that Katoch was able to generate with Tony on his back. Chengiz Khan was still another eighteen hundred metres away.

'Fox this is Tango. You need to haul ass. The Snakes and the Ground Bandits are barely eight hundred metres away now. One of the ground bandits teams is moving on a direct intercept path.'

'Are they between us already?'

'No, but they will be if you guys don't shake a leg fast.'

'Roger that Tango.'

The three men reached within themselves and called up every reserve available. 'Katoch, here let me take him now.' Tiwathia quickly took Tony on his back and they raced on. Seven hundred metres away Katoch again took on Tony as Tiwathia started to tire and slow down. By now the blood from Sami's ear had soaked the handkerchief and was starting to seep down his collar.

'The finish line is close...almost in touching reach.' Gritting his teeth he ignored the spasms of pain that coursed from his ear to his neck as he ran on. 'So are the damn Pakis.'

He did not know it but at that precise moment one of the Pakistan Rangers had finished deploying the battlefield surveillance radar and had begun to scan the desert. It took him barely a minute to locate Fox as it raced towards the border. The excited Ranger was on the set and screaming within seconds. Luckily he had no means of communicating directly with the chopper above and his message had to be routed through his Company Commander.

Even so, almost immediately the hunters changed course and began to close in on the Force 22 commandos. The commandos only got wind of this when the first volley of shots rang out. Racing through the desert the commandos felt the whiplash of hot lead whine past them. None of the shots were aimed, but all of them were lethal enough in any case. Carrying Tony on his back as he ran, Katoch felt one of them hit his right arm. He stumbled as it slashed past. It must have been a graze since he did not feel any pain. Tossing up a silent prayer he raced on towards the border and the safety of Chengiz Khan.

At Chengiz Khan, the same group of people who had seen them off, now awaited the return of the four commandos. This time however there were more combat dress uniforms to be seen than labourers' attire; the need and time for pretence was fast receding. Also in evidence were a lot of automatic weapons. The thunder of gunfire and the roar of the choppers were clearly audible to them all.

'Chengiz this is Tango. Fox is blown. They are heading your way...bandits close behind.' The Krishnas overhead were watching everything unblinkingly. They saw the hunters alter course and knew the curtain was coming down fast. The slim window of opportunity had begun to close.

'Roger that Tango. We're hot now and ready to move in.'

'No Chengiz. Don't cross the IB till we confirm. Instead just buzz the bird and get it away from Fox. It is almost on their backs right now. In fact if it hadn't been for the darkness they'd be toast by now.'

'Chengiz this is Tiger.' Watching from afar, Anbu cut in smoothly. 'You are cleared to cross the IB. Do whatever it takes but get Fox back.'

The Chengiz team leader assimilated the input. *'This is serious shit, man. Nobody crosses the IB lightly...especially not armed men.'* He shrugged. *'Thank God, we have a serious dude backing the play.'*

'Roger Tiger, leave it to me. Fox is coming back in one piece.'

'Team One, get ready to move.' Tossing the radio handset to the operator the Chengiz leader raced out of the tent. 'Team Two stand by for fire support. Move, *move....*'

There was a flurry of activity as men raced out cocking their weapons. The Chengiz team leader grabbed the Igla-1S MANPAD missile and ran to the top of the nearest dune.

The Soviet made Igla-1S is an excellent surface to air missile with all aspect capability. It also has IFF capability to ensure friendly aircraft are not fired upon. The officer aligned the Igla-1S towards the Pakistani chopper hovering a little over a kilometre away. At that range and in such conditions it was a sitting duck.

'I have movement there.' The Indian soldier manning the battlefield surveillance radar at Chengiz pointed out. 'About seven hundred metres now and closing. There are three in front and about ten behind. There are another ten angling in from the right…about five hundred metres away.'

'Three? Only three men? We have four men out there.' The officer paused and turned towards him. 'Ajit!' He called out to the Team Two leader. 'Get your guys ready.' He turned back to the Igla and zeroed in on the Pakistani helicopter. At that moment it was the most potent threat on their horizon. 'I have to neutralize the bastard. Another minute or two and our boys will be done for.'

A silent beam shot out from the Igla's IFF system as it queried the helicopter.

'Friend or foe? Identify yourself.' The beam seemed to ask.

'Shit!' The Pakistani chopper pilot breathed as his systems bleeped a warning. 'We're being tracked…. These bloody Indians! What the fuck is wrong with them…how far are we from the border?' Then deciding that he didn't want to wait and find out he whirled the bird around and, dropping height, headed northwards. 'Control this is Mike Two. What the hell is happening here? We are being hit upon with a missile track. Is there something going on that we haven't been told?'

'Mike Two what are you talking about? Stay low and pull back a little. Let me check this out.' The Controller immediately got on to the hotline to check with his boss what they needed to do next.

The Pakistan Rangers on ground saw the chopper pull away and move homewards. That confused the already perplexed men.

'What's going on here? Where is that joker going?'

'Wait…let me check.' The patrol leader was not an exceptionally bright man. He was also not at the age where one could expect any major surges of initiative from him. His tired patrol clustered around him as he got on to the horn with the Company Commander. They were all fed up of chasing ghosts in the desert.

'Tango for Chengiz. That was neat. The bird has pulled back a bit. Enough for the moment. The ground bandits also seem to have halted for the time being.' Pause. 'Fox is closing in now.'

'Thanks, Tango. We have got Fox on the charts…but only three of them. What's happening out there?'

'Fox for Chengiz.' The radio crackled before Tango could reply

'Fox this is Chengiz. We are reading you strength five.' The operator manning the set was right on the ball.

'Chengiz keep your guns tight. We are coming in now.'

'Come on in Fox. Confirm guns tight. I repeat we are guns tight now. Over.' The radio operator raced out.

'Hey! Guys! They are coming in now. Hold your fire. Oye you...hold your fire.'

He had barely shouted out the warning when three figures raced out of the darkness and across the gap in the fence.

'We have a man wounded here!' Tiwathia called out as he led the way in. His breath came in ragged spurts. The other two tumbled in behind him, bleeding and exhausted. 'Do you guys have a medic around?'

'Coming right up,' the Chengiz leader yelled as the team medic rushed forward.

Katoch heaved a sigh of relief and grinned as the medic team eased the wounded Tony off his back. 'What the hell, Tony! I never knew you're so full of shit. I should be getting overtime for this.'

Fox was home.

The hunt had gone well after all.

IQBAL

Even though there was dense foliage around the small knoll behind which he had taken position, Iqbal had a decent view of the complete camp from his perch at the edge of the small cluster of trees. He felt no sense of connect as he surveyed the training camp. It was as if the young man who had left the camp barely ten days ago had nothing in common with the man crouching in the undergrowth three hundred metres away.

Twenty minutes after Iqbal moved into position he glimpsed Maulana Fazlur Rehman heading towards the hut that housed the radio set. An hour later he came out from the communications hut and walked up and down the camp a couple of times. The Maulana was stretching his legs. Iqbal followed him through the sights of his rifle. He had several opportunities to take a shot at him. But that was not the aim. Iqbal wanted to see him die. Up-close, and personal. *I want you to see it coming. I want you to feel the fear, you bastard. I want you to know why you have to be killed.*

Iqbal wanted Rehman to understand why he needed to die, even though he knew he would not be able to make the Maulana see things differently. The

Maulana was a man deeply handicapped by the poverty of limited judgement; the one-sided vision of the zealot. He would never be able to see or accept any other point of view.

It was becoming hard to stay still in the cold. Iqbal could feel his extremities starting to freeze. Movement was necessary to keep the blood circulating. But motion would give him away. Iqbal forced himself to ignore the cold. Despite his best efforts, by the time night arrived, the increasing cold and the lack of motion had sapped him badly. Iqbal's numbed hands, nose and ears were losing sensation. Yet, Iqbal resisted the temptation to get up and make his move as soon as it grew dark. That would be tactically stupid. He needed to let people settle down for the night. He needed to let the silent darkness of the cold night dull the alertness of the sentries.

Iqbal recalled that the camp had two sentries. The first sentry guarded the communications hut and the second the weapons hut. This was reconfirmed when he saw the first set of sentries move into position just as darkness began to fall. Iqbal noted the time. It was almost 1800 hours. When the sentries moved into position there was a brief window of opportunity when the outskirts of the camp went unobserved. In any case, during the first five to ten minutes of sentry duty their eyes would still not be acclimatized to the darkness.

Iqbal used this opportunity to rapidly crawl ahead to the second position that he had picked out during the day's vigil. Now he was barely a hundred and seventy metres from the outer perimeter of the camp.

Each sentry duty shift would be of the standard two hours duration unless things had changed drastically. They hadn't. Precisely at 2000 hours Iqbal heard more than saw the guards changing. Hearing the new sentries moving in, Iqbal remembered how they had all hated night guard duty when they were undergoing training. Especially in winter. After an hour in the mind-numbing cold all you could think of was getting warm again. 'The worst thing is the bloody pointlessness of the whole thing.' In his mind Iqbal could hear Omar complain. 'Nothing ever happens that can justify standing there and freezing your nuts off. Not here in the back of beyond.'

That's what they had all thought, Iqbal remembered.

As the night deepened Iqbal began to flex his fingers and move his limbs more and more, rubbing his face with his hands to restore some semblance of feeling and warmth to his body. The chances of being spotted reduced as the shroud of darkness deepened.

At midnight, Iqbal heard the sentries change again. He gave the new pair of sentries another thirty minutes to settle down. Then he got up and, moving in a wide loop, circled around till he was at the point where it was easiest to access the hut that housed the Maulana. The walk not only warmed Iqbal's body and loosened his limbs it also adjusted his eyes completely to the darkness and primed him for silent motion in the dark. It was precisely 0125 hours by his watch when Iqbal emerged from the foliage and silently slithered into the camp. Moving imperceptibly with great stealth it took him about ten minutes to cross the open area that lay all around the camp and reach the hut where his target slept.

He was just twenty feet away when he heard a tiny metallic clang. He froze for a few seconds and listened. It was the sentry by the weapons hut who had changed his position. Iqbal could hear him stamping his feet as he moved around. He listened for a bit longer. The poor sod seemed to be trying to stay warm. Iqbal began to move again.

Almost diagonally opposite from the weapons hut, about ninety feet away, sat the second sentry. There was no sound from him. Iqbal guessed that the man was asleep; a lot of them tended to nap when they thought they could get away with it, which they did invariably, as the instructors couldn't be bothered to come out and brave the chill. In any case, Iqbal knew from experience that this was the time of the night when sleep was deepest.

Reaching the Maulana's hut, Iqbal quickly merged with the deeper shadows immediately around the walls. Shouldering his rifle carefully he held his knife in one hand and reached for the door with the other. *I hope the damn door does not creak,* he thought grimly as he gently pulled it open.

REACTION

'How could those wimpy Indians have done this?' The General's temper was as short as his vision and political horizon. 'How could they have even thought of doing it? Who do they think we are?'

'It couldn't have been anyone else, sir.' The ISI Director spoke warily. 'That much is obvious from the people who have been eliminated.'

'I know that, dammit! I want to know how we were caught with our pants down!' The dictator gave his security chief a filthy look. 'What were your idiots doing?'

The security chief looked away. This was not the time to tell the General that there was little they could have done; it was simply not possible to foresee every possible reaction and protect every possible target. But now was neither the time nor place to tell him that. The days of due process were over for the people of Pakistan. Those who crossed the dictator or rubbed him the wrong way tended to vanish without a trace.

'What are the losses like?' The General finally gave an angry snort and turned back to the ISI Director.

'Just those three or four men.'

'Who gives a shit for men? Men die all the time. What is the damage like to the...the...pipeline?' The

General chose his words with great care. Although they were in the safe confines of his office and the offices were swept electronically every morning these days one could never be too careful. In any case, it was always wiser not to talk openly about things like the narco-nuclear-terror trail.

'The damage is substantial,' the ISI chief replied softly. He did not like being the bearer of bad tidings and cursed the wimpy security chief for not taking on these questions. This shit was his domain, after all. 'Especially with the scientist under house arrest, the man in Karachi was vital, we were using his conduits extensively.'

'Bloody hell!'

The ISI chief was careful to keep the contempt off his face as he watched the dictator pace up and down the room. All he had lost was money. Shitloads of it no doubt, but they were the ones hit hardest. All those years of work had gone down the shitter with that guy in Karachi. His loss would substantially affect their capability to carry out strikes inside India.

'What do you suggest?'

'We will have to develop his Second in Command to take over.'

'How much time?'

'Who can say for sure?' The ISI chief shrugged. 'A few months maybe. The Second in Command is not that bright…but then that is also a big plus for us. It makes it easier for us to control him.'

The General stopped pacing the room and looked at him. 'Good! That's good. So we are not that badly off?'

'Well...not that we have too many options open to us right now,' the ISI chief shrugged. 'The scientist is on a global shit list. If he even steps out of Pakistan God knows who will take him down...or even worse, whisk him away for questioning.'

'But what about the Indians? We must send out a strong message to them. The buggers shouldn't get the feeling that they can get away with these James Bond stunts on our territory.'

'There is nothing we can do overtly. We cannot even admit to those men having been killed on our territory. After all, the Indians have been asking for them to be extradited all these years and we have been denying they are in Pakistan.'

'That's true.'

The security chief was glad to have something other than matters pertaining to security being talked about. 'The damn Indians even handed over a list and dossiers of the infamous twenty to us the day before...Interpol alerts and all.'

'What are the other options?' The General looked pointedly at the ISI Director.

Surprisingly, the security chief spoke before anyone else could: 'To begin with we should lodge a protest over the intrusion of our air space by the Indian Air Force. We know for a fact that they have used a UAV at Mari. Otherwise there is no way those missiles could have taken out the house at Mari. We have recovered enough from the debris to establish that.'

'The missiles were Indian?'

'No.' The security chief squirmed uncomfortably again. 'They were American, but they had been modified. That's for sure.'

'American missiles! You think they are helping them?'

'Not necessarily. You know the Americans. Those pimps will sell weapons to anyone who has money. In any case, there are a million ways to buy those things with no one being any wiser.'

'Who cares?' General Haque, the ISI Director, butted in. 'It is not as if we have to prove anything in court. You go ahead and make the right diplomatic noises. I'll give the Indians something to think about.'

The Pakistanis lodged a strong protest with the Indian Government the next morning. A press conference was called and Indian involvement in terrorist activities in Pakistan was spoken about at great length.

'You're being ridiculous. Please don't make baseless allegations,' a calm and polite Indian spokeswoman told the surprised Pakistanis as the Indians took a leaf out of the ISI's own book. 'We would be more than happy to bring to justice any person or persons involved in any criminal acts in Pakistan. Just let us have the proof, please. Meanwhile,' she added, 'would you please hand over the twenty terrorists being harboured by Pakistan so that we can try them here in India? You may also like to hand over Brigadier Murad Salim, Maulana Fazlur Rehman and the others who were involved in the Delhi bombings. They are criminals and must be tried as such.'

'What nonsense! You Indians blame us even if bird flu strikes your country. Do you have any proof to support what you are alleging?'

'Actually, we do. Switch on your televisions a couple of hours from now and you will get to see most of it.'

Sure enough, a few hours later, the Indian Government aired telecasts of the captured terrorists over all major television channels and invited the FBI and MI5 to be a part of the interrogation of these men. Finding no other option available, Pakistan fell back on its time-tested pattern of brazen denials and blatant lies, with the rabid General making some really asinine threats.

'We have no recourse now,' the Indian PM told the press conference that had been convened to address these threats. 'The community of nations must realize that our neighbours leave us with no choice; we have to defend ourselves.'

The Pakistani dictator was a little taken aback when the Indians responded by mobilizing their army along the entire border and line of control. Both the Indian Naval battle groups along with the newly-inducted aircraft carriers set sail to take up position on the approach to Karachi. Tension in the region ratcheted up considerably.

A whole platoon of spy satellites and HUMINT sources from all over the globe watched as a storm of activity erupted in Indian Army cantonments all over the country. A dozen different types of camouflaged battle dresses replaced the staid olive green peacetime Army uniforms. Long convoys of fighting and troop-carrying vehicles began to stream out of the cantonments as they headed for their designated operational posts.

Pointing at the two thick black lines on the White House crisis room board the intelligence man briefing the US President said, 'These photos are in real-time, sir. You are seeing things as they happen. That is the Indian strike corps moving out of their peacetime locations.'

'How long before they get operational?' the President asked.

'Barring the forces based in South India the others are garrisoned almost on the borders. So I would say not more than a few hours, Mr President. They are already on high alert and all defensive formations are already in their positions.'

'Shit!' said the President, a man not famous for his erudition or keen intellect. 'We need to talk to the Indians and cool them down.'

'They are not in the mood to talk, Mr President,' the Secretary of State intervened. 'They want blood.'

'Tell the Indians to cool off, we have troops in that area hunting down the terrorists.'

'We did. They asked us to pull them out for the time being so that they could also sort out some terrorists.'

'How the hell can we do that? Don't they know we stand on the threshold of elections? We can't be seen to be weak; not at this time.'A longer and more thoughtful pause invaded the room. 'Tell them the nuke deal is at stake.'

'We did that too.'

'And?'

'They listened to us politely.'

'Paradigms are shifting, sir,' the Secretary of State cut in again. 'The Indians know they are sitting on one of the fastest growing economies of the world. They know we need access to their markets. Worse, neither Russia nor China want us hanging around in their parts of the world. These three countries together have more clout than we can…' his voice trailed away. These were areas where few of them dared to tread.

The Pakistani Armed Forces responded by also mobilizing to their operational locations. The mobilization was a hugely expensive exercise for both nations. It was definitely not one that the Pakistani economy was in a position to withstand. For a nation already on the brink of a teetering economy the effects were immediate and devastating. The Indian economy was far better poised to take the hit.

'Let us maintain the Army on the borders for a month or so, sir.' The Indian PM was advised. 'It is going to cost us a bomb but the economic shock will literally smother those buggers across the border. Let the bastards bleed.'

The Indian PM was an ardent economics man himself; he loved the idea. It was a simple strategy that allowed them to maintain the moral high ground while simultaneously inflicting a crippling blow on the enemy.

'Isn't that what Sun Tzu would have advocated? The primary aim of a war after all is to degrade the enemy's will and ability to fight.'

What could be better than starving them to death?

'Let us do it,' he ordered.

The don't-mess-with-us message was driven home when the PM again addressed the nation the next morning:

'Brothers and Sisters, I would like to assure you that the Indian Armed Forces stand ready not just to protect, but also to take the battle deep into the enemy heartland should the need arise. India will no longer take such acts of terrorism and war lying down.' His tone was strong and firm. 'Let me also state unequivocally that although India will stand by its doctrine of no-first-use, there will be no hesitation on our part to retaliate with nuclear weapons in case of any nuclear threat against the motherland.'

His words sent cold shivers down the spines of the world. It was the first time that an Indian head of state had made so direct or potent a threat. Indeed, paradigms had altered.

As hours turned into days the Indian Armed Forces continued a hard offensive stance all along the borders with Pakistan. Aggressive patrols on ground and continuous sorties by the Indian Air Force and the Indian Navy became a matter of routine.

Rhetoric mounted at a dizzying pace. So did the cost and the tension, not just on both sides of the border, but in state capitals all over the world. The horror of a nuclear holocaust was something the world was not even ready to contemplate. Trigger-happy Pakistan was not a nation known for being reasonable or mature enough to handle nukes. They inspired little confidence in other nations. A posse of politicians from all over the globe began to exert whatever pull or push they could on the Pakistani dictator. Some heads had to roll. Some did.

1000 hours, 04 November, 2005, Office of the Director, ISI, Islamabad, Pakistan.

The Director of the ISI, General Haque, put down the phone. The expression on his face was grim. He sat for a long time and mulled over what the General had told him to do. *It is not fair! Salim has given most of his life to us, to the cause. Just because he made a mistake and got caught doesn't mean we lynch him.*

Abruptly, he made up his mind and leaning forward picked up the phone; but this time he chose the small satellite phone lying on the table before him and he dialled the number of another satellite phone. 'Listen, very carefully,' the Director said. 'Things have gone very wrong. I just got off the phone with the big man. The writing on the wall is clear; you are going to be left holding the baby.'

There was a short angry outburst from the other side.

'No!' the Director cut in vehemently. 'Not right now. This is not the time...we are not ready yet. I will be the first one to tell you when we are ready, and it will not be long now. We will strike before that man drives our country into the ground.' The Director's tone was harsh. 'The man is definitely losing it. Can you imagine he is releasing his memoirs? The stupid jerk is actually going to talk about things that...'

Another angry outburst erupted from the phone. The Director winced and delicately held the phone away from his ear.

When he spoke again his tone was still soft but the steel of command was unmistakable. 'Yes, I know. I have had the pleasure of reading the draft.' The ISI Director's voice was heavy with sarcasm. He forced himself to speak patiently. 'Salim, you have to trust me. I know that in your line of work trust does not come easily, but this time you will have to trust me. I promise you, we will strike, but at the time and place of our choice. We will strike when we are ready; when they least expect us. But for now it is time for you to do an Osama – drop out of sight and lie low for some time.'

He spoke softly for another minute before he disconnected the call. Then returning the satellite phone to a drawer in the table he picked up the intercom and called in his aide.

'Call up Brigadier Salim and tell him to come down to meet me. Tell him a chopper is on the way to Lahore. Then ask Ali to send him a bird immediately.'

Thirty minutes later, the helicopter was on its way to Lahore.

A black, unmarked car with dark film on the windows waited at the small helipad on the fringes of Lahore. As the chopper's rotors slowed down a short stocky man got out of the car and walked briskly into the chopper. Right behind him was a tall, broad-shouldered man in his early thirties who walked with a marked military gait.

A man standing on the roof of the tall building watched the helicopter diminish in the distance through the powerful binoculars in his hands. He saw the yellow fiery trail rise up from the ground and snake its way up towards the helicopter. From a distance it looked like a firework rocket. Suddenly a ball of fire ballooned around the space that had been occupied by the chopper. It was too far away for the man to be able to hear the sound, but he could almost feel the blast of the Stinger missile as it decimated the chopper. For a very brief moment a blackish cloud of debris hung in the air then it too disappeared. A moment later the man turned and headed for the elevator that would take him down to the waiting car. He had an odd expression on his face.

Brigadier Murad Salim of the ISI had just watched himself die in the chopper that had gone down in flames. He could visualize the headlines in tomorrow's newspapers. As far as the world was concerned Brigadier Murad Salim and his aide Captain Azam Cheema had ceased to exist.

The driver started the engine as soon as Salim emerged from the building. The car headed out for the town of Faislabad to the plush, well-appointed house on the outskirts that awaited Salim.

'How did it go, sir?' Without turning back or taking his attention off the road Captain Azam Cheema asked from the driver's seat.

'Well! It went well.'

'Bit of a pity about Rashid though. The other man was new, but Rashid was a good chap,' Cheema said.

'The casualties of war, Cheema, just the casualties of war. Happens every time.' Salim paused. 'Their sacrifice will not go waste. Remember to send some money to their families.' With that the Brigadier ticked off another task performed in his metal checklist and returned to his reminiscing; about the days gone by and those that lay ahead. *General Haque is right. I'm going to lie low for some time and then decide what to do.* He was not too worried about the future. With the kind of money and resources available to him there was no dearth of options as far as he was concerned. Brigadier Murad Salim knew that no matter what happened or where he went to live his work was not over. *The kafir must be made to pay.*

The supposedly dead man closed his eyes and leaned back against the soft cushions of the car.

IQBAL

Sliding inside like a wraith, Iqbal slowly pulled the door shut behind him and stood stock-still. He waited patiently as his eyes adjusted to the deeper darkness within. Except for a faint sliver of moonlight that lacerated the bed it was pitch dark. The fire in the angeethi had deadened to a dull glow. It gave a faint light.

Iqbal saw a figure asleep on the narrow wooden cot towards the rear of the hut, the image of him sharpening as Iqbal's eyes adjusted to the dark. Fazlur Rehman lay on his side with his face towards the wall. Iqbal waited for another few moments. Till such time that the placement of the furniture inside the hut was firmly embedded in his mind. Finally, moving forward stealthily till he was crouching beside the sleeping man, he raised his rifle and brought the butt down hard on his head. The crack of the rifle striking hard bone reverberated through the silent hut. Iqbal was sure it must have been heard outside. He froze with his head cocked to one side, listening for the sound of movement. There was none. The man jerked spasmodically before his body went limp.

Leaning the rifle against the wall Iqbal pulled out the length of rope and tape he was carrying. Trussing up the unconscious man's hands tightly behind him, Iqbal tied his legs together and secured them to the wooden cot. Then he yanked off one of the thick woollen socks the man was wearing and stuffed it into his mouth before taping it tightly shut. Iqbal wrapped the tape around Rehman's head a couple of times to make sure he would not be able to free his mouth no matter how hard he struggled when he regained consciousness.

When he was finally satisfied with his efforts Iqbal returned to the door and opening it a crack, scoped out things carefully. He was about to pull the door shut when he heard the rustle of movement outside. He froze as the sound continued, faint but persistent. Then he threw a glance at his watch. *Two o'clock. It must be the shift changing.*

Iqbal stood near the slightly open door. Almost twenty minutes lapsed as he let the new sentries settle down to the tedium of the night. He would have waited a few more minutes, but just then there was a faint moan behind him. Iqbal realized the man on the bed was regaining consciousness.

Quietly pulling the door shut, Iqbal moved across the hut. The time to kill was upon him now. The man he had travelled so far for lay helplessly before him.

Maulana Fazlur Rehman was a proud man. He had walked hard and relentlessly on the path that he knew Allah had wanted him to tread.

Rehman had built up the jihadi outfit almost single-handedly. There had been substantial help from the ISI of course, but the Maulana was loath to acknowledge it. He never denigrated the ISI and was very careful in the way he responded and interacted with it, but in his heart of hearts he hated the slimy, drug-dealing, self-centred ISI bastards. He knew they had their own secret agenda, but Rehman did not care. 'As long as they serve the purpose we will use them,' he would tell his cronies. 'The jihad must go on.'

His jihadis had been responsible for sending many a kafir to the hell that they rightly deserved. Of course, in the wake of the American interference he had been forced by the treacherous, two-faced General to change the name of his organization. He had even lost a lot of money when those white-skinned bastards froze the bank accounts of his organization. Inshahallah. So be it. The Maulana had accepted all this as the will of Allah as yet another test that he had to suffer and survive. And survive he had. So far.

The cold shock of the rifle butt that had slammed into his head had befuddled Rehman. The pain in his head made him want to scream, but he was not able to open his mouth. He wanted to press down on his throbbing temple and still the pain, but he was unable to move his hands. The shock and confusion deepened when he realized that he was unable to move his legs either. And whatever was stuck in his mouth not only prevented him from shouting it cut off his breathing too. Then a hand clamped down on his throat. A moment later, a man's face came out of the darkness and stopped a few inches away from his. The dim light in the hut was enough for the Maulana to recognize Iqbal.

Iqbal scrutinized him carefully for a very long time. It seemed as though he wanted to absorb every fleeting expression on the Maulana's face. Bewilderment seemed to be paramount. *The fucker is not afraid. He will be though. Soon.*

Then Iqbal began to talk. Speaking in a flat staccato Iqbal told the bound and gagged man his story. It took all of five minutes. It did not move the Maulana. There was a long pause as Iqbal again studied the face before him. Still no fear, no remorse. 'Have you understood anything that I have said?' Iqbal asked him.

Rehman inclined his head.

'Good. Then you will have no difficulty in understanding why I am going to kill you.' Even now there was no heat or high decibel energy in the hut. Iqbal held the knife in the air, close to the man's face.

That is when the fear came.

Out of nowhere. Like a pot of milk suddenly boiling over. Pure terror gleamed in Rehman's eyes, which were now riveted on the cold steel. Iqbal raised the knife a little higher. The fear mounted. He could see it glittering in the eyes of the man lying before him. An endless silent scream stormed through the hut. Shards of cold comfort drove through Iqbal. 'You deserve it...you bastard,' he hissed.

Iqbal was about to drive the knife into the soft flesh of the man's belly when an unbidden memory intruded. There was still one more man alive who needed to die.

'Do you want to live old man?' Iqbal whispered.

Sudden hope flared in Rehman's fear- struck eyes. He nodded.

'Then I need you to talk to me. If you tell me what I want I may let you...'

The man nodded vehemently. He would have agreed to anything.

'Good!' Iqbal reached out. 'I am going to remove the gag from your mouth, but I promise that if you make one sound I will kill you...no one can reach you before my knife. Do you understand?'

Another swift nod. Iqbal reached out and removed the gag from his mouth. The man gasped and spluttered breathing greedy mouthfuls of air into his starved lungs.

'The man in the hut with you that day...when you showed us the television coverage of the Delhi blasts...Salim...didn't he mastermind the mission?'

The man nodded. 'Brigadier Murad Salim of the ISI.'

'Salim. Brigadier Murad Salim.' Iqbal whispered the name to himself softly. 'Salim must die.' He thought for a moment then prodded Rehman with his knife. 'Where can I find him?'

'He has many houses and offices. I have all the addresses in that diary there.' The man motioned to a small table in the corner. His voice was getting stronger now. Iqbal could see the man's confidence return. 'But they will do you no good. Salim was killed last week.'

'Killed? How?' Iqbal felt cheated.

'Salim's helicopter was shot down a few days back.'

'By whom?'

'A Stinger missile.'

Iqbal shrugged. 'I hope he died screaming in pain.'

Then Iqbal reached out for him again. The Maulana tried to resist as Iqbal's hands picked up the gag and shoved it back in his mouth. Rehman's eyes bulged in confusion. 'I watched a gut-shot man die a few days ago. I know how slow and painful such a death can be.' Iqbal whispered harshly. 'That is the kind of death you deserve.'

Iqbal's hand flashed up and descended in a vicious arc. The knife entered the man's belly with a heavy sucking sound. A soundless scream ripped through him. As he writhed in pain, Iqbal withdrew the knife and carefully wiped it clean on the man's clothes.

'Die slowly, old man...and give a thought to those hundreds of innocents you have sentenced to death. Maybe Allah will forgive you.'

Iqbal walked up to a table in the corner and picked up the small telephone book lying on it. Right next to the phone book was a sleek, almost new satellite phone. On an impulse he picked that up too. Just before leaving the hut, Iqbal taped his last grenade tightly to Rehman's torso. He tied a string to the grenade's pin and attached the other end to the inner handle of the door.

This was to be his parting gift. The next man who pulled open the door would be in for the shock of his life.

Pulling the door gently behind him Iqbal dropped silently to the ground again and melted into the jungles surrounding the camp.

FULL CIRCLE

Despite all their howling and screaming the Pakistanis knew that nothing concrete was going to come of the whole exercise. Maintaining the Armed Forces in the current state of readiness was slowly but deftly starting to strangle an already weak economy. But they could not afford to take the offensive lying down. From the madrassas to the offices of the various jihadi outfits there was a massive clamour at the failure of the Pakistani Government to protect them.

A reaction was imminent. The Pakistanis continued with their political posturing while word was quietly sent out to the tribe of terror groups that the ISI controlled: 'The Indians must be made to pay for this.'

The coming days saw a spate of terrorist attacks and suicide bombings erupt in the Kashmir Valley and many other Indian cities as the ISI activated several sleeper cells.

The Indians had been expecting something pretty much on these lines. Luckily, most of the attacks did not cause substantial damage. Of course, some of them did succeed.

The number of ISI- sponsored terrorists that came in to India with the constant inflow of refugees from Bangladesh and Nepal was far higher than normal in the coming weeks. Many of them were apprehended at the borders and sent back or jailed.

Some foreign tourists were unlucky enough to be picnicking on the banks of the Dal Lake when a suicide bomber took them out. Two of them happened to be American. This did not go down well with the American public; there were just too many body bags being flown back from all over the world.

A party of Hindu pilgrims in the Kashmir Valley was met by two jihadi snipers who managed to cut down three of them before the security man carrying the rocket launcher was able to get a fix on the snipers and blow them to bits.

A pressure-cooker bomb exploded in the temple city of Varanasi. Sixteen devotees were killed.

Another bomb placed in a trashcan near the Akshardham temple in Gujarat was defused minutes before it was set to explode.

Three Indian ministers also got unlucky as their security men failed to prevent an attack on them. Barring the loss of face to the Indian Government, their demise caused no significant loss since they were from the standard corrupt pool of politicians; two of them were facing charges for their involvement in the kind of scams that rock Indian polity every so often. In fact, their untimely departure from earth proved to be a blessing in disguise. It saved the Indian exchequer a lot of money that would have been spent needlessly prosecuting them, since it is almost certain that they would eventually have got away scot-free.

IQBAL

Somewhere along the LOC, POK.

He felt neither elation nor satisfaction; neither rewarded nor redeemed. All he felt was an emptiness. Inside him was an emotional wasteland. Whatever it was that had been pushing him these past few days seemed at last to have been stilled. At least for the moment.

In the distance was the snow-clad mountain peak that marked the path that Iqbal had to take today. Just along the base of that mountain lay the twisting path that would take him back home. Back to Abbu and Ashraf.

It was a long journey and by no means an easy one. His legs moved of their own accord. As feet turned to yards and yards into miles Iqbal felt the relentless images in his mind recede. A blank white numbness engulfed his mind. Somewhere, far away he saw his mother and sister calling him home... *Allaa-hummaf-tah Lee Abwaaba Rahmatik...*

It was not the soldier manning the battlefield surveillance radar who spotted the movement. It was the Machine-Gunner who first heard the sound and alerted the Section Commander. The Section

Commander immediately pointed out the positions and gave the required field signals. Silently, the section moved into position. Barely eighty seconds later, all six rifles of the section were trained on the narrow winding mountain trail. So was the section's machine-gun. The ambush was firmly in place. Every gun was cocked and poised to unleash a hail of leaden death.

'No one will fire till I give the signal,' the Section Commander whispered. Nobody nodded or spoke to acknowledge the command. Every man's attention was focused on the barely audible sounds coming from the trail and they all tensed as the target suddenly appeared over the crest. He was not making much noise but neither was he taking many precautions. Like a zombie, like a man walking in his sleep. *Stupid shit!* the Section Commander thought. *One of those newly-trained morons coming back to save the world.*

The man had descended almost twenty metres down the rocky slope. Another eighty metres and he would be almost at the base of the defile and within easy striking range of the waiting guns. So would the rest of the infiltrating party that was sure to be behind him. The Section Commander had been told during his induction training that there were normally eight to ten of them in each infiltration party. By now the man had descended another fifty metres and the Section Commander was starting to get a little concerned. *How come none of the others are visible yet? You never maintain such a large distance between each other when moving in such rough terrain.*

The man had almost reached the centre of the killing ground. Another few moments and he would be out of it, lost forever behind the bend in the mountain trail. The Section Commander pondered the dilemma briefly. In the end it was a pretty simple choice. A bird in the hand is worth two in the bush. The Section Commander nodded to his men: 'Get ready, guys,' he whispered softly. 'I am going to hail him once, if he doesn't stop blow him away.'

Guns steadied as he raised the small hailer to his mouth. Experience had shown that a sudden loud voice booming out of the mountainside more often than not froze the unsuspecting person for a few seconds. In such conditions those few seconds were more than critical. They made the difference between life and death.

'Stop! Stop right there and raise your hands in the air!'

Amplified by the hailer the Section Commander's voice blasted out of the undergrowth shattering the uneasy calm that prevailed along the LOC.

But it was not half as loud or disruptive as the gunfire waiting to be unleashed…

Please turn the page
for an exciting preview of
Mukul Deva's sequel to *Lashkar*

Salim Must Die

Coming in 2009

Male Airport, Maldives

The man squinted as the bright clear sunlight struck him. After the fog-laden climate of Murree, the bright sun was a shocker. Groping in the laptop bag slung on his shoulder, he pulled out a pair of dark sunglasses and put them on as he walked up to the edge of the ocean. The old man was watching the water lap against the low concrete wall running all along the edge when his younger companion from Murree emerged from the airport building and walked up to him.

In his mid-thirties, the second man was tall and broad-shouldered. He sported a distinctly military haircut and his eyes were hidden behind dark wraparound shades like those worn by cricketers on the field. He was sweating profusely. He, too, must have been feeling the sharp change in climate after the long stay at Murree.

Walking just behind him, pushing a luggage trolley, was a muscular young man with a healthy tanned complexion, in a sparkling white T-shirt with 'Sunshine Travels' emblazoned across his muscular chest.

'We are ready, sirs,' the young man with the luggage trolley called out brightly. 'Please follow me. That's our boat.' He pushed the trolley around them and made his way to a speedboat bobbing gently alongside the wooden jetty. The trolley made a hollow trundling sound as it lumbered over the long wooden slats of the jetty. The duo from Murree waited till the luggage was on board and then jumped onto the speedboat. A few minutes later it pulled away from the jetty and headed out into the vastness of the brilliant blue ocean. The nose of the speedboat lifted into the air as it gathered speed. A fine spray arced out in the wind, gently dousing the two men standing leewards of the tiny cockpit-like cabin. It felt pleasant and refreshing.

'Our hotel, the Blue Moon Resort, is there.' The enthusiastic young man from Sunshine Travels gestured at the distant horizon. 'It will take us about forty minutes to reach. The Blue Moon is one of the finest resorts in Maldives. I can assure you that both of you will have a wonderful time.' He was shouting, but his voice was blown away in the wind that whipped past the speeding boat.

'What is that?' Cheema pointed at the huge gleaming golden dome sparkling in the sun.

'That is the Islamic Centre. You can see it no matter which direction you approach Male from. We must come down and see it one of these days. Believe me, sirs, it is really beautiful.'

The two men from Murree watched the huge, shining facade recede rapidly in the distance. Their escort prattled on about the islands and the wonders of Maldives.

The younger of the two seemed to be listening intently, but his older colleague was clearly disinterested in his surroundings. The lad's constant drone was starting to get on his nerves. Closing his mind to it, the old man turned his thoughts inwards.

Ex-Brigadier Murad Salim of the Pakistani ISI was not here on a holiday jaunt. He was a man with a mission, though officially he was a dead man, like his younger companion and aide, ex-Captain Azam Cheema. They had both been declared dead after they had engineered their own deaths in a helicopter crash in the wake of the Delhi bomb blasts of October 2005.

Salim was impatient to reach the hotel and meet the men and women who were gathering there from all points of the compass. They were a diverse group from different countries, of different nationalities. But they all had one thing in common. They were gathering to plot death.

Death for a great many people...

ACKNOWLEDGMENTS

This writing of this book has been a fascinating journey for me and not one, I might add, that I have always enjoyed. It is sad to see the kind of pain and misery that we humans are capable of inflicting on each other in the name of religion.

I owe a huge debt of gratitude to many officers of the Indian Armed Forces who have been kind enough to ensure I did not make any major blunders when writing about tactics, weapons and weapon systems. I must also mention here that all technical data used in this book is freely and easily available on the Internet and has not been provided to me by any person or persons.

Any errors (factual or technical) that still exist in this book are solely my fault *or* have been deliberately left in there by me to prevent any misuse of the technology.

This book would definitely not have been possible without the tremendous support and expert guidance that I received from my editor Nandita Aggarwal.

I would also like to thank V.K. Karthika, Yogesh Sharma and Amit Sharma at HarperCollins for their help and support.